Agatha Christie, is known throughout the world as the Queen of Crime. Her seventy-six detective novels and books of stories have been translated into every major language, and her sales are calculated in tens of millions.

She began writing at the end of the First World War, when she created Hercule Poirot, the little Belgian detective with the egg-shaped head and the passion for order – the most popular sleuth in fiction since Sherlock Holmes. Poirot, Miss Marple and her other detectives have appeared in films, radio programmes, television films and stage plays based on her books.

Agatha Christie also wrote six romantic novels under the pseudonym Mary Westmacott, several plays and a book of poems; as well, she assisted her archaeologist husband Sir Max Mallowan on many expeditions to the Near East. She was awarded the DBE in 1971.

Postern of Fate was the last book she wrote before her death in 1976, but since its publication two books Agatha Christie wrote in the 1940s have appeared: *Curtain: Poirot's Last Case* and *Sleeping Murder*, the last Miss Marple book.

Agatha Christie's *Autobiography* was published by Fontana in 1978.

AGATHA CHRISTIE

Passenger to Frankfurt

An Extravaganza

FONTANA/Collins

To Margaret Guillaume

First published by William Collins 1970
First issued in Fontana Books 1973
Eighteenth impression September 1987

Printed and bound in Great Britain by
Cox & Wyman Ltd, Reading

CONTENTS

'Leadership, besides being a great creative
force, can be diabolical ...'
JAN SMUTS

INTRODUCTION

The Author speaks:

The first question put to an author, personally, or through the post, is:

'Where do you get your ideas from?'

The temptation is great to reply: 'I always go to Harrods,' or 'I get them mostly at the Army & Navy Stores,' or, snappily, 'Try Marks and Spencer.'

The universal opinion seems firmly established that there is a magic source of ideas which authors have discovered how to tap.

One can hardly send one's questioners back to Elizabethan times, with Shakespeare's:

> Tell me, where is fancy bred,
> Or in the heart or in the head,
> How begot, how nourished?
> Reply, reply.

You merely say firmly: 'My own head.'

That, of course, is no help to anybody. If you like the look of your questioner you relent and go a little further.

'If one idea in particular seems attractive, and you feel you could do something with it, then you toss it around, play tricks with it, work it up, tone it down, and gradually get it into shape. Then, of course, you have to start writing it. That's not nearly such fun – it becomes hard work. Alternatively, you can tuck it carefully away, in storage, for perhaps using in a year or two years' time.'

A second question – or rather a statement – is then likely to be:

'I suppose you take most of your characters from real life?'

7

An indignant denial to that monstrous suggestion.

'No, I don't. I invent them. They are *mine*. They've got to be *my* characters – doing what I want them to do, being what I want them to be – coming alive for me, having their own ideas sometimes, but only because I've made them become *real*.'

So the author has produced the ideas, and the characters – but now comes the third necessity – the setting. The first two come from inside sources, but the third is outside – it must be there – waiting – in existence already. You don't invent that – it's there – it's real.

You have been perhaps for a cruise on the Nile – you remember it all – just the setting you want for this particular story. You have had a meal at a Chelsea café. A quarrel was going on – one girl pulled out a handful of another girl's hair. An excellent start for the book you are going to write next. You travel on the Orient Express. What fun to make it the scene for a plot you are considering. You go to tea with a friend. As you arrive her brother closes a book he is reading – throws it aside, says: 'Not bad, but why on earth didn't they ask Evans?'

So you decide immediately a book of yours shortly to be written will bear the title, *Why Didn't They Ask Evans?*

You don't know yet who Evans is going to be. Never mind. Evans will come in due course – the title is fixed.

So, in a sense, you don't invent your settings. They are outside you, all around you, in existence – you have only to stretch out your hand and pick and choose. A railway train, a hospital, a London hotel, a Caribbean beach, a country village, a cocktail party, a girls' school.

But one thing only applies – they must be there – in existence. Real people, real places. A definite place in time and space. If here and now – how shall you get full information – apart from the evidence of your own eyes and ears? The answer is frighteningly simple.

It is what the Press brings to you every day, served up in your morning paper under the general heading of News. Collect it from the front page. What is going on in the world today? What is everyone saying, thinking, doing? Hold up a mirror to 1970 in England.

Look at that front page every day for a month, make notes, consider and classify.

Every day there is a killing.

A girl strangled.

Elderly woman attacked and robbed of her meagre savings.

Young men or boys – attacking or attacked.

Buildings and telephone kiosks smashed and gutted.

Drug smuggling.

Robbery and assault.

Children missing and children's murdered bodies found not far from their homes.

Can this be England? Is England *really* like this? One feels – no – not yet, *but it could be*.

Fear is awakening – fear of what may be. Not so much because of actual happenings but because of the possible causes behind them. Some known, some unknown, but *felt*. And not only in our own country. There are smaller paragraphs on other pages – giving news from Europe – from Asia – from the Americas – Worldwide News.

Hi-jacking of planes.

Kidnapping.

Violence.

Riots.

Hate.

Anarchy – all growing stronger.

All seeming to lead to worship of destruction, pleasure in cruelty.

What does it all mean? An Elizabethan phrase echoes from the past, speaking of Life:

> … it is a tale
> Told by an idiot, full of sound and fury,
> Signifying nothing.

And yet one knows – of one's own knowledge – how much

goodness there is in this world of ours – the kindnesses done, the goodness of heart, the acts of compassion, the kindness of neighbour to neighbour, the helpful actions of girls and boys.

Then why this fantastic atmosphere of daily news – of things that happen – that are actual *facts*?

To write a story in this year of Our Lord 1970 – you must come to terms with your background. If the background is fantastic, then the story must accept its background. It, too, must be a fantasy – an extravaganza. The setting must include the fantastic facts of daily life.

Can one envisage a fantastic cause? A secret Campaign for Power? Can a maniacal desire for destruction create a new world? Can one go a step further and suggest deliverance by fantastic and impossible-sounding means?

Nothing is impossible, science has taught us that.

This story is in essence a fantasy. It pretends to be nothing more.

But most of the things that happen in it are happening, or giving promise of happening in the world of today.

It is not an impossible story – it is only a fantastic one.

BOOK 1

Interrupted Journey

CHAPTER 1

Passenger To Frankfurt

'Fasten your seat-belts, please.' The diverse passengers in the plane were slow to obey. There was a general feeling that they couldn't possibly be arriving at Geneva yet. The drowsy groaned and yawned. The more than drowsy had to be gently roused by an authoritative stewardess.

'Your seat-belts, please.'

The dry voice came authoritatively over the Tannoy. It explained in German, in French, and in English that a short period of rough weather would shortly be experienced. Sir Stafford Nye opened his mouth to its full extent, yawned and pulled himself upright in his seat. He had been dreaming very happily of fishing an English river.

He was a man of forty-five, of medium height, with a smooth, olive, clean-shaven face. In dress he rather liked to affect the bizarre. A man of excellent family, he felt fully at ease indulging any such sartorial whims. If it made the more conventionally dressed of his colleagues wince occasionally, that was merely a source of malicious pleasure to him. There was something about him of the eighteenth-century buck. He liked to be noticed.

His particular kind of affectation when travelling was a kind of bandit's cloak which he had once purchased in Corsica. It was of a very dark purply-blue, had a scarlet lining and had a kind of burnous hanging down behind which he could draw up over his head when he wished to, so as to obviate draughts.

Sir Stafford Nye had been a disappointment in diplomatic circles. Marked out in early youth by his gifts for great things, he had singularly failed to fulfil his early promise. A peculiar and diabolical sense of humour was wont to afflict him in what should have been his most serious moments. When it came to the point, he found that he always preferred to indulge his delicate Puckish malice to boring himself. He was a well-known figure in public life without ever having reached eminence. It was felt that Stafford Nye, though definitely brilliant, was not – and presumably never would be – a safe man. In these days of tangled politics and tangled foreign relations, safety, especially if one were to reach ambassadorial rank, was preferable to brilliance. Sir Stafford Nye was relegated to the shelf, though he was occasionally entrusted with such missions as needed the art of intrigue, but were not of too important or public a nature. Journalists sometimes referred to him as the dark horse of diplomacy.

Whether Sir Stafford himself was disappointed with his own career, nobody ever knew. Probably not even Sir Stafford himself. He was a man of a certain vanity, but he was also a man who very much enjoyed indulging his own proclivities for mischief.

He was returning now from a commission of inquiry in Malaya. He had found it singularly lacking in interest. His colleagues had, in his opinion, made up their minds beforehand what their findings were going to be. They saw and they listened, but their preconceived views were not affected. Sir Stafford had thrown a few spanners into the works, more for the hell of it than from any pronounced convictions. At all events, he thought, it had livened things up. He wished there were more possibilities of doing that sort of thing. His fellow members of the commission had been sound, dependable fellows, and remarkably dull. Even the well-known Mrs Nathaniel Edge, the only woman member, well known as having bees in her bonnet, was no fool when it came down to plain facts. She saw, she listened and she played safe.

He had met her before on the occasion of a problem to be solved in one of the Balkan capitals. It was there that Sir Stafford Nye had not been able to refrain from embarking on a few interesting suggestions. In that scandal-loving periodical *Inside News* it was insinuated that Sir Stafford Nye's presence in that Balkan capital was intimately connected with Balkan problems, and that his mission was a secret one of the greatest delicacy. A kind of friend had sent Sir Stafford a copy of this with the relevant passage marked. Sir Stafford was not taken aback. He read it with a delighted grin. It amused him very much to reflect how ludicrously far from the truth the journalists were on this occasion. His presence in Sofiagrad had been due entirely to a blameless interest in the rarer wild flowers and to the urgencies of an elderly friend of his, Lady Lucy Cleghorn, who was indefatigable in her quest for these shy floral rarities, and who at any moment would scale a rock cliff or leap joyously into a bog at the sight of some flowerlet, the length of whose Latin name was in inverse proportion to its size.

A small band of enthusiasts had been pursuing this botanical search on the slopes of mountains for about ten days when it occurred to Sir Sir Stafford that it was a pity the paragraph was not true. He was a little – just a little – tired of wild flowers and, fond as he was of dear Lucy, her ability despite her sixty-odd years to race up hills at top speed, easily outpacing him, sometimes annoyed him. Always just in front of him he saw the seat of those bright royal blue trousers and Lucy, though scraggy enough elsewhere, goodness knows, was decidedly too broad in the beam to wear royal blue corduroy trousers. A nice little international pie, he had thought, in which to dip his fingers, in which to play about ...

In the aeroplane the metallic Tannoy voice spoke again. It told the passengers that owing to heavy fog at Geneva, the plane would be diverted to Frankfurt airport and proceed from there to London. Passengers to Geneava would be re-routed from Frankfurt as soon as possible. It made no difference to Sir Stafford Nye. If there was fog in London, he supposed they would re-route the plane to Prestwick. He hoped that would not happen. He had been to Prestwick once or twice too often. Life, he thought, and journeys by air, were really excessively boring. If only – he didn't know – if only – *what*?

It was warm in the Transit Passenger Lounge at Frankfurt, so Sir Stafford Nye slipped back his cloak, allowing its crimson lining to drape itself spectacularly round his shoulders. He was drinking a glass of beer and listening with half an ear to the various announcements as they were made.

'Flight 4387. Flying to Moscow. Flight 2381 bound for Egypt and Calcutta.'

Journeys all over the globe. How romantic it ought to be. But there was something about the atmosphere of a Passengers' Lounge in an airport that chilled romance. It was too full of people, too full of things to buy, too full of similarly coloured seats, too full of plastic, too full of human beings, too full of crying children. He tried to remember who had said:

> I wish I loved the Human Race;
> I wish I loved its silly face.

Chesterton perhaps? It was undoubtedly true. Put enough people together and they looked so painfully alike that one could hardly bear it. An interesting face now, thought Sir Stafford. What a difference it would make. He looked disparagingly at two young women, splendidly made up, dressed in the national uniform of their country – England he presumed – of shorter and shorter miniskirts, and another young woman, even better made up – in fact quite good-looking – who was wearing what he believed to be called a culotte suit. She had gone a little further along the road of fashion.

He wasn't very interested in nice-looking girls who looked like all the other nice-looking girls. He would like someone to be different. Someone sat down beside him on the plastic-covered artificial leather settee on which he was sitting. Her face attracted his attention at once. Not precisely because it was different, in fact he almost seemed to recognize it as a face he knew. Here was someone he had seen before. He couldn't remember where or when but it was certainly familiar. Twenty-five or six, he thought, possibly, as to age. A delicate high-bridged aquiline nose, a black heavy bush of hair reaching to her shoulders. She had a magazine in front of her but she was

16

not paying attention to it. She was, in fact, looking with something that was almost eagerness at him. Quite suddenly she spoke. It was a deep contralto voice, almost as deep as a man's. It had a very faint foreign accent. She said,

'Can I speak to you?'

He studied her for a moment before replying. No – not what one might have thought – this wasn't a pick-up. This was something else.

'I see no reason,' he said, 'why you should not do so. We have time to waste here, it seems.'

'Fog,' said the woman, 'fog in Geneva, fog in London, perhaps. Fog everywhere. I don't know what to do.'

'Oh, you mustn't worry,' he said reassuringly, 'they'll land you somewhere all right. They're quite efficient, you know. Where are you going?'

'I was going to Geneva.'

'Well, I expect you'll get there in the end.'

'I have to get there *now*. If I can get to Geneva, it will be all right. There is someone who will meet me there. I can be safe.'

'Safe?' He smiled a little.

She said, 'Safe is a four-letter word but not the kind of four-letter word that people are interested in nowadays. And yet it can mean a lot. It means a lot to me.' Then she said, 'You see, if I can't get to Geneva, if I have to leave this plane here, or go on in this plane to London with no arrangements made, I shall be killed.' She looked at him sharply. 'I suppose you don't believe that.'

'I'm afraid I don't.'

'It's quite true. People can be. They are, every day.'

'Who wants to kill you?'

'Does it matter?'

'Not to me.'

'You can believe me if you wish to believe me. I am speaking the truth. I want help. Help to get to London safely.'

'And why should you select me to help you?'

'Because I think that you know something about death. You have known of death, perhaps seen death happen.'

17

He looked sharply at her and then away again.

'Any other reason?' he said.

'Yes. This.' She stretched out her narrow olive-skinned hand and touched the folds of the voluminous cloak. 'This,' she said.

For the first time his interest was aroused.

'Now what do you mean by that?'

'It's unusual – characteristic. It's not what everyone wears.'

'True enough. It's one of my affectations, shall we say?'

'It's an affectation that could be useful to me.'

'What do you mean?'

'I am asking you something. Probably you will refuse but you might not refuse because I think you are a man who is ready to take risks. Just as I am a woman who takes risks.'

'I'll listen to your project,' he said, with a faint smile.

'I want your cloak to wear. I want your passport. I want your boarding ticket for the plane. Presently, in twenty minutes or so, say, the flight for London will be called. I shall have your passport, I shall wear your cloak. And so I shall travel to London and arrive safely.'

'You mean you'll pass yourself off as me? My dear girl.'

She opened a handbag. From it she took a small square mirror.

'Look there,' she said. 'Look at me and then look at your own face.'

He saw then, saw what had been vaguely nagging at his mind. His sister, Pamela, who had died about twenty years ago. They had always been very alike, he and Pamela. A strong family resemblance. She had had a slightly masculine type of face. His face, perhaps, had been, certainly in early life, of a slightly effeminate type. They had both had the high-bridged nose, the tilt of eyebrows, the slightly sideways smile of the lips. Pamela had been tall, five foot eight, he himself five foot ten. He looked at the woman who had tendered him the mirror.

'There is a facial likeness between us, that's what you mean, isn't it? But my dear girl, it wouldn't deceive anyone who knew me or knew you.'

18

'Of course it wouldn't. Don't you understand? It doesn't need to. I am travelling wearing slacks. You have been travelling with the hood of your cloak drawn up round your face. All I have to do is to cut off my hair, wrap it up in a twist of newspaper, throw it in one of the litter-baskets here. Then I put on your burnous, I have your boarding card, ticket, and passport. Unless there is someone who knows you well on this plane, and I presume there is not or they would have spoken to you already, then I can safely travel as you. Showing your passport when it's necessary, keeping the burnous and cloak drawn up so that my nose and eyes and mouth are about all that are seen. I can walk out safely when the plane reaches its destination because no one will know I have travelled by it. Walk out safely and disappear into the crowds of the city of London.'

'And what do I do?' asked Sir Stafford, with a slight smile.

'I can make a suggestion if you have the nerve to face it.'

'Suggest,' he said. 'I always like to hear suggestions.'

'You get up from here, you go away and buy a magazine or a newspaper, or a gift at the gift counter. You leave your cloak hanging here on the seat. When you come back with whatever it is, you sit down somewhere else – say at the end of that bench opposite here. There will be a glass in front of you, this glass still. In it there will be something that will send you to sleep. Sleep in a quiet corner.'

'What happens next?'

'You will have been presumably the victim of a robbery,' she said. 'Somebody will have added a few knock-out drops to your drink, and will have stolen your wallet from you. Something of that kind. You declare your identity, say that your passport and things are stolen. You can easily establish your identity.'

'You know who I am? My name, I mean?'

'Not yet,' she said. 'I haven't seen your passport yet. I've no idea who you are.'

'And yet you say I can establish my identity easily.'

'I am a good judge of people. I know who is important or who isn't. You are an important person.'

19

'And why should I do all this?'

'Perhaps to save the life of a fellow human being.'

'Isn't that rather a highly coloured story?'

'Oh yes. Quite easily not believed. Do you believe it?'

He looked at her thoughtfully. 'You know what you're talking like? A beautiful spy in a thriller.'

'Yes, perhaps. But I am not beautiful.'

'And you're not a spy?'

'I might be so described, perhaps. I have certain information. Information I want to preserve. You will have to take my word for it, it is information that would be valuable to your country.'

'Don't you think you're being rather absurd?'

'Yes I do. If this was written down it would look absurd. But so many absurd things are true, aren't they?'

He looked at her again. She was very like Pamela. Her voice, although foreign in intonation, was like Pamela's. What she proposed was ridiculous, absurd, quite impossible, and probably dangerous. Dangerous to him. Unfortunately, though, that was what attracted him. To have the nerve to suggest such a thing to him! What would come of it all? It would be interesting, certainly, to find out.

'What do I get out of it?' he said. 'That's what I'd like to know.'

She looked at him consideringly. 'Diversion,' she said. 'Something out of the everyday happenings? An antidote to boredom, perhaps. We've not got very long. It's up to you.'

'And what happens to *your* passport? Do I have to buy myself a wig, if they sell such a thing, at the counter? Do I have to impersonate a female?'

'No. There's no question of exchanging places. You have been robbed and drugged but you remain yourself. Make up your mind. There isn't long. Time is passing very quickly. I have to do my own transformation.'

'You win,' he said. 'One mustn't refuse the unusual, if it is offered to one.'

'I hoped you might feel that way, but it was a toss-up.'

From his pocket Stafford Nye took out his passport. He slipped it into the outer pocket of the cloak he had been wearing. He rose to his feet, yawned, looked round him, looked at his watch, and strolled over to the counter where various goods were displayed for sale. He did not even look back. He bought a paperback book and fingered some small woolly animals, a suitable gift for some child. Finally he chose a panda. He looked round the lounge, came back to where he had been sitting. The cloak was gone and so had the girl. A half glass of beer was on the table still. Here, he thought, is where I take the risk. He picked up the glass, moved away a little, and drank it. Not quickly. Quite slowly. It tasted much the same as it had tasted before.

'Now I wonder,' said Sir Stafford. 'Now I wonder.'

He walked across the lounge to a far corner. There was a somewhat noisy family sitting there, laughing and talking together. He sat down near them, yawned, let his head fall back on the edge of the cushion. A flight was announced leaving for Teheran. A large number of passengers got up and went to queue by the requisite numbered gate. The lounge still remained half full. He opened his paperback book. He yawned again. He was really sleepy now, yes, he was very sleepy ... He must just think out where it was best for him to go off to sleep. Somewhere he could remain ...

Trans-European Airways announced the departure of their plane, Flight 309 for London.

Quite a good sprinkling of passengers rose to their feet to obey the summons. By this time though, more passengers had entered the transit lounge waiting for other planes. Announcements followed as to fog at Geneva and other disabilities of travel. A slim man of middle height wearing a dark blue cloak with its red lining showing and with a hood drawn up over a close-cropped head, not noticeably more untidy than many of the heads of young men nowadays, walked across the floor to take his place in the queue for the plane. Showing a boarding ticket, he passed out through gate No. 9.

More announcements followed. Swissair flying to Zürich. BEA to Athens and Cyprus – And then a different type of announcement.

'Will Miss Daphne Theodofanous, passenger to Geneva, kindly come to the flight desk. Plane to Geneva is delayed owing to fog. Passengers will travel by way of Athens. The aeroplane is now ready to leave.'

Other announcements followed dealing with passengers to Japan, to Egypt, to South Africa, air lines spanning the world. Mr Sidney Cook, passenger to South Africa, was urged to come to the flight desk where there was a message for him. Daphne Theodofanous was called for again.

'This is the last call before the departure of Flight 309.'

In a corner of the lounge a little girl was looking up at a man in a dark suit who was fast asleep, his head resting against the cushion of the red settee. In his hand he held a small woolly panda.

The little girl's hand stretched out towards the panda. Her mother said:

'Now, Joan, don't touch that. The poor gentleman's asleep.'

'Where is he going?'

'Perhaps he's going to Australia too,' said her mother, 'like we are.'

'Has he got a little girl like me?'

'I think he must have,' said her mother.

The little girl sighed and looked at the panda again. Sir Stafford Nye continued to sleep. He was dreaming that he was trying to shoot a leopard. A very dangerous animal, he was saying to the safari guide who was accompanying him. 'A very dangerous animal, so I've always heard. You can't trust a leopard.'

The dream switched at that moment, as dreams have a habit of doing, and he was having tea with his Great-Aunt Matilda, and trying to make her hear. She was deafer than ever! He had not heard any of the announcements except the first one for Miss Daphne Theodofanous. The little girl's mother said:

'I've always wondered, you know, about a passenger that's

missing. Nearly always, whenever you go anywhere by air, you hear it. Somebody they can't find. Somebody who hasn't heard the call or isn't on the plane or something like that. I always wonder who it is and what they're doing, and *why* they haven't come. I suppose this Miss What's-a-name or whatever it is will just have missed her plane. What will they do with her then?'

Nobody was able to answer her question because nobody had the proper information.

CHAPTER 2

London

Sir Stafford Nye's flat was a very pleasant one. It looked out upon Green Park. He switched on the coffee percolator and went to see what the post had left him this morning. It did not appear to have left him anything very interesting. He sorted through the letters, a bill or two, a receipt and letters with rather uninteresting postmarks. He shuffled them together and placed them on the table where some mail was already lying, accumulating from the last two days. He'd have to get down to things soon, he supposed. His secretary would be coming in some time or other this afternoon.

He went back to the kitchen, poured coffee into a cup and brought it to the table. He picked up the two or three letters that he had opened late last night when he arrived. One of them he referred to, and smiled a little as he read it.

'Eleven-thirty,' he said. 'Quite a suitable time. I wonder now. I expect I'd better just think things over, and get prepared for Chetwynd.'

Somebody pushed something through the letter-box. He went out into the hall and got the morning paper. There was very little news in the paper. A political crisis, an item of foreign news which might have been disquieting, but he didn't think it was. It was merely a journalist letting off steam and trying to make things rather more important than they were. Must give the people something to read. A girl had been strangled in the park. Girls were always being strangled. One a day, he thought callously. No child had been kidnapped or raped this morning. That was a nice surprise. He made himself a piece of toast and drank his coffee.

Later, he went out of the building, down into the street, and walked through the park in the direction of Whitehall. He was smiling to himself. Life, he felt, was rather good this morning. He began to think about Chetwynd. Chetwynd was a silly fool if there ever was one. A good façade, important-seeming, and a nicely suspicious mind. He'd rather enjoy talking to Chetwynd.

He reached Whitehall a comfortable seven minutes late. That was only due to his own importance compared with that of Chetwynd, he thought. He walked into the room. Chetwynd was sitting behind his desk and had a lot of papers on it and a secretary there. He was looking properly important, as he always did when he could make it.

'Hullo, Nye,' said Chetwynd, smiling all over his impressively handsome face. 'Glad to be back? How was Malaya?'

'Hot,' said Stafford Nye.

'Yes. Well, I suppose it always is. You meant atmospherically, I suppose, not politically?'

'Oh, purely atmospherically,' said Stafford Nye.

He accepted a cigarette and sat down.

'Get any results to speak of?'

'Oh, hardly. Not what you'd call results. I've sent in my report. All a lot of talky-talky as usual. How's Lazenby?'

'Oh, a nuisance as he always is. He'll never change,' said Chetwynd.

'No, that would seem too much to hope for. I haven't served on anything with Bascombe before. He can be quite fun when he likes.'

'Can he? I don't know him very well. Yes. I suppose he can.'

24

'Well, well, well. No other news, I suppose?'

'No, nothing. Nothing I think that would interest you.'

'You didn't mention in your letter quite why you wanted to see me.'

'Oh, just to go over a few things, that's all. You know, in case you'd brought any special dope home with you. Anything we ought to be prepared for, you know. Questions in the House. Anything like that.'

'Yes, of course.'

'Came home by air, didn't you? Had a bit of trouble, I gather.'

Stafford Nye put on the face he had been determined to put on beforehand. It was slightly rueful, with a faint tinge of annoyance.

'Oh, so you heard about that, did you?' he said. 'Silly business.'

'Yes. Yes, must have been.'

'Extaordinary,' said Stafford Nye, 'how things always get into the press. There was a paragraph in the stop press this morning.'

'You'd rather they wouldn't have, I suppose?'

'Well, makes me look a bit of an ass, doesn't it?' said Stafford Nye. 'Got to admit it. At my age too!'

'What happened exactly? I wondered if the report in the paper had been exaggerating.'

'Well, I suppose they made the most of it, that's all. You know what these journeys are. Damn boring. There was fog at Geneva so they had to re-route the plane. Then there was two hours' delay at Frankfurt.'

'Is that when it happened?'

'Yes. One's bored stiff in these airports. Planes coming, planes going. Tannoy going full steam ahead. Flight 302 leaving for Hong Kong, Flight 109 going to Ireland. This, that and the other. People getting up, people leaving. And you just sit there yawning.'

'What happened exactly?' said Chetwynd.

'Well, I'd got a drink in front of me, Pilsner as a matter of

25

fact, then I thought I'd got to get something else to read. I'd read everything I'd got with me so I went over to the counter and bought some wretched paperback or other. Detective story, I think it was, and I bought a woolly animal for one of my nieces. Then I came back, finished my drink, opened my paperback and then I went to sleep.'

'Yes, I see. You went to sleep.'

'Well, a very natural thing to do, isn't it? I suppose they called my flight but if they did I didn't hear it. I didn't hear it apparently for the best of reasons. I'm capable of going to sleep in an airport any time but I'm also capable of hearing an announcement that concerns me. This time I didn't. When I woke up, or came to, however you like to put it, I was having a bit of medical attention. Somebody apparently had dropped a Mickey Finn or something or other in my drink. Must have done it when I was away getting the paperback.'

'Rather an extraordinary things to happen, wasn't it?' said Chetwynd.

'Well, it's never happened to me before,' said Stafford Nye. 'I hope it never will again. It makes you feel an awful fool, you know. Besides having a hangover. There was a doctor and some nurse creature, or something. Anyway, there was no great harm done apparently. My wallet had been pinched with some money in it and my passport. It was awkward of course. Fortunately, I hadn't got much money. My travellers' cheques were in an inner pocket. There always has to be a bit of red tape and all that if you lose your passport. Anyway, I had letters and things and identification was not difficult. And in due course things were squared up and I resumed my flight.'

'Still, very annoying for you,' said Chetwynd. 'A person of your status, I mean.' His tone was disapproving.

'Yes,' said Stafford Nye. 'It doesn't show me in a very good light, does it? I mean, not as bright as a fellow of my – er – status ought to be.' The idea seemed to amuse him.

'Does this often happen, did you find out?'

'I don't think it's a matter of general occurrence. It could be. I suppose any person with a pick-pocket trend could notice a

26

fellow asleep and slip a hand into a pocket, and if he's accomplished in his profession, get hold of a wallet or a pocket-book or something like that, and hope for some luck.'

'Pretty awkward to lose a passport.'

'Yes, I shall have to put in for another one now. Make a lot of explanations, I suppose. As I say, the whole thing's a damn silly business. And let's face it, Chetwynd, it doesn't show me in a very favourable light, does it?'

'Oh, not your fault, my dear boy, not your fault. It could happen to anybody, anybody at all.'

'Very nice of you to say so,' said Stafford Nye, smiling at him agreeably. 'Teach me a sharp lesson, won't it?'

'You don't think anyone wanted *your* passport specially?'

'I shouldn't think so,' said Stafford Nye. 'Why should they want my passport. Unless it was a matter of someone who wished to annoy me and that hardly seems likely. Or somebody who took a fancy to my passport photo – and that seems even less likely!'

'Did you see anyone you knew at this – where did you say you were – Frankfurt?'

'No, no. Nobody at all.'

'Talk to anyone?'

'Not particularly. Said something to a nice fat woman who'd got a small child she was trying to amuse. Came from Wigan, I think. Going to Australia. Don't remember anybody else.'

'You're sure?'

'There was some woman or other who wanted to know what she did if she wanted to study archaeology in Egypt. Said I didn't know anything about that. I told her she'd better go and ask the British Museum. And I had a word or two with a man who I think was an anti-vivisectionist. Very passionate about it.'

'One always feels,' said Chetwynd, 'that there might be something *behind* things like this.'

'Things like what?'

'Well, things like what happened to you.'

'I don't see what can be behind this,' said Sir Stafford. 'I daresay journalists could make up some story, they're so clever at that sort of thing. Still, it's a silly business. For goodness' sake, let's forget it. I suppose now it's been mentioned in the press, all my friends will start asking me about it. How's old Leyland? What's he up to nowadays? I heard one or two things about him out there. Leyland always talks a bit too much.'

The two men talked amiable shop for ten minutes or so, then Sir Stafford got up and went out.

'I've got a lot of things to do this morning,' he said. 'Presents to buy for my relations. The trouble is that if one goes to Malaya, all one's relations expect you to bring exotic presents to them. I'll go round to Liberty's, I think. They have a nice stock of Eastern goods there.'

He went out cheerfully, nodding to a couple of men he knew in the corridor outside. After he had gone, Chetwynd spoke through the telephone to his secretary.

'Ask Colonel Munro if he can come to me.'

Colonel Munro came in, bringing another tall middle-aged man with him.

'Don't know whether you know Horsham,' he said, 'in Security.'

'Think I've met you,' said Chetwynd.

'Nye's just left you, hasn't he?' said Colonel Munro. 'Anything in this story about Frankfurt? Anything, I mean, that we ought to take any notice of?'

'Doesn't seem so,' said Chetwynd. 'He's a bit put out about it. Thinks it makes him look a silly ass. Which it does, of course.'

The man called Horsham nodded his head. 'That's the way he takes it, is it?'

'Well, he tried to put a good face upon it,' said Chetwynd.

'All the same, you know,' said Horsham, 'he's not really a silly ass, is he?'

Chetwynd shrugged his shoulders. 'These things happen,' he said.

'I know,' said Colonel Munro, 'yes, yes, I know. All the same, well, I've always felt in some ways that Nye is a bit

28

unpredictable. That in some ways, you know, he mightn't be really *sound* in his views.'

The man called Horsham spoke. 'Nothing against him,' he said. 'Nothing at all as far as *we* know.'

'Oh, I didn't mean there was. I didn't mean that at all,' said Chetwynd. 'It's just – how shall I put it? – he's not always very serious about things.'

Mr Horsham had a moustache. He found it useful to have a moustache. It concealed moments when he found it difficult to avoid smiling.

'He's not a stupid man,' said Munro. 'Got brains, you know. You don't think that – well, I mean you don't think there could be anything at all doubtful about this?'

'On his part? It doesn't seem so.'

'You've been into it all, Horsham?'

'Well, we haven't had very much time yet. But as far as it goes it's all right. But his passport *was* used.'

'Used? In what way?'

'It passed through Heathrow.'

'You mean someone represented himself as Sir Stafford Nye?'

'No, no,' said Horsham, 'not in so many words. We could hardly hope for that. It went through with other passports. There was no alarm out, you know. He hadn't even woken up, I gather, at that time, from the dope or whatever it was he was given. He was still at Frankfurt.'

'But someone could have stolen that passport and come on the plane and so got into England?'

'Yes,' said Munro, 'that's the presumption. Either someone took a wallet which had money in it and a passport, or else someone wanted a passport and settled on Sir Stafford Nye as a convenient person to take it from. A drink was waiting on a table, put a pinch in that, wait till the man went off to sleep, take the passport and chance it.'

'But after all, they look at a passport. Must have seen it wasn't the right man,' said Chetwynd.

'Well, there must have been a certain resemblance, certainly,' said Horsham. 'But it isn't as though there was any notice of his being missing, any special attention drawn to that particular passport in any way. A large crowd comes through on a plane that's overdue. A man looks reasonably like the photograph in his passport. That's all. Brief glance, handed back, pass it on. Anyway what they're looking for usually is the *foreigners* that are coming in, not the British lot. Dark hair, dark blue eyes, clean shaven, five foot ten or whatever it is. That's about all you want to see. Not on a list of undesirable aliens or anything like that.'

'I know, I know. Still, you'd say if anybody wanted merely to pinch a wallet or some money or that, they wouldn't use the passport, would they. Too much risk.'

'Yes,' said Horsham. 'Yes, that is the interesting part of it. Of course,' he said, 'we're making investigations, asking a few questions here and there.'

'And what's your own opinion?'

'I wouldn't like to say yet,' said Horsham. 'It takes a little time, you know. One can't hurry things.'

'They're all the same,' said Colonel Munro, when Horsham had left the room. 'They never will tell you anything, those damned security people. If they think they're on the trail of anything, they won't admit it.'

'Well, that's natural,' said Chetwynd, 'because they might be wrong.'

It seemed a typically political view.

'Horsham's a pretty good man,' said Munro. 'They think very highly of him at headquarters. He's not likely to be wrong.'

CHAPTER 3

The Man From The Cleaners

Sir Stafford Nye returned to his flat. A large woman bounced out of the small kitchen with welcoming words.

'See you got back all right, sir. Those nasty planes. You never know, do you?'

'Quite true, Mrs Worrit,' said Sir Stafford Nye. 'Two hours late, the plane was.'

'Same as cars, aren't they,' said Mrs Worrit. 'I mean, you never know, do you, what's going to go wrong with *them*. Only it's more worrying, so to speak, being up in the air, isn't it? Can't just draw up to the kerb, not the same way, can you? I mean, there you are. I wouldn't go by one myself, not if it was ever so.' She went on, 'I've ordered in a few things. I hope that's all right. Eggs, butter, coffee, tea –' She ran off the words with the loquacity of a Near Eastern guide showing a Pharaoh's palace. 'There,' said Mrs Worrit, pausing to take breath, 'I think that's all as you're likely to want. I've ordered the French mustard.'

'Not Dijon, is it? They always try and give you Dijon.'

'I don't know who *he* was, but it's Esther Dragon, the one you like, isn't it?'

'Quite right,' said Sir Stafford, 'you're a wonder.'

Mrs Worrit looked pleased. She retired into the kitchen again, as Sir Stafford Nye put his hand on his bedroom door handle preparatory to going into the bedroom.

'All right to give your clothes to the gentleman what called for them, I suppose, sir? You hadn't said or left word or anything like that.'

'What clothes?' said Sir Stafford Nye, pausing.

'Two suits, it was, the gentleman said as called for them. Twiss and Bonywork it was, think that's the same name as

31

called before. We'd had a bit of a dispute with the White Swan laundry if I remember rightly.'

'Two suits?' said Sir Stafford Nye. 'Which suits?'

'Well, there was the one you travelled home in, sir. I made out that would be one of them. I wasn't quite so sure about the other, but there was the blue pinstripe that you didn't leave no orders about when you went away. It could do with cleaning, and there was a repair wanted doing to the right-hand cuff, but I didn't like to take it on myself while you were away. I never likes to do that,' said Mrs Worrit with an air of palpable virtue.

'So the chap, whoever he was, took those suits away?'

'I hope I didn't do wrong, sir.' Mrs Worrit became worried.

'I don't mind the blue pinstripe. I daresay it's all for the best. The suit I came home in, well –'

'It's a bit thin, that suit, sir, for this time of year, you know, sir. All right for those parts as you've been in where it's hot. And it could do with a clean. He said as you'd rung up about them. That's what the gentleman said as called for them.'

'Did he go into my room and pick them out himself?'

'Yes, sir. I thought that was best.'

'Very interesting,' said Sir Stafford. 'Yes, very interesting.'

He went into his bedroom and looked round it. It was neat and tidy. The bed was made, the hand of Mrs Worrit was apparent, his electic razor was on charge, the things on the dressing-table were neatly arranged.

He went to the wardrobe and looked inside. He looked in the drawers of the tallboy that stood against the wall near the window. It was all quite tidy. It was tidier indeed than it should have been. He had done a little unpacking last night and what little he had done had been of a cursory nature. He had thrown underclothing and various odds and ends in the appropriate drawer but he had not arranged them neatly. He would have done that himself either today or tomorrow. He would not have expected Mrs Worrit to do it for him. He expected her merely to keep things as she found them. Then, when he came back from abroad, there would be a time for rearrangements and readjustments because of climate and other matters. So someone had looked round here, someone had taken out drawers, looked through them quickly, hurriedly, had replaced things, partly because of his hurry, more tidily and neatly than he should have done. A quick careful job and he had gone away with two suits and a plausible explanation. One suit obviously worn by Sir Stafford when travelling and a suit of thin material which might have been one taken abroad and brought home. So why?

'Because,' said Sir Stafford thoughtfully, to himself, 'because somebody was looking for something. But what? And who? And also perhaps why?' Yes, it was interesting.

He sat down in a chair and thought about it. Presently his eyes strayed to the table by the bed on which sat, rather pertly, a small furry panda. It started a train of thought. He went to the telephone and rang a number.

'That you, Aunt Matilda?' he said. 'Stafford here.'

'Ah, my dear boy, so you're back. I'm so glad. I read in the paper they'd got cholera in Malaya yesterday, at least I think it was Malaya. I always get so mixed up with those places. I hope you're coming to see me soon? Don't pretend you're busy. You can't be busy all the time. One really only accepts that sort of thing from tycoons, people in industry, you know, in the middle of mergers and takeovers. I never know what it all really means. It used to mean doing your work properly but now it means things all tied up with atom bombs and factories in concrete,' said Aunt Matilda, rather wildly. 'And those terrible computers that get all one's figures wrong, to say nothing of making them the wrong shape. Really, they have made life so difficult for us nowadays. You wouldn't believe the things they've done to my bank account. And to my postal address too. Well, I suppose I've lived too long.'

'Don't you believe it! All right if I come down next week?'

'Come down tomorrow if you like. I've got the vicar coming to dinner, but I can easily put him off.'

'Oh, look here, no need to do that.'

'Yes there is, every need. He's a most irritating man and he wants a new organ too. This one does quite well as it is. I mean

33

the trouble is with the organist, really, not the organ. An absolutely abominable musician. The vicar's sorry for him because he lost his mother whom he was very fond of. But really, being fond of your mother doesn't make you play the organ any better, does it? I mean, one has to look at things as they are.'

'Quite right. It will have to be next week – I've got a few things to see to. How's Sybil?'

'Dear child! Very naughty but such fun.'

'I brought her home a woolly panda,' said Sir Stafford Nye.

'Well, that was very nice of you, dear.'

'I hope she'll like it,' said Sir Stafford, catching the panda's eye and feeling slightly nervous.

'Well, at any rate, she's got very good manners,' said Aunt Matilda, which seemed a somewhat doubtful answer, the meaning of which Sir Stafford did not quite appreciate.

Aunt Matilda suggested likely trains for next week with the warning that they very often did not run, or changed their plans, and also commanded that he should bring her down a Camembert cheese and half a Stilton.

'Impossible to get anything down here now. Our own grocer – such a nice man, so thoughtful and such good taste in what we all liked – turned suddenly into a supermarket, six times the size, all rebuilt, baskets and wire trays to carry round and try to fill up with things you don't want and mothers always losing their babies, and crying and having hysterics. Most exhausting. Well, I'll be expecting you, dear boy.' She rang off.

The telephone rang again at once.

'Hullo? Stafford? Eric Pugh here. Heard you were back from Malaya – what about dining tonight?'

'Like to very much.'

'Good – Limpits Club – eight-fifteen?'

Mrs Worrit panted into the room as Sir Stafford replaced the receiver.

'A gentleman downstairs wanting to see you, sir,' she said. 'At least I mean, I suppose he's that. Anyway he said he was sure you wouldn't mind.'

'What's his name?'

'Horsham, sir, like the place on the way to Brighton.'

'Horsham.' Sir Stafford Nye was a little surprised.

He went out of his bedroom, down a half flight of stairs that led to the big sitting-room on the lower floor. Mrs Worrit had made no mistake. Horsham it was, looking as he had looked half an hour ago, stalwart, trustworthy, cleft chin, rubicund cheeks, bushy grey moustache and a general air of imperturbability.

'Hope you don't mind,' he said agreeably, rising to his feet.

'Hope I don't mind what?' said Sir Stafford Nye.

'Seeing me again so soon. We met in the passage outside Mr Gordon Chetwynd's door – if you remember?'

'No objections at all,' said Sir Stafford Nye.

He pushed a cigarette-box along the table.

'Sit down. Something forgotten, something left unsaid?'

'Very nice man, Mr Chetwynd,' said Horsham. 'We've got him quietened down, I think. He and Colonel Munro. They're a bit upset about it all, you know. About you, I mean.'

'Really?'

Sit Stafford Nye sat down too. He smiled, he smoked, and he looked thoughtfully at Henry Horsham. 'And where do we go from here?' he asked.

'I was just wondering if I might ask, without undue curiosity, where you're going from here?'

'Delighted to tell you,' said Sir Stafford Nye. 'I'm going to stay with an aunt of mine, Lady Matilda Cleckheaton. I'll give you the address if you like.'

'I know it,' said Henry Horsham. 'Well, I expect that's a very good idea. She'll be glad to see you've come home safely all right. Might have been a near thing, mightn't it?'

'Is that what Colonel Munro thinks and Mr Chetwynd?'

'Well, you know what it is, sir,' said Horsham. 'You know well enough. They're always in a state, gentlemen in that department. They're not sure whether they trust you or not.'

'Trust me?' said Sir Stafford Nye in an offended voice. 'What do you mean by that, Mr Horsham?'

Mr Horsham was not taken aback. He merely grinned.

'You see,' he said, 'you've got a reputation for not taking things seriously.'

'Oh. I thought you meant I was a fellow traveller or a convert to the wrong side. Something of that kind.'

'Oh no, sir, they just don't think you're serious. They think you like having a bit of a joke now and again.'

'One cannot go entirely through life taking oneself and other people seriously,' said Sir Stafford Nye, disapprovingly.

'No. But you took a pretty good risk, as I've said before, didn't you?'

'I wonder if I know in the least what you are talking about.'

'I'll tell you. Things go wrong, sir, sometimes, and they don't always go wrong because people have made them go wrong. What you might call the Almighty takes a hand, or the other gentleman – the one with the tail, I mean.'

Sir Stafford Nye was slightly diverted.

'Are you referring to fog at Geneva?' he said.

'Exactly, sir. There was fog at Geneva and that upset people's plans. Somebody was in a nasty hole.'

'Tell me all about it,' said Sir Stafford Nye. 'I really would like to know.'

'Well, a passenger was missing when that plane of yours left Frankfurt yesterday. You'd drunk your beer and you were sitting in a corner snoring nicely and comfortably by yourself. One passenger didn't report and they called her and they called her again. In the end, presumably, the plane left without her.'

'Ah. And what had happened to her?'

'It would be interesting to know. In any case, your passport arrived at Heathrow even if you didn't.'

'And where is it now? Am I supposed to have got it?'

'No. I don't think so. That would be rather too quick work. Good reliable stuff, that dope. Just right, if I may say so. It put you out and it didn't produce any particularly bad effects.'

'It gave me a very nasty hangover,' said Sir Stafford.

'Ah well, you can't avoid that. Not in the circumstances.'

'What would have happened,' Sir Stafford asked, 'since you

seem to know all about everything, if I had refused to accept the proposition that may – I will only say may – have been put up to me?'

'It's quite possible that it would have been curtains for Mary Ann.'

'Mary Ann? Who's Mary Ann?'

'Miss Daphne Theodofanous.'

'That's the name I do seem to have heard – being summoned as a missing traveller?'

'Yes, that's the name she was travelling under. We call her Mary Ann.'

'Who is she – just as a matter of interest?'

'In her own line she's more or less the tops.'

'And what is her line? Is she ours or is she theirs, if you know who "theirs" is? I must say I find a little difficulty myself when making my mind up about that.'

'Yes, it's not so easy, is it? What with the Chinese and the Russkies and the rather queer crowd that's behind all the student troubles and the New Mafia and the rather odd lot in South America. And the nice little nest of financiers who seem to have got something funny up their sleeves. Yes, it's not easy to say.'

'Mary Ann,' said Sir Stafford Nye thoughtfully. 'It seems a curious name to have for her if her real one is Daphne Theodofanous.'

'Well, her mother's Greek, her father was an Englishman, and her grandfather was an Austrian subject.'

'What would have happened if I hadn't made her a – loan of a certain garment?'

'She might have been killed.'

'Come, come. Not really?'

'We're worried about the airport at Heathrow. Things have happened there lately, things that need a bit of explaining. If the plane had gone via Geneva as planned, it would have been all right. She'd have had full protection all arranged. But this other way – there wouldn't have been time to arrange anything and you don't know who's who always, nowadays. Everyone's playing a double game or a treble or a quadruple one.'

'You alarm me,' said Sir Stafford Nye. 'But she's all right, is she? Is that what you're telling me?'

'I hope she's all right. We haven't heard anything to the contrary.'

'If it's any help to you,' said Sir Stafford Nye, 'somebody called here this morning while I was out talking to my little pals in Whitehall. He represented that I telephoned a firm of cleaners and he removed the suit that I wore yesterday, and also another suit. Of course it may have been merely that he took a fancy to the other suit, or he may have made a practice of collecting various gentlemen's suitings who have recently returned from abroad. Or – well, perhaps you've got an "or" to add?'

'He might have been looking for something.'

'Yes, I think he was. Somebody's been looking for something. All very nice and tidily arranged again. Not the way I left it. All right, he was looking for something. What was he looking for?'

'I'm not sure myself,' said Horsham, slowly. 'I wish I was. There's something going on – somewhere. There are bits of it sticking out, you know, like a badly done up parcel. You get a peep here and a peep there. One moment you think it's going on at the Bayreuth Festival and the next minute you think it's tucking out of a South American estancia and then you get a bit of a lead in the USA. There's a lot of nasty business going on in different places, working up to something. Maybe politics, maybe something quite different from politics. It's probably money.' He added: 'You know Mr Robinson, don't you? Or rather Mr Robinson knows you, I think he said.'

'Robinson?' Sir Stafford Nye considered. 'Robinson. Nice English name.' He looked across to Horsham. 'Large, yellow face?' he said. 'Fat? Finger in financial pies generally?' He asked: 'Is he, too, on the side of the angels – is that what you're telling me?'

'I don't know about angels,' said Henry Horsham. 'He's

38

pulled us out of a hole in this country more than once. People like Mr Chetwynd don't go for him much. Think he's too expensive, I suppose. Inclined to be a mean man, Mr Chetwynd. A great one for making enemies in the wrong place.'

'One used to say "Poor but honest",' said Sir Stafford Nye thoughtfully. 'I take it that you would put it differently. You would describe our Mr Robinson as expensive but honest. Or shall we put it, honest but expensive.' He sighed. 'I wish you could tell me what all this is about,' he said plaintively. 'Here I seem to be mixed up in something and no idea what it is.' He looked at Henry Horsham hopefully, but Horsham shook his head.

'None of us knows. Not exactly,' he said.

'What am I supposed to have got hidden here that someone comes fiddling and looking for?'

'Frankly, I haven't the least idea, Sir Stafford.'

'Well, that's a pity because I haven't either.'

'As far as *you* know you haven't got anything. Nobody gave you anything to keep, to take anywhere, to look after?'

'Nothing whatsoever. If you mean Mary Ann, she said she wanted her life saved, that's all.'

'And unless there's a paragraph in the evening papers, you *have* saved her life.'

'It seems rather the end of the chapter, doesn't it? A pity. My curiosity is rising. I find I want to know very much what's going to happen next. All you people seem very pessimistic.'

'Frankly, we are. Things are going badly in this country. Can you wonder?'

'I know what you mean. I sometimes wonder myself –'

CHAPTER 4

Dinner With Eric

'Do you mind if I tell you something, old man?' said Eric Pugh.

Sir Stafford Nye looked at him. He had known Eric Pugh for a good many years. They had not been close friends. Old Eric, or so Sir Stafford thought, was rather a boring friend. He was, on the other hand, faithful. And he was the type of man who, though not amusing, had a knack of knowing things. People said things to him and he remembered what they said and stored them up. Sometimes he could push out a useful bit of information.

'Come back from that Malay Conference, haven't you?'

'Yes,' said Sir Stafford.

'Anything particular turn up there?'

'Just the usual,' said Sir Stafford.

'Oh. I wondered if something had – well, you know what I mean. Anything had occurred to put the cat among the pigeons.'

'What, at the Conference? No, just painfully predictable. Everyone said just what you thought they'd say only they said it unfortunately at rather greater length than you could have imagined possible. I don't know why I go on these things.'

Eric Pugh made a rather tedious remark or two as to what the Chinese were really up to.

'I don't think they're really up to anything,' said Sir Stafford. 'All the usual rumours, you know, about the diseases poor old Mao has got and who's intriguing against him and why.'

'And what about the Arab-Israeli business?'

'That's proceeding according to plan also. Their plan, that is to say. And anyway, what's that got to do with Malaya?'

'Well, I didn't really mean so much Malaya.'

'You're looking rather like the Mock Turtle,' said Sir

Stafford Nye. ' "Soup of the evening, beautiful soup."
Wherefore this gloom?'

'Well, I just wondered if you'd – you'll forgive me, won't
you? – I mean you haven't done anything to blot your
copybook, have you, in any way?'

'Me?' said Sir Stafford, looking highly surprised.

'Well, you know what you're like, Staff. You like giving
people a jolt sometimes, don't you?'

'I have behaved impeccably of late,' said Sir Stafford. 'What
have you been hearing about me?'

'I hear there was some trouble about something that
happened in a plane on your way home.'

'Oh?' Who did you hear that from?'

'Well, you know, I saw old Cartison.'

'Terrible old bore. Always imagining things that haven't
happened.'

'Yes, I know. I know he is like that. But he was just saying
that somebody or other – Winterton, at least – seemed to think
you'd been up to something.'

'Up to something? I wish I had,' said Sir Stafford Nye.

'There's some espionage racket going on somewhere and he
got a bit worried about certain people.'

'What do they think I am – another Philby, something of
that kind?'

'You know you're very unwise sometimes in the things you
say, the things you make jokes about.'

'It's very hard to resist sometimes,' his friend told him. 'All
these politicians and diplomats and the rest of them. They're so
bloody solemn. You'd like to give them a bit of a stir up now
and again.'

'Your sense of fun is very distorted, my boy. It really is. I
worry about you sometimes. They wanted to ask you some
questions about something that happened on the flight back
and they seem to think that you didn't, well – that perhaps you
didn't exactly speak the truth about it all.'

'Ah, that's what they think, is it? Interesting. I think I must
work that up a bit.'

41

'Now don't do anything rash.'

'I must have my moments of fun sometimes.'

'Look here, old fellow, you don't want to go and ruin your career just by indulging your sense of humour.'

'I am quickly coming to the conclusion that there is nothing so boring as having a career.'

'I know, I know. You are always inclined to take that point of view, and you haven't got on as far as you ought to have, you know. You were in the running for Vienna at one time. I don't like to see you muck up things.'

'I am behaving with the utmost sobriety and virtue, I assure you,' said Sir Stafford Nye. He added, 'Cheer up, Eric. You're a good friend, but really, I'm not guilty of fun and games.'

Eric shook his head doubtfully.

It was a fine evening. Sir Stafford walked home across Green Park. As he crossed the road in Birdcage Walk, a car leaping down the street missed him by a few inches. Sir Stafford was an athletic man. His leap took him safely on to the pavement. The car disappeared down the street. He wondered. Just for a moment he could have sworn that that car had deliberately tried to run him down. An interesting thought. First his flat had been searched, and now he himself might have been marked down. Probably a mere coincidence. And yet, in the course of his life, some of which had been spent in wild neighbourhoods and places, Sir Stafford Nye had come in contact with danger. He knew, as it were, the touch and feel and smell of danger. He felt it now. Someone, somewhere was gunning for him. But why? For what reason? As far as he knew, he had not stuck his neck out in any way. He wondered.

He let himself into his flat and picked up the mail that lay on the floor inside. Nothing much. A couple of bills and copy of *Lifeboat* periodical. He threw the bills on to his desk and put a finger through the wrapper of *Lifeboat*. It was a cause to which he occasionally contributed. He turned the pages without much attention because he was still absorbed in what he was thinking. The he stopped the action of his fingers abruptly. Something was taped between two of the pages. Taped with

42

adhesive tape. He looked at it closely. It was his passport returned to him unexpectedly in this fashion. He tore it free and looked at it. The last stamp on it was the arrival stamp at Heathrow the day before. She had used his passport, getting back here safely, and had chosen this way to return it to him. Where was she now? He would like to know.

He wondered if he would ever see her again. Who was she? Where had she gone, and why? It was like waiting for the second act of a play. Indeed, he felt the first act had hardly been played yet. What had he seen? An old-fashioned curtain-raiser, perhaps. A girl who had ridiculously wanted to dress herself up and pass herself off as of the male sex, who had passed the passport control of Heathrow without attracting suspicion of any kind to herself and who had now disappeared through that gateway into London. No, he would probably never see her again. It annoyed him. But why, he thought, why do I want to? She wasn't particularly attractive, she wasn't anything. No, that wasn't quite true. She was something, or someone, or she could not have induced him, with no particular persuasion, with no overt sex stimulation, nothing except a plain demand for help, to do what she wanted. A demand from one human being to another human being because, or so she had intimated, not precisely in words, but nevertheless it was what she *had* intimated, she knew people and she recognized in him a man who was willing to take a risk to help another human being. And he had taken a risk, too, thought Sir Stafford Nye. She could have put anything in that beer glass of his. He could have been found, if she had so willed it, found as a dead body in a seat tucked away in the corner of a departure lounge in an airport. And if she had, as no doubt she must have had, a knowledgeable recourse to drugs, his death might have been passed off as an attack of heart trouble due to altitude or difficult pressurizing – something or other like that. Oh well, why think about it? He wasn't likely to see her again and he was annoyed.

Yes, he was annoyed, and he didn't like being annoyed. He considered the matter for some minutes. Then he wrote out an

43

advertisement, to be repeated three times. '*Passenger to Frankfurt. November 3rd. Please communicate with fellow traveller to London.*' No more than that. Either she would or she wouldn't. If it ever came to her eyes she would know by whom that advertisement had been inserted. She had had his passport, she knew his name. She could look him up. He might hear from her. He might not. Probably not. If not, the curtain-raiser would remain a curtain-raiser, a silly little play that received late-comers to the theatre and diverted them until the real business of the evening began. Very useful in pre-war times. In all probability, though, he would not hear from her again and one of the reasons might be that she might have accomplished whatever it was she had come to do in London, and have now left the country once more, flying abroad to Geneva, or the Middle East, or to Russia or to China or to South America, or to the United States. And why, thought Sir Stafford, do I include South America? There must be a reason. She had not mentioned South America. Nobody had mentioned South America. Except Horsham, that was true. And even Horsham had only mentioned South America among a lot of other mentions.

On the following morning as he walked slowly homeward, after handing in his advertisement, along the pathway across St James's Park his eye picked out, half unseeing, the autumn flowers. The chrysanthemums looking by now stiff and leggy with their button tops of gold and bronze. Their smell came to him faintly, a rather goatlike smell, he had always thought, a smell that reminded him of hillsides in Greece. He must remember to keep his eye on the Personal Column. Not yet. Two or three days at least would have to pass before his own advertisement was put in and before there had been time for anyone to put in one in answer. He must not miss it if there was an answer because, after all, it was irritating not to know – not to have any idea what all this was about.

He tried to recall not the girl at the airport but his sister Pamela's face. A long time since her death. He remembered her. Of course he remembered her, but he could not somehow

44

picture her face. It irritated him not to be able to do so. He had paused just when he was about to cross one of the roads. There was no traffic except for a car jigging slowly along with the solemn demeanour of a bored dowager. An elderly car, he thought. An old-fashioned Daimler limousine. He shook his shoulders. Why stand here in this idiotic way, lost in thought?

He took an abrupt step to cross the road and suddenly with surprising vigour the dowager limousine, as he had thought of it in his mind, accelerated. Accelerated with a sudden astonishing speed. It bore down on him with such swiftness that he only just had time to leap across on to the opposite pavement. It disappeared with a flash, turning round the curve of the road further on.

'I wonder,' said Sir Stafford to himself. 'Now I wonder. Could it be that there *is* someone that doesn't like me? Someone following me, perhaps, watching me take my way home, waiting for an opportunity?'

Colonel Pikeaway, his bulk sprawled out in his chair in the small room in Bloomsbury where he sat from ten to five with a short interval for lunch, was surrounded as usual by an atmosphere of thick cigar smoke; with his eyes closed, only an occasional blink showed that he was awake and not asleep. He seldom raised his head. Somebody had said that he looked like a cross between an ancient Buddha and a large blue frog, with perhaps, as some impudent youngster had added, just a touch of a bar sinister from a hippopotamus in his ancestry.

The gentle buzz of the intercom on his desk roused him. He blinked three times and opened his eyes. He stretched forth a rather weary-looking hand and picked up the receiver.

'Well?' he said.

His secretary's voice spoke.

'The Minister is here waiting to see you.'

'Is he now?' said Colonel Pikeaway. 'And what Minister is that? The Baptist minister from the church round the corner?'

'Oh no, Colonel Pikeaway, it's Sir George Packham.'

'Pity,' said Colonel Pikeaway, breathing asthmatically.

'Great pity. The Reverend McGill is far more amusing. There's a splendid touch of hell fire about him.'

'Shall I bring him in, Colonel Pikeaway?'

'I suppose he will expect to be brought in at once. Under Secretaries are far more touchy than Secretaries of State,' said Colonel Pikeaway gloomily. 'All these Ministers insist on coming in and having kittens all over the place.'

Sir George Packham was shown in. He coughed and wheezed. Most people did. The windows of the small room were tightly closed. Colonel Pikeaway reclined in his chair, completely smothered in cigar ash. The atmosphere was almost unbearable and the room was known in official circles as the 'small cat-house'.

'Ah, my dear fellow,' said Sir George, speaking briskly and cheerfully in a way that did not match his ascetic and sad appearance. 'Quite a long time since we've met, I think.'

'Sit down, sit down do,' said Pikeaway. 'Have a cigar?'

Sir George shuddered slightly.

'No, thank you,' he said, 'no, thanks very much.'

He looked hard at the windows. Colonel Pikeaway did not take the hint. Sir George cleared his throat and coughed again before saying:

'Er – I believe Horsham has been to see you.'

'Yes, Horsham's been and said his piece,' said Colonel Pikeaway, slowly allowing his eyes to close again.

'I thought it was the best way. I mean, that he should call upon you here. It's most important that things shouldn't get round anywhere.'

'Ah,' said Colonel Pikeaway, 'but they will, won't they?'

'I beg your pardon?'

'They will,' said Colonel Pikeaway.

'I don't know how much you – er – well, know about this last business.'

'We know everything here,' said Colonel Pikeaway. 'That's what we're for.'

'Oh – oh yes, yes certainly. About Sir S.N. – you know who I mean?'

'Recently a passenger from Frankfurt,' said Colonel Pikeaway.

'Most extraordinary business. Most extraordinary. One wonders – one really does not know, one can't begin to imagine ...'

Colonel Pikeaway listened kindly.

'What is one to think?' pursued Sir George. 'Do you know him personally?'

'I've come across him once or twice,' said Colonel Pikeaway.

'One really cannot help wondering –'

Colonel Pikeaway subdued a yawn with some difficulty. He was rather tired of Sir George's thinking, wondering, and imagining. He had a poor opinion anyway of Sir George's process of thought. A cautious man, a man who could be relied upon to run his department in a cautious manner. Not a man of scintillating intellect. Perhaps, thought Colonel Pikeaway, all the better for that. At any rate, those who think and wonder and are not quite sure are reasonably safe in the place where God and the electors have put them.

'One cannot quite forget,' continued Sir George, 'the disillusionment we have suffered in the past.'

Colonel Pikeaway smiled kindly.

'Charleston, Conway and Courtfold,' he said. 'Fully trusted, vetted and approved of. All beginning with C, all crooked as sin.'

'Sometimes I wonder if we can trust anyone,' said Sir George unhappily.

'That's easy,' said Colonel Pikeaway, 'you can't.'

'Now take Stafford Nye,' said Sir George. 'Good family, excellent family, knew his father, his grandfather.'

'Often a slip-up in the third generation,' said Colonel Pikeaway.

The remark did not help Sir George.

'I cannot help doubting – I mean, sometimes he doesn't really seem serious.'

'Took my two nieces to see the châteaux of the Loire when I was a young man,' said Colonel Pikeaway unexpectedly.

47

'Man fishing on the bank. I had my fishing-rod with me, too. He said to me, "*Vous n'êtes pas un pêcheur sérieux. Vous avez des femmes avec vous.*"'

'You mean you think Sir Stafford –?'

'No, no, never been mixed up with women much. Irony's his trouble. Likes surprising people. He can't help liking to score off people.'

'Well, that's not very satisfactory, is it?'

'Why not?' said Colonel Pikeaway. 'Liking a private joke is much better than having some deal with a defector.'

'If one could feel that he was really sound. What would you say – your personal opinion?'

'Sound as a bell,' said Colonel Pikeaway. 'If a bell is sound. It makes a sound, but that's different, isn't it?' He smiled kindly. 'Shouldn't worry, if I were you,' he said.

Sir Stafford Nye pushed aside his cup of coffee. He picked up the newspaper, glancing over the headlines, then he turned it carefully to the page which gave Personal advertisements. He'd looked down that particular column for seven days now. It was disappointing but not surprising. Why on earth should he expect to find an answer? His eye went slowly down miscellaneous peculiarities which had always made that particular page rather fascinating in his eyes. They were not so strictly personal. Half of them or even more than half were disguised advertisements or offers of things for sale or wanted for sale. They should perhaps have been put under a different heading but they had found their way here considering that they were more likely to catch the eye that way. They included one or two of the hopeful variety.

'Young man who objects to hard work and who would like an easy life would be glad to undertake a job that would suit him.'

'Girl wants to travel to Cambodia. Refuses to look after children.'

'Firearm used at Waterloo. What offers.'

'Glorious fun-fur coat. Must be sold immediately. Owner going abroad.'

'Do you know Jenny Capstan? Her cakes are superb. Come to 14 Lizzard Street, S.W.3.'

For a moment Stafford Nye's finger came to a stop. Jenny Capstan. He liked the name. Was there any Lizzard Street? He supposed so. He had never heard of it. With a sigh, the finger went down the column and almost at once was arrested once more.

'Passenger from Frankfurt, Thursday Nov. 11, Hungerford Bridge 7.20.'

Thursday, November 11th. That was – yes, that was today. Sir Stafford Nye leaned back in his chair and drank more coffee. He was excited, stimulated. Hungerford. Hungerford Bridge. He got up and went into the kitchenette. Mrs Worrit was cutting potatoes into strips and throwing them into a large bowl of water. She looked up with some slight surprise.

'Anything you want, sir?'

'Yes,' said Sir Stafford Nye. 'If anyone said Hungerford Bridge to you, where would you go?'

'Where should I go?' Mrs Worrit considered. 'You mean if I wanted to go, do you?'

'We can proceed on that assumption.'

'Well, then, I suppose I'd go to Hungerford Bridge, wouldn't I?'

'You mean you would go to Hungerford in Berkshire?'

'Where is that?' said Mrs Worrit.

'Eight miles beyond Newbury.'

'I've heard of Newbury. My old man backed a horse there last year. Did well, too.'

'So you'd go to Hungerford near Newbury?'

'No, of course I wouldn't,' said Mrs Worrit. 'Go all that way – what for? I'd go to Hungerford Bridge, of course.'

'You mean –?'

'Well, it's near Charing Cross. You know where it is. Over the Thames.'

'Yes,' said Sir Stafford Nye. 'Yes, I do know where it is quite well. Thank you, Mrs Worrit.'

It had been, he felt, rather like tossing a penny heads or tails. An advertisement in a morning paper in London meant Hungerford Railway Bridge in London. Presumably therefore that is what the advertiser meant, although about this particular advertiser Sir Stafford Nye was not at all sure. Her ideas, from the brief experience he had had of her, were original ideas. They were not the normal responses to be expected. But still, what else could one do. Besides, there were probably other Hungerfords, and possibly they would also have bridges, in various parts of England. But today, well, today he would see.

It was a cold windy evening with occasional bursts of thin misty rain. Sir Stafford Nye turned up the collar of his mackintosh and plodded on. It was not the first time he had gone across Hungerford Bridge, but it had never seemed to him a walk to take for pleasure. Beneath him was the river and crossing the bridge were large quantities of hurrying figures like himself. Their mackintoshes pulled round them, their hats pulled down and on the part of one and all of them an earnest desire to get home and out of the wind and rain as soon as possible. It would be, thought Sir Stafford Nye, very difficult to recognize anybody in this scurrying crowd. 7.20. Not a good moment to choose for a rendezvous of any kind. Perhaps it was Hungerford Bridge in Berkshire. Anyway, it seemed very odd.

He plodded on. He kept an even pace, not overtaking those ahead of him, pushing past those coming the opposite way. He went fast enough not to be overtaken by the others behind him, though it would be possible for them to do so if they wanted to. A joke, perhaps, thought Stafford Nye. Not quite his kind of joke, but someone else's.

And yet – not her brand of humour either, he would have thought. Hurrying figures passed him again, pushing him slightly aside. A woman in a mackintosh was coming along, walking heavily. She collided with him, slipped, dropped to her knees. He assisted her up.

50

'All right?'

'Yes, thanks.'

She hurried on, but as she passed him, her wet hand, by which he had held her as he pulled her to her feet, slipped something into the palm of his hand, closing the fingers over it. Then she was gone, vanishing behind him, mingling with the crowd. Stafford Nye went on. He couldn't overtake her. She did not wish to be overtaken, either. He hurried on and his hand held something firmly. And so, at long last it seemed, he came to the end of the bridge on the Surrey side.

A few minutes later he had turned into a small café and sat there behind a table, ordering coffee. Then he looked at what was in his hand. It was a very thin oilskin envelope. Inside it was a cheap quality white envelope. That too he opened. What was inside surprised him. It was a ticket.

A ticket for the Festival Hall for the following evening.

CHAPTER 5

Wagnerian Motif

Sir Stafford Nye adjusted himself more comfortably in his seat and listened to the persistent hammering of the Nibelungen, with which the programme began.

Though he enjoyed Wagnerian opera, *Siegfried* was by no means his favourite of the operas composing the Ring. *Rheingold* and *Götterdämmerung* were his two preferences. The music of the young Siegfried, listening to the songs of the birds, had always for some strange reason irritated him instead of filling him with melodic satisfaction. It might have been because he went to a performance in Munich in his young days which had displayed a magnificent tenor of unfortunately over-magnificent proportions, and he had been too young to divorce

51

the joy of music from the visual joy of seeing a young Siegfried that looked even passably young. The fact of an outsized tenor rolling about on the ground in an access of boyishness had revolted him. He was also not particularly fond of birds and forest murmurs. No, give him the Rhine Maidens every time, although in Munich even the Rhine Maidens in those days had been of fairly solid proportions. But that mattered less. Carried away by the melodic flow of water and the joyous impersonal song, he had not allowed visual appreciation to matter.

From time to time he looked about him casually. He had taken his seat fairly early. It was a full house, as it usually was. The intermission came. Sir Stafford rose and looked about him. The seat beside his had remained empty. Someone who was supposed to have arrived had not arrived. Was that the answer, or was it merely a case of being excluded because someone had arrived late, which practice still held on the occasions when Wagnerian music was listened to.

He went out, strolled about, drank a cup of coffee, smoked a cigarette, and returned when the summons came. This time, as he drew near, he saw that the seat next to his was filled. Immediately his excitement returned. He regained his seat and sat down. Yes, it was the woman of the Frankfurt Air Lounge. She did not look at him, she was looking straight ahead. Her face in profile was as clean-cut and pure as he remembered it. Her head turned slightly, and her eyes passed over him but without recognition. So intent was that non-recognition that it was as good as a word spoken. This was a meeting that was not to be acknowledged. Not now, at any event. The lights began to dim. The woman beside him turned.

'Excuse me, could I look at your programme? I have dropped mine, I'm afraid, coming to my seat.'

'Of course,' he said.

He handed over the programme and she took it from him. She opened it, studied the items. The lights went lower. The second half of the programme began. It started with the overture to *Lohengrin*. At the end of it she handed back the programme to him with a few words of thanks.

'Thank you so much. It was very kind of you.'

The next item was the Siegfried forest murmur music. He consulted the programme she had returned to him. It was then that he noticed something faintly pencilled at the foot of a page. He did not attempt to read it now. Indeed, the light would have not been sufficient. He merely closed the programme and held it. He had not, he was quite sure, written anything there himself. Not, that is, in his own programme. She had, he thought, had her own programme ready, folded perhaps in her handbag and had already written some message ready to pass to him. Altogether, it seemed to him, there was still that atmosphere of secrecy, of danger. The meeting on Hungerford Bridge and the envelope with the ticket forced into his hand. And now the silent woman who sat beside him. He glanced at her once or twice with the quick, careless glance that one gives to a stranger sitting next to one. She lolled back in her seat; her high-necked dress was of dull black crêpe, an antique torque of gold encircled her neck. Her dark hair was cropped closely and shaped to her head. She did not glance at him or return any look. He wondered. Was there someone in the seats of the Festival Hall watching her – or watching him? Noting whether they looked or spoke to each other? Presumably there must be, or there must be at least the possibility of such a thing. She had answered his appeal in the newspaper advertisement. Let that be enough for him. His curiosity was unimpaired, but he did at least know now that Daphne Theodofanous – alias Mary Ann – was here in London. There were possibilities in the future of his learning more of what was afoot. But the plan of campaign must be left to her. He must follow her lead. As he had obeyed her in the airport, so he would obey her now and – let him admit it – life had become suddenly more interesting. This was better than the boring conferences of his political life. Had a car really tried to run him down the other night? He thought it had. Two attempts – not only one. It was easy enough to imagine that one was the target of assault, people drove so recklessly nowadays that you could easily fancy malice afore-thought when it was not so. He folded his programme, did not

53

look at it again. The music came to its end. The woman next to him spoke. She did not turn her head or appear to speak to him, but she spoke aloud, with a little sigh between the words as though she was communing with herself or possibly to her neighbour on the other side.

'The young Siegfried,' she said, and sighed again.

The programme ended with the March from *Die Meistersinger*. After enthusiastic applause, people began to leave their seats. He waited to see if she would give him any lead, but she did not. She gathered up her wrap, moved out of the row of chairs, and with a slightly accelerated step, moved along with other people and disappeared in the crowd.

Stafford Nye regained his car and drove home. Arrived there, he spread out the Festival Hall programme on his desk and examined it carefully, after putting the coffee to percolate.

The programme was disappointing to say the least of it. There did not appear to be any message inside. Only on one page above the list of the items, were the pencil marks that he had vaguely observed. But they were not words or letters or even figures. They appeared to be merely a musical notation. It was as though someone had scribbled a phrase of music with a somewhat inadequate pencil. For a moment it occurred to Stafford Nye there might perhaps be a secret message he could bring out by applying heat. Rather gingerly, and in a way rather ashamed of his melodramatic fancy, he held it towards the bar of the electric fire but nothing resulted. With a sigh he tossed the programme back on to the table. But he felt justifiably annoyed. All this rigmarole, a rendezvous on a windy and rainy bridge overlooking the river! Sitting through a concert by the side of a woman of whom he yearned to ask at least a dozen questions – and at the end of it? Nothing! No further on. Still, she *had* met him. But why? If she didn't want to speak to him, to make further arrangements with him, why had she come at all?

His eyes passed idly across the room to his bookcase which he reserved for various thrillers, works of detective fiction and an occasional volume of science fiction; he shook his head.

Fiction, he thought, was infinitely superior to real life. Dead bodies, mysterious telephone calls, beautiful foreign spies in profusion! However, this particular elusive lady might not have done with him yet. Next time, he thought, he would make some arrangements of his own. Two could play at the game that she was playing.

He pushed aside the programme and drank another cup of coffee and went to the window. He had the programme still in his hand. As he looked out towards the street below his eyes fell back again on the open programme in his hand and he hummed to himself, almost unconsciously. He had a good ear for music and he could hum the notes that were scrawled there quite easily. Vaguely they sounded familiar as he hummed them. He increased his voice a little. What was it now? Tum, tum, tum tum ti-tum. Tum. Yes, definitely familiar.

He started opening his letters.

They were mostly uninteresting. A couple of invitations, one from the American Embassy, one from Lady Athelhampton, a Charity Variety performance which Royalty would attend and for which it was suggested five guineas would not be an exorbitant fee to obtain a seat. He threw them aside lightly. He doubted very much whether he wished to accept any of them. He decided that instead of remaining in London he would without more ado go and see his Aunt Matilda, as he had promised. He was fond of his Aunt Matilda though he did not visit her very often. She lived in a rehabilitated apartment consisting of a series of rooms in one wing of a large Georgian manor house in the country which she had inherited from his grandfather. She had a large, beautifully proportioned sitting-room, a small oval dining-room, a new kitchen made from the old housekeeper's room, two bedrooms for guests, a large comfortable bedroom for herself with an adjoining bathroom, and adequate quarters for a patient companion who shared her daily life. The remains of a faithful domestic staff were well provided for and housed. The rest of the house remained under dust sheets with periodical cleaning. Stafford Nye was fond of the place, having spent holidays there as a boy. It had been a gay house then. His eldest uncle had lived there with his wife and their two children. Yes, it had been pleasant there then. There had been money and a sufficient staff to run it. He had not specially noticed in those days the portraits and pictures. There had been large-sized examples of Victorian art occupying pride of place – overcrowding the walls, but there had been other masters of an older age. Yes, there had been some good portraits there. A Raeburn, two Lawrences, a Gainsborough, a Lely, two rather dubious Vandykes. A couple of Turners, too. Some of them had had to be sold to provide the family with money. He still enjoyed when visiting there strolling about and studying the family pictures.

His Aunt Matilda was a great chatterbox but she always enjoyed his visits. He was fond of her in a desultory way, but he was not quite sure why it was that he had suddenly wanted to visit her now. And what it was that had brought family portraits into his mind? Could it have been because there was a portrait of his sister Pamela by one of the leading artists of the day twenty years ago. He would like to see that portrait of Pamela and look at it more closely. See how close the resemblance had been between the stranger who had disrupted his life in this really outrageous fashion and his sister.

He picked up the Festival Hall programme again with some irritation and began to hum the pencilled notes. Tum, tum, ti tum – Then it came to him and he knew what it was. It was the Siegfried motif. Siegfried's Horn. The Young Siegfried motif. That was what the woman had said last night. Not apparently to him, not apparently to anybody. But it had been the message, a message that would have meant nothing to anyone around since it would have seemed to refer to the music that had just been played. And the motif had been written on his programme also in musical terms. The Young Siegfried. It must have meant something. Well, perhaps further enlightenment would come. The Young Siegfried. What the hell *did* that mean? Why and how and when and what? Ridiculous! All those questioning words.

He rang the telephone and obtained Aunt Matilda's number.

'But of course, Staffy dear, it will be lovely to have you. Take the four-thirty train. It still runs, you know, but it gets here an hour and a half later. And it leaves Paddington later – five-fifteen. That's what they mean by improving the railways, I suppose. Stops at several most absurd stations on the way. All right. Horace will meet you at King's Marston.'

'He's still there then?'

'Of course he's still there.'

'I suppose he is,' said Sir Stafford Nye.

Horace, once a groom, then a coachman, had survived as a chauffeur, and apparently was still surviving. 'He must be at least eighty,' said Sir Stafford. He smiled to himself.

CHAPTER 6

Portrait Of A Lady

'You look very nice and brown, dear,' said Aunt Matilda, surveying him appreciatively. 'That's Malaya, I suppose. If it *was* Malaya you went to? Or was it Siam or Thailand? They change the names of all these places and really it makes it very difficult. Anyway, it wasn't Vietnam, was it? You know, I don't like the sound of Vietnam *at all*. It's all very confusing, North Vietnam and South Vietnam and the Viet-Cong and the Viet – whatever the other thing is and all wanting to fight each other and nobody wanting to stop. They won't go to Paris or wherever it is and sit round tables and talk sensibly. Don't you think really, dear – I've been thinking it over and I thought it would be a very nice solution – couldn't you make a lot of football fields and then they could all go and fight each other there, but with less lethal weapons. Not that nasty palm burning stuff. You know. Just hit each other and punch each other and all that. They'd enjoy it, everyone would enjoy it and you could charge admission for people to go and see them do it. I do think really that we don't understand giving people the things they really want.'

'I think it's a very fine idea of yours, Aunt Matilda,' said Sir Stafford Nye as he kissed a pleasantly perfumed, pale pink wrinkled cheek. 'And how are you, my dear?'

'Well, I'm old,' said Lady Matilda Cleckheaton. 'Yes, I'm old. Of course you don't know what it is to be old. If it isn't one thing it's another. Rheumatism or arthritis or a nasty bit of asthma or a sore throat or an ankle you've turned. Always *something*, you know. Nothing very important. But there it is. Why have you come to see me, dear?'

Sir Stafford was slightly taken aback by the directness of the query.

'I usually come and see you when I return from a trip abroad.'

'You'll have to come one chair nearer,' said Aunt Matilda. 'I'm just that bit deafer since you saw me last. You look different ... Why do you look different?'

'Because I'm more sunburnt. You said so.'

'Nonsense, that's not what I mean at all. Don't tell me it's a girl at last.'

'A girl?'

'Well, I've always felt it might be one some day. The trouble is you've got too much sense of humour.'

'Now why should you think that?'

'Well, it's what people do think about you. Oh yes, they do. Your sense of humour is in the way of your career, too. You know, you're all mixed up with all these people. Diplomatic and political. What they call younger statesmen and elder statesmen and middle statesmen too. And all those different Parties. Really I think it's too silly to have too many Parties. First of all those awful, awful Labour people.' She raised her Conservative nose into the air. 'Why, when I was a girl there wasn't such a thing as a *Labour* Party. Nobody would have

58

known what you meant by it. They'd have said "nonsense". Pity it wasn't nonsense, too. And then there's the Liberals, of course, but they're terribly wet. And then there are the Tories, or the Conservatives as they call themselves again now.'

'And what's the matter with them?' asked Stafford Nye, smiling slightly.

'Too many earnest women. Makes them lack gaiety, you know.'

'Oh well, no political party goes in for gaiety much nowadays.'

'Just so,' said Aunt Matilda. 'And then of course that's where you go wrong. You want to cheer things up. You want to have a little gaiety and so you make a little gentle fun at people and of course they don't like it. They say "Ce n'est pas un garçon sérieux," like that man in the fishing.'

Sir Stafford Nye laughed. His eyes were wandering round the room.

'What are you looking at?' said Lady Matilda.

'Your pictures.'

'You don't want me to sell them, do you? Everyone seems to be selling their pictures nowadays. Old Lord Grampion, you know. He sold his Turners and he sold some of his ancestors as well. And Geoffrey Gouldman. All those lovely horses of his. By Stubbs, weren't they? Something like that. Really, the prices one gets!

'But I don't want to sell my pictures. I like them. Most of them in this room have a real interest because they're ancestors. I know nobody wants ancestors nowadays but then I'm old-fashioned. I like ancestors. My own ancestors, I mean. What are you looking at? Pamela?'

'Yes, I was. I was thinking about her the other day.'

'Astonishing how alike you two are. I mean, it's not even as though you were twins, though they say that different sex twins, even if they are twins, can't be identical, if you know what I mean.'

'So Shakespeare must have made rather a mistake over Viola and Sebastian.'

'Well, ordinary brothers and sisters can be alike, can't they? You and Pamela were always very alike – to look at, I mean.'

'Not in any other way? Don't you think we were alike in character?'

'No, not in the least. That's the funny part of it. But of course you and Pamela have what I call the family face. Not a Nye face. I mean the Baldwen-White face.'

Sir Stafford Nye had never quite been able to compete when it came down to talking on a question of genealogy with his great-aunt.

'I've always thought that you and Pamela both took after Alexa,' she went on.

'Which was Alexa?'

'Your great-great – I think one more great – grandmother. Hungarian. A Hungarian countess or baroness or something. Your great-great-grandfather fell in love with her when he was at Vienna in the Embassy. Yes. Hungarian. That's what she was. Very sporting too. They are sporting, you know, Hungarians. She rode to hounds, rode magnificently.'

'Is she in the picture gallery?'

'She's on the first landing. Just over the head of the stairs, a little to the right.'

'I must go and look at her when I go to bed.'

'Why don't you go and look at her now and then you can come back and talk about her.'

'I will if you like.' He smiled at her.

He ran out of the room and up the staircase. Yes, she had a sharp eye, old Matilda. That was the face. That was the face that he had seen and remembered. Remembered not for its likeness to himself, not even for its likeness to Pamela, but for a closer resemblance still to this picture here. A handsome girl brought home by his Ambassador great-great-great-grandfather if that was enough greats. Aunt Matilda was never satisfied with only a few. About twenty she had been. She had come here and been high-spirited and rode a horse magnificently and danced divinely and men had fallen in love with her. But she had been faithful, so it was always said, to great-great-

great-grandfather, a very steady and sober member of the Diplomatic Service. She had gone with him to foreign Embassies and returned here and had had children – three or four children, he believed. Through one of those children the inheritance of her face, her nose, the turn of her neck had been passed down to him and to his sister, Pamela. He wondered if the young woman who had doped his beer and forced him to lend her his cloak and who had depicted herself as being in danger of death unless he did what she asked, had been possibly related as a fifth or sixth cousin removed, a descendant of the woman pictured on the wall at which he looked. Well, it could be. They had been of the same nationality, perhaps. Anyway their faces had resembled each other a good deal. How upright she'd sat at the opera, how straight that profile, the thin, slightly arched aquiline nose. And the atmosphere that hung about her.

'Find it?' asked Lady Matilda, when her nephew returned to the white drawing-room, as her sitting-room was usually called. 'Interesting face, isn't it?'

'Yes, quite handsome, too.'

'It's much better to be interesting than handsome. But you haven't been in Hungary or Austria, have you? You wouldn't meet anyone like her out in Malaya? She wouldn't be sitting around a table there making little notes or correcting speeches or things like that. She was a wild creature, by all accounts. Lovely manners and all the rest of it. But wild. Wild as a wild bird. She didn't know what danger was.'

'How do you know so much about her?'

'Oh, I agree I wasn't a contemporary of hers, I wasn't born until several years after she was dead. All the same, I've always been interested in her. She was adventurous, you know. Very adventurous. Very queer stories were told about her, about things she was mixed up in.'

'And how did my great-great-great-grandfather react to that?'

'I expect it worried him to death,' said Lady Matilda. 'They say he was devoted to her, though. By the way, Staffy, did you ever read *The Prisoner of Zenda*?'

'Prisoner of Zenda? Sounds very familiar.'

'Well, of course it's familiar, it's a book.'

'Yes, yes, I realize it's a book.'

'You wouldn't know about it, I expect. After your time. But when I was a girl – that's about the first taste of romance we got. Not pop singers or Beatles. Just a romantic novel. We weren't allowed to read novels when I was young. Not in the morning anyway. You could read them in the afternoon.'

'What extraordinary rules,' said Sir Stafford. 'Why is it wrong to read novels in the morning and not in the afternoon?'

'Well, in the mornings, you see, girls were supposed to be doing something useful. You know, doing the flowers or cleaning the silver photograph frames. All the things we girls did. Doing a bit of studying with the governess – all that sort of thing. In the afternoon we were allowed to sit down and read a story book and *The Prisoner of Zenda* was usually one of the first ones that came our way.'

'A very nice, respectable story, was it? I seem to remember something about it. Perhaps I did read it. All very pure, I suppose. Not too sexy?'

'Certainly not. We didn't have sexy books. We had romance. *The Prisoner of Zenda* was very romantic. One fell in love, usually, with the hero, Rudolf Rassendyll.'

'I seem to remember that name too. Bit florid, isn't it?'

'Well, I still think it was rather a romantic name. Twelve years old, I must have been. It made me think of it, you know, your going up and looking at that portrait. Princess Flavia,' she added.

Stafford Nye was smiling at her.

'You look young and pink and very sentimental,' he said.

'Well, that's just what I'm feeling. Girls can't feel like that nowadays. They're swooning with love, or they're fainting when somebody plays the guitar or sings in a very loud voice, but they're not sentimental. But I wasn't in love with Rudolf Rassendyll. I was in love with the other one – his double.'

'Did he have a double?'

'Oh yes, a king. The King of Ruritania.'

'Ah, of course, now I know. That's where the word Ruritania comes from: one is always throwing it about. Yes, I think I did read it, you know. The King of Ruritania, and Rudolf Rassendyll was stand-in for the King and fell in love with Princess Flavia to whom the King was officially betrothed.'

Lady Matilda gave some more deep sighs.

'Yes. Rudolf Rassendyll had inherited his red hair from an ancestress, and somewhere in the book he bows to the portrait and says something about the – I can't remember the name now – the Countess Amelia or something like that from whom he inherited his looks and all the rest of it. So I looked at you and thought of you as Rudolf Rassendyll and you went out and looked at a picture of someone who might have been an ancestress of yours and saw whether she reminded you of someone. So you're mixed up in a romance of some kind, are you?'

'What on earth makes you say that?'

'Well, there aren't so many patterns in life, you know. One recognizes patterns as they come up. It's like a book on knitting. About sixty-five different fancy stitches. Well, you know a particular stitch when you see it. Your stitch, at the moment, I should say, is the romantic adventure.' She sighed. 'But you won't tell me about it, I suppose.'

'There's nothing to tell,' said Sir Stafford.

'You always were quite an accomplished liar. Well, never mind. You bring her to see me some time. That's all I'd like, before the doctors succeed in killing me with yet another type of antibiotic that they've just discovered. The different coloured pills I've had to take by this time! You wouldn't believe it.'

'I don't know why you say "she" and "her" –'

'Don't you? Oh, well, I know a she when I come across a she. There's a she somewhere dodging about in your life. What beats me is how you found her. In Malaya, at the conference table? Ambassador's daughter or minister's daughter? Good-looking secretary from the Embassy pool? No, none of it seems to fit. Ship coming home? No, you don't use ships nowadays. Plane, perhaps.'

'You are getting slightly nearer,' Sir Stafford Nye could not help saying.

'Ah!' She pounced. 'Air hostess?'

He shook his head.

'Ah well. Keep your secret. I shall find out, mind you. I've always had a good nose for things going on where you're concerned. Things generally as well. Of course I'm out of everything nowadays, but I meet my old cronies from time to time and it's quite easy, you know, to get a hint or two from them. People are worried. Everywhere – they're worried.'

'You mean there's a general kind of discontent – upset?'

'No, I didn't mean that at all. I mean the highups are worried. Our awful governments are worried. The dear old sleepy Foreign Office is worried. There are things going on, things that shouldn't be. Unrest.'

'Student unrest?'

'Oh, student unrest is just one flower on the tree. It's blossoming everywhere and in every country, or so it seems. I've got a nice girl who comes, you know, and reads the papers to me in the mornings. I can't read them properly myself. She's got a nice voice. Takes down my letters and she reads things from the papers and she's a good kind girl. She reads the things I want to know, not the things that she thinks are right for me to know. Yes, everyone's worried, as far as I can make out and this, mind you, came more or less from a very old friend of mine.'

'One of your old military cronies?'

'He's a major-general, if that's what you mean, retired a good many years ago but still in the know. Youth is what you might call the spearhead of it all. But that's not really what's so worrying. They – whoever *they* are – work through youth. Youth in every country. Youth urged on. Youth chanting slogans, slogans that sound exciting, though they don't always

64

know what they mean. So easy to start a revolution. That's natural to youth. All youth has always rebelled. You rebel, you pull down, you want the world to be different from what it is. But you're blind, too. There are bandages over the eyes of youth. They can't see where things are taking them. What's going to come next? What's in front of them? And who it is behind them, urging them on? That's what's frightening about it. You know, someone holding out the carrot to get the donkey to come along and at the same time there is someone behind the donkey urging it on with a stick.'

'You've got some extraordinary fancies.'

'They're not only fancies, my dear boy. That's what people said about Hitler. Hitler and the Hitler Youth. But it was a long careful preparation. It was a war that was worked out in detail. It was a fifth column being planted in different countries all ready for the supermen. The supermen were to be the flower of the German nation. That's what they thought and believed in passionately. Somebody else is perhaps believing something like that now. It's a creed that they'll be willing to accept – if it's offered cleverly enough.'

'Who are you talking about? Do you mean the Chinese or the Russians? What do you mean?'

'I don't know. I haven't the faintest idea. But there's something somewhere, and it's running on the same lines. Pattern again, you see. Pattern! The Russians? Bogged down by Communism, I should think they're considered old-fashioned. The Chinese? I think they've lost their way. Too much Chairman Mao, perhaps. I don't know who these people are who are doing the planning. As I said before, it's why and where and when and *who*.'

'Very interesting.'

'It's so frightening, this same idea that always recurs. History repeating itself. The young hero, the golden superman that all must follow.' She paused, then said, 'Same idea, you know. The young Siegfried.'

CHAPTER 7

Advice From Great-Aunt Matilda

Great-Aunt Matilda looked at him. She had a very sharp and shrewd eye. Stafford Nye had noticed that before. He noticed it particularly at this moment.

'So you've heard that term before,' she said. 'I see.'

'What does it mean?'

'You don't know?' She raised her eyebrows.

'Cross my heart and wish to die,' said Sir Stafford, in nursery language.

'Yes, we always used to say that, didn't we,' said Lady Matilda. 'Do you really mean what you're saying?'

'I don't know anything about it.'

'But you'd heard the term before.'

'Yes. Someone said it to me.'

'Anyone important?'

'It could be. I suppose it could be. What do you mean by "anyone important"?'

'Well, you've been involved in various Government missions lately, haven't you? You've represented this poor, miserable country as best you could, which I shouldn't wonder wasn't rather better than many others could do, sitting round a table and talking. I don't know whether anything's come of all that.'

'Probably not,' said Stafford Nye. 'After all, one isn't optimistic when one goes into these things.'

'One does one's best,' said Lady Matilda correctively.

'A very Christian principle. Nowadays if one does one's worst one often seems to get on a good deal better. What does all this mean, Aunt Matilda?'

'I don't suppose *I* know,' said his aunt.

'Well, you very often do know things.'

'Not exactly. I just pick up things here and there.'

'Yes?'

'I've got a few old friends left, you know. Friends who are in the know. Of course most of them are either practically stone deaf or half blind or a little bit gone in the top storey or unable to walk straight. But something still functions. Something, shall we say, up here.' She hit the top of her neatly arranged white head. 'There's a good deal of alarm and despondency about. More than usual. That's one of the things I've picked up.'

'Isn't there always?'

'Yes, yes, but this is a bit more than that. Active instead of passive, as you might say. For a long time, as I have noticed from the outside, and you, no doubt, from the inside, we have felt that things are in a mess. A rather bad mess. But now we've got to a point where we feel that perhaps something might have been done about the mess. There's an element of danger in it. Something is going on – something is brewing. Not just in one country. In quite a lot of countries. They've recruited a service of their own and the danger about that is that it's a service of young people. And the kind of people who will go anywhere, do anything, unfortunately believe anything, and so long as they are promised a certain amount of pulling down, wrecking, throwing spanners in the works, then they think the cause must be a good one and that the world will be a different place. They're not creative, that's the trouble – only destructive. The creative young write poems, write books, probably compose music, paint pictures just as they always have done. They'll be all right – But once people learn to love destruction for its own sake, evil leadership gets its chance.'

'You say "they" or "them". Who do you mean?'

'Wish I knew,' said Lady Matilda. 'Yes, I wish I knew. Very much indeed. If I hear anything useful, I'll tell you. Then you can do something about it.'

'Unfortunately, *I* haven't got anyone to tell, I mean to pass it on to.'

'Yes, don't pass it on to just anyone. You can't trust people. Don't pass it on to any one of those idiots in the Government, or connected with government or hoping to be participating in government after this lot runs out. Politicians don't have time to look at the world they're living in. They see the country they're living in and they see it as one vast electoral platform. That's quite enough to put on their plates for the time being. They do things which they honestly believe will make things better and then they're surprised when they don't make things better because they're not the things that people want to have. And one can't help coming to the conclusion that politicians have a feeling that they have a kind of divine right to tell lies in a good cause. It's not really so very long ago since Mr Baldwin made his famous remark – 'If I had spoken the truth, I should have lost the election.' Prime Ministers still feel like that. Now and again we have a great man, thank God. But it's rare.'

'Well, what do you suggest ought to be done?'

'Are you asking my advice? Mine? Do you know how old I am?'

'Getting on for ninety,' suggested her nephew.

'Not quite as old as that,' said Lady Matilda, slightly affronted. 'Do I look it, my dear boy?'

'No, darling. You look a nice, comfortable sixty-six.'

'That's better,' said Lady Matilda. 'Quite untrue. But better. If I get a tip of any kind from one of my dear old admirals or an old general or even possibly an air marshal – they do hear things, you know – they've got cronies still and the old boys get together and talk. And so it gets around. There's always been the grapevine and there still is a grapevine, no matter how elderly the people are. The young Siegfried. We want a clue to just what that means – I don't know if he's a person or a password or the name of a Club or a new Messiah or a Pop singer. But that term covers *something*. There's the musical motif too. I've rather forgotten my Wagnerian days.' Her aged voice croaked out a partially recognizable melody. 'Siegfried's horn call, isn't that it? Get a recorder, why don't you? Do I mean a recorder. I don't mean a record that you put on a gramophone – I mean the things that schoolchildren play. They have classes for them. Went to a talk the other day. Our vicar got it up. Quite interesting. You know, tracing the history of the recorder and the kind of recorders there were from the Elizabethan age onwards. Some big, some small, all different notes and sounds. Very interesting. Interesting hearing in two senses. The recorders themselves. Some of them give out lovely noises. And the history. Yes. Well, what was I saying?'

'You told me to get one of these instruments, I gather.'

'Yes. Get a recorder and learn to blow Siegfried's horn call on that. You're musical, you always were. You can manage that, I hope?'

'Well, it seems a very small part to play in the salvation of the world, but I dare say I could manage that.'

'And have the thing ready. Because, you see –' she tapped on the table with her spectacle case – 'you might want it to impress the wrong people some time. Might come in useful. They'd welcome you with open arms and then you might learn a bit.'

'You certainly have ideas,' said Sir Stafford admiringly.

'What else can you have when you're my age?' said his great-aunt. 'You can't get about. You can't meddle with people much, you can't do any gardening. All you *can* do is sit in your chair and have ideas. Remember that when you're forty years older.'

'One remark you made interested me.'

'Only one?' said Lady Matilda. 'That's rather poor measure considering how much I've been talking. What was it?'

'You suggested that I might be capable of impressing the wrong people with my recorder – did you mean that?'

'Well, it's one way, isn't it? The right people don't matter. But the wrong people – well, you've got to find out things, haven't you? You've got to permeate things. Rather like a death-watch beetle,' she said thoughtfully.

'So I should make significant noises in the night?'

'Well, that sort of thing, yes. We had death-watch beetle in the east wing here once. Very expensive it was to put it right. I dare say it will be just as expensive to put the world right.'

'In fact a good deal more expensive,' said Stafford Nye.

'That won't matter,' said Lady Matilda. 'People never mind

spending a great deal of money. It impresses them. It's when you want to do things economically, they won't play. We're the same people, you know. In this country, I mean. We're the same people we always were.'

'What do you mean by that?'

'We're capable of doing big things. We were good at running an empire. We weren't good at *keeping* an empire running, but then you see we didn't need an empire any more And we recognized that. Too difficult to keep up. Robbie made me see that,' she added.

'Robbie?' It was faintly familiar.

'Robbie Shoreham. Robert Shoreham. He's a very old friend of mine. Paralysed down the left side. But he can talk still and he's got a moderately good hearing-aid.'

'Besides being one of the most famous physicists in the world,' said Stafford Nye. 'So he's another of your old cronies, is he?'

'Known him since he was a boy,' said Lady Matilda. 'I suppose it surprises you that we should be friends, have a lot in common and enjoy talking together?'

'Well, I shouldn't have thought that –'

'That we had much to talk about? It's true I could never do mathematics. Fortunately, when I was a girl one didn't even try. Mathematics came easily to Robbie when he was about four years old, I believe. They say nowadays that that's quite natural. He's got plenty to talk about. He liked me always because I was frivolous and made him laugh. And I'm a good listener, too. And really, he says some very interesting things sometimes.'

'So I suppose,' said Stafford Nye drily.

'Now don't be superior. Molière married his housemaid, didn't he, and made a great success of it – if it *is* Molière I mean. If a man's frantic with brains he doesn't really want a woman who's also frantic with brains to talk to. It would be exhausting. He'd much prefer a lovely nitwit who can make him laugh. I wasn't bad-looking when I was young,' said Lady Matilda complacently. 'I know I have no academic distinctions. I'm not in the least intellectual. But Robert has always said that I've got a great deal of common sense, of intelligence.'

'You're a lovely person,' said Sir Stafford Nye. 'I enjoy coming to see you and I shall go away remembering all the things you've said to me. There are a good many more things, I expect, that you could tell me but you're obviously not going to.'

'Not until the right moment comes,' said Lady Matilda, 'but I've got your interests at heart. Let me know what you're doing from time to time. You're dining at the American Embassy, aren't you, next week?'

'How did you know that? I've been asked.'

'And you've accepted, I understand.'

'Well, it's all in the course of duty.' He looked at her curiously. 'How do you manage to be so well informed?'

'Oh, Milly told me.'

'Milly?'

'Milly Jean Cortman. The American Ambassador's wife. A most attractive creature, you know. Small and rather perfect-looking.'

'Oh, you mean Mildred Cortman.'

'She was christened Mildred but she preferred Milly Jean. I was talking to her on the telephone about some Charity Matinée or other – she's what we used to call a pocket Venus.'

'A most attractive term to use,' said Stafford Nye.

CHAPTER 8

An Embassy Dinner

As Mrs Cortman came to meet him with outstretched hand, Stafford Nye recalled the term his great-aunt had used. Milly Jean Cortman was a woman of between thirty-five and forty.

She had delicate features, big blue-grey eyes, a very perfectly shaped head with bluish-grey hair tinted to a particularly attractive shade which fitted her with a perfection of grooming. She was very popular in London. Her husband, Sam Cortman, was a big, heavy man, slightly ponderous. He was very proud of his wife. He himself was one of those slow, rather over-emphatic talkers. People found their attention occasionally straying when he was elucidating at some length a point which hardly needed making.

'Back from Malaya, aren't you, Sir Stafford? It must have been quite interesting to go out there, though it's not the time of year I'd have chosen. But I'm sure we're all glad to see you back. Let me see now. You know Lady Aldborough and Sir John, and Herr von Roken, Frau von Roken. Mr and Mrs Staggenham.'

They were all people known to Stafford Nye in more or less degree. There was a Dutchman and his wife whom he had not met before, since they had only just taken up their appointment. The Staggenhams were the Minister of Social Security and his wife. A particularly uninteresting couple, he had always thought.

'And the Countess Renata Zerkowski. I think she said she'd met you before.'

'It must be about a year ago. When I was last in England,' said the Countess.

And there she was, the passenger from Frankfurt again. Self-possessed, at ease, beautifully turned out in faint grey-blue with a touch of chinchilla. Her hair dressed high (a wig?) and a ruby cross of antique design round her neck.

'Signor Gasparo, Count Reitner, Mr and Mrs Arbuthnot.'

About twenty-six in all. At dinner Stafford Nye sat between the dreary Mrs Staggenham and Signora Gasparo on the other side of him. Renata Zerkowski sat exactly opposite him.

An Embassy dinner. A dinner such as he so often attended, holding much of the same type of guests. Various members of the Diplomatic Corps, junior ministers, one or two industrialists, a sprinkling of socialites usually included because they were good conversationalists, natural, pleasant people to meet, though one or two, thought Stafford Nye, one or two were maybe different. Even while he was busy sustaining his conversation with Signora Gasparo, a charming person to talk to, a chatterbox, slightly flirtatious; his mind was roving in the same way that his eye also roved, though the latter was not very noticeable. As it roved round the dinner table, you would not have said that he was summing up conclusions in his own mind. He had been asked here. Why? For any reason or for no reason in particular. Because his name had come up automatically on the list that the secretaries produced from time to time with checks against such members as were due for their turn. Or as the extra man or the extra woman required for the balancing of the table. He had always been in request when an extra was needed.

'Oh yes,' a diplomatic hostess would say, 'Stafford Nye will do beautifully. You will put him next to Madame So-and-so, or Lady Somebody else.'

He had been asked perhaps to fill in for no further reason than that. And yet, he wondered. He knew by experience that there were certain other reasons. And so his eye with its swift social amiability, its air of not looking really at anything in particular, was busy.

Amongst these guests there was someone perhaps who for some reason mattered, was important. Someone who had been asked – not to fill in – on the contrary – someone who had had a selection of other guests invited to fit in round him – or her. Someone who mattered. He wondered – he wondered which of them it might be.

Cortman knew, of course. Milly Jean, perhaps. One never really knew with wives. Some of them were better diplomats than their husbands. Some of them could be relied upon merely for their charm, for their adaptability, their readiness to please, their lack of curiosity. Some again, he thought ruefully to himself, were, as far as their husbands were concerned, disasters. Hostesses who, though they may have brought prestige or money to a diplomatic marriage, were yet capable at any moment of saying or doing the wrong thing, and creating an unfortunate situation. If that was to be guarded against, it would need one of the guests, or two or even three of the guests, to be what one might call professional smoothers-over.

Did this dinner party this evening mean anything but a social event? His quick and noticing eye had by now been round the dinner table picking out one or two people whom so far he had not entirely taken in. An American business man. Pleasant, not socially brilliant. A professor from one of the universities of the Middle West. A married couple, the husband German, the wife predominantly, almost aggressively American. A very beautiful woman, too. Sexually, highly attractive, Sir Stafford thought. Was one of them important? Initials floated through his mind. FBI. CIA. The business man perhaps a CIA man, there for a purpose. Things were like that nowadays. Not as they used to be. How had the formula gone? Big Brother is watching you. Yes, well it went further than that now. Transatlantic Cousin is watching you. High Finance for Middle Europe is watching you. A diplomatic difficulty has been asked here for *you* to watch *him*. Oh yes. There was often a lot behind things nowadays. But was that just another formula, just another fashion? Could it really mean more than that, something vital, something real? How did one talk of events in Europe nowadays? The Common Market. Well, that was fair enough, that dealt with trade, with economics, with the inter-relationships of countries.

That was the stage to set. But behind the stage. Back-stage. Waiting for the cue. Ready to prompt if prompting were needed. What was going on? Going on in the big world and behind the big world. He wondered.

Some things he knew, some things he guessed at, some things, he thought to himself, I know nothing about and nobody wants me to know anything about them.

His eyes rested for a moment on his vis-à-vis, her chin tilted upward, her mouth just gently curved in a polite smile, and their eyes met. Those eyes told him nothing, the smile told him nothing. What was she doing here? She was in her element, she

74

fitted in, she knew this world. Yes, she was at home here. He could find out, he thought, without much difficulty where she figured in the diplomatic world, but would that tell him where she really had her place?

The young woman in the slacks who had spoken to him suddenly at Frankfurt had had an eager intelligent face. Was that the real woman, or was this casual social acquaintance the real woman? Was one of those personalities a part being played? And if so, which one? And there might be more than just those two personalities. He wondered. He wanted to find out.

Or had the fact that he had been asked to meet her been pure coincidence? Milly Jean was rising to her feet. The other ladies rose with her. Then suddenly an unexpected clamour arose. A clamour from outside the house. Shouts. Yells. The crash of breaking glass in a window. Shouts. Sounds – surely pistol shots. Signora Gasparo spoke, clutching Stafford Nye's arm.

'What again!' she exclaimed. '*Dio*! – again it is those terrible students. It is the same in our country. Why do they attack Embassies? They fight, resist the police – go marching, shouting idiotic things, lie down in the streets. *Si, si*. We have them in Rome – in Milan – We have them like a pest everywhere in Europe. Why are they never happy, these young ones? What do they want?'

Stafford Nye sipped his brandy and listened to the heavy accents of Mr Charles Staggenham, who was being pontifical and taking his time about it. The commotion had subsided. It would seem that the police had marched off some of the hotheads. It was one of those occurrences which once would have been thought extraordinary and even alarming but which were now taken as a matter of course.

'A larger police force. That's what we need. A larger police force. It's more than these chaps can deal with. It's the same everywhere, they say. I was talking to Herr Lurwitz the other day. They have their troubles, so have the French. Not quite so much of it in the Scandinavian countries. What do they all want – just trouble? I tell you if I had my way –'

75

Stafford Nye removed his mind to another subject while keeping up a flattering pretence as Charles Staggenham explained just what his way would be, which in any case was easily to be anticipated beforehand.

'Shouting about Vietnam and all that. What do any of them know about Vietnam. None of them have ever been there, have they?'

'One would think it very unlikely,' said Sir Stafford Nye.

'Man was telling me earlier this evening, they've had a lot of trouble in California. In the universities – If we had a sensible policy ...'

Presently the men joined the ladies in the drawing-room. Stafford Nye, moving with that leisurely grace, that air of complete lack of purpose he found so useful, sat down by a golden-haired, talkative woman whom he knew moderately well, and who could be guaranteed seldom to say anything worth listening to as regards ideas or wit, but who was excessively knowledgeable about all her fellow creatures within the bounds of her acquaintance. Stafford Nye asked no direct questions but presently, without the lady being even aware of the means by which he had guided the subject of conversation, he was hearing a few remarks about the Countess Renata Zerkowski.

'Still very good-looking isn't she? She doesn't come over here very often nowadays. Mostly New York, you know, or that wonderful island place. You know the one I mean. Not Minorca. One of the other ones in the Mediterranean. Her sister's married to that soap king, at least I think it's a soap king. Not the Greek one. He's Swedish, I think. Rolling in money. And then of course, she spends a lot of time in some castle place in the Dolomites – or near Munich – very musical, she always has been. She said you'd met before, didn't she?'

'Yes. A year or two years ago, I think.'

'Oh yes, I suppose when she was over in England before. They say she was mixed up in the Czechoslovakian business. Or do I mean the Polish trouble? Oh dear, it's so difficult, isn't it. All the names, I mean. They have so many z's and k's. Most peculiar, and so hard to spell. She's very literary. You know, gets up petitions for people to sign. To give writers asylum here, or whatever it is. Not that anyone really pays much attention. I mean, what else can one think of nowadays except how one can possibly pay one's own taxes. The travel allowance makes things a little better but not much. I mean, you've got to get the money, haven't you, before you can take it abroad. I don't know how anyone manages to have money now, but there's a lot of it about. Oh yes, there's a lot of it about.'

She looked down in a complacent fashion at her left hand, on which were two solitaire rings, one a diamond and one an emerald, which seemed to prove conclusively that a considerable amount of money had been spent upon her at least.

The evening drew on to its close. He knew very little more about his passenger from Frankfurt than he had known before. He knew that she had a façade, a façade it seemed to him, very highly faceted, if you could use those two alliterative words together. She was interested in music. Well, he had met her at the Festival Hall, had he not? Fond of outdoor sports. Rich relations who owned Mediterranean islands. Given to supporting literary charities. Somebody in fact who had good connections, was well related, had entries to the social field. Not apparently highly political and yet, quietly perhaps, affiliated to some group. Someone who moved about from place to place and country to country. Moving among the rich, amongst the talented, about the literary world.

He thought of espionage for a moment or two. That seemed the most likely answer. And yet he was not wholly satisfied with it.

The evening drew on. It came at last to be his turn to be collected by his hostess. Milly Jean was very good at her job.

'I've been longing to talk to you for ages. I wanted to hear about Malaya. I'm so stupid about all these places in Asia, you know, I mix them up. Tell me, what happened out there? Anything interesting or was everything terribly boring?'

'I'm sure you can guess the answer to that one.'

77

'Well, I should guess it was very boring. But perhaps you're not allowed to say so.'

'Oh yes, I can think it, and I can say it. It wasn't really my cup of tea, you know.'

'Why did you go then?'

'Oh well, I'm always fond of travelling, I like seeing countries.'

'You're such an intriguing person in many ways. Really, of course, all diplomatic life is very boring, isn't it? *I* oughtn't to say so. I only say it to you.'

Very blue eyes. Blue like bluebells in a wood. They opened a little wider and the black brows above them came down gently at the outside corners while the inside corners went up a little. It made her face look like a rather beautiful Persian cat. He wondered what Milly Jean was really like. Her soft voice was that of a southerner. The beautifully shaped little head, her profile with the perfection of a coin – what was she really like? No fool, he thought. One who could use social weapons when needed, who could charm when she wished to, who could withdraw into being enigmatic. If she wanted anything from anyone she would be adroit in getting it. He noticed the intensity of the glance she was giving him now. Did she want something of him? He didn't know. He didn't think it could be likely. She said, 'Have you met Mr Staggenham?'

'Ah yes. I was talking to him at the dinner table. I hadn't met him before.'

'He is said to be very important,' said Milly Jean. 'He's the President of PBF as you know.'

'One should know all those things,' said Sir Stafford Nye. 'PBF and DCV. LYH. And all the world of initials.'

'Hateful,' said Milly Jean. 'Hateful. All these initials, no personalities, no *people* any more. Just initials. What a hateful world! That's what I sometimes think. What a hateful world. I want it to be different, quite, quite different –'

Did she mean that? He thought for one moment that perhaps she did. Interesting …

Grosvenor Square was quietness itself. There were traces of broken glass still on the pavements. There were even eggs, squashed tomatoes and fragments of gleaming metal. But above, the stars were peaceful. Car after car drove up to the Embassy door to collect the home-going guests. The police were there in the corners of the square but without ostentation. Everything was under control. One of the political guests leaving spoke to one of the police officers. He came back and murmured, 'Not too many arrests. Eight. They'll be up at Bow Street in the morning. More or less the usual lot. Petronella was here, of course, and Stephen and his crowd. Ah well. One would think they'd get tired of it one of these days.'

'You live not very far from here, don't you?' said a voice in Sir Stafford Nye's ear. A deep contralto voice. 'I can drop you on my way.'

'No, no. I can walk perfectly. It's only ten minutes or so.'

'It will be no trouble to me, I assure you,' said the Countess Zerkowski. She added, 'I'm staying at the St James's Tower.'

The St James's Tower was one of the newer hotels.

'You are very kind.'

It was a big, expensive-looking hire car that waited. The chauffeur opened the door, the Countess Renata got in and Sir Stafford Nye followed her. It was she who gave Sir Stafford Nye's address to the chauffeur. The car drove off.

'So you know where I live?' he said.

'Why not?'

He wondered just what that answer meant: Why not?

'Why not indeed,' he said. 'You know so much, don't you?' He added, 'It was kind of you to return my passport.'

'I thought it might save certain inconveniences. It might be simpler if you burnt it. You've been issued with a new one, I presume –'

'You presume correctly.'

'Your bandit's cloak you will find in the bottom drawer of your tallboy. It was put there tonight. I believed that perhaps to purchase another one would not satisfy you, and indeed that to find one similar might not be possible.'

'It will mean more to me now that it has been through certain – adventures,' said Stafford Nye. He added, 'It has served its purpose.'

The car purred through the night.

The Countess Zerkowski said:

'Yes. It has served its purpose since I am here – alive ...'

Sir Stafford Nye said nothing. He was assuming, rightly or not, that she wanted him to ask questions, to press her, to know more of what she had been doing, of what fate she had escaped. She wanted him to display curiosity, but Sir Stafford Nye was not going to display curiosity. He rather enjoyed not doing so. He heard her laugh very gently. Yet he fancied, rather surprisingly, that it was a pleased laugh, a laugh of satisfaction, not of stalemate.

'Did you enjoy your evening?' she said.

'A good party, I think, but Milly Jean always gives good parties.'

'You know her well then?'

'I knew her when she was a girl in New York before she married. A pocket Venus.'

She looked at him in faint surprise.

'Is that your term for her?'

'Actually, no. It was said to me by an elderly relative of mine.'

'Yes, it isn't a description that one hears given often of a woman nowadays. It fits her, I think, very well. Only –'

'Only what?'

'Venus is seductive, is she not? Is she also ambitious?'

'You think Milly Jean Cortman is ambitious?'

'Oh yes. That above all.'

'And you think to be the wife of the Ambassador to St James's is insufficient to satisfy ambition?'

'Oh no,' said the Countess. 'That is only the beginning.'

He did not answer. He was looking out through the car window. He began to speak, then stopped himself. He noted her quick glance at him, but she too was silent. It was not till

80

they were going over a bridge with the Thames below them that he said:

'So you are not giving me a lift home and you are not going back to the St James's Tower. We are crossing the Thames. We met there once before, crossing a bridge. Where are you taking me?'

'Do you mind?'

'I think I do.'

'Yes, I can see you might.'

'Well of course you are quite in the mode. Hi-jacking is the fashion nowadays, isn't it? You have hi-jacked me. Why?'

'Because, like once before, I have need of you.' She added, 'And others have need of you.'

'Indeed.'

'And that does not please you.'

'It would please me better to be asked.'

'If I had asked, would you have come?'

'Perhaps yes, perhaps no.'

'I am sorry.'

'I wonder.'

They drove on through the night in silence. It was not a drive through lonely country, they were on a main road. Now and then the lights picked up a name or a signpost so that Stafford Nye saw quite clearly where their route lay. Through Surrey and through the first residential portions of Sussex. Occasionally he thought they took a detour or a side road which was not the most direct route, but even of this he could not be sure. He almost asked his companion whether this was being done because they might possibly have been followed from London. But he had determined rather firmly on his policy of silence. It was for her to speak, for her to give information. He found her, even with the additional information he had been able to get, an enigmatic character.

They were driving to the country after a dinner party in London. They were, he was pretty sure, in one of the more expensive types of hire car. This was something planned beforehand. Reasonable, nothing doubtful or unexpected about it. Soon, he imagined, he would find out where it was they were going. Unless, that is, they were going to drive as far as the coast. That also was possible, he thought. Haslemere, he saw on a signpost. Now they were skirting Godalming. All very plain and above board. The rich countryside of moneyed suburbia. Agreeable woods, handsome residences. They took a few side turns and then as the car finally slowed, they seemed to be arriving at their destination. Gates. A small white lodge by the gates. Up a drive, well-kept rhododendrons on either side of it. They turned round a bend and drew up before a house. 'Stockbroker Tudor,' murmured Sir Stafford Nye, under his breath. His companion turned her head inquiringly.

'Just a comment,' said Stafford Nye. 'Pay no attention. I take it we are now arriving at the destination of your choice?'

'And you don't admire the look of it very much.'

'The grounds seem well-kept up,' said Sir Stafford, following the beam of the headlights as the car rounded the bend. 'Takes money to keep these places up and in good order. I should say this was a comfortable house to live in.'

'Comfortable but not beautiful. The man who lives in it prefers comfort to beauty, I should say.'

'Perhaps wisely,' said Sir Stafford. 'And yet in some ways he is very appreciative of beauty, of some kinds of beauty.'

They drew up before the well-lighted porch. Sir Stafford got out and tendered an arm to help his companion. The chauffeur had mounted the steps and pressed the bell. He looked inquiringly at the woman as she ascended the steps.

'You won't be requiring me again tonight, m'lady?'

'No. That's all for now. We'll telephone down in the morning.'

'Good night. Good night, sir.'

There were footsteps inside and the door was flung open. Sir Stafford had expected some kind of butler, but instead there was a tall grenadier of a parlour-maid. Grey-haired, tight-lipped, eminently reliable and competent, he thought. An invaluable asset and hard to find nowadays. Trustworthy, capable of being fierce.

'I am afraid we are a little late,' said Renata.

'The master is in the library. He asked that you and the gentleman should come to him there when you arrived.'

CHAPTER 9

The House Near Godalming

She led the way up the broad staircase and the two of them followed her. Yes, thought Stafford Nye, a very comfortable house. Jacobean paper, a most unsightly carved oak staircase but pleasantly shallow treads. Pictures nicely chosen but of no particular artistic interest. A rich man's house, he thought. A man, not of bad taste, a man of conventional tastes. Good thick pile carpet of an agreeable plum-coloured texture.

On the first floor, the grenadier-like parlour-maid went to the first door along it. She opened it and stood back to let them go in but she made no announcement of names. The Countess went in first and Sir Stafford Nye followed her. He heard the door shut quietly behind him.

There were four people in the room. Sitting behind a large desk which was well covered with papers, documents, an open map or two and presumably other papers which were in the course of discussion, was a large, fat man with a very yellow face. It was a face Sir Stafford Nye had seen before, though he could not for the moment attach the proper name to it. It was a man whom he had met only in a casual fashion, and yet the occasion had been an important one. He should know, yes, definitely he should know. But why – why wouldn't the name come?

With a slight struggle, the figure sitting at the desk rose to his feet. He took the Countess Renata's outstretched hand.

'You've arrived,' he said, 'splendid.'

'Yes. Let me introduce you, though I think you already know him. Sir Stafford Nye, Mr Robinson.'

Of course. In Sir Stafford Nye's brain something clicked like a camera. That fitted in, too, with another name. Pikeaway. To say that he knew all about Mr Robinson was not true. He knew about Mr Robinson all that Mr Robinson permitted to be known. His name, as far as anyone knew, *was* Robinson, though it might have been any name of foreign origin. No one had ever suggested anything of that kind. Recognition came also of his personal appearance. The high forehead, the melancholy dark eyes, the large generous mouth, and the impressive white teeth – false teeth, presumably, but at any rate teeth of which it might have been said, like in Red Riding Hood, 'the better to eat you with, child!'

He knew, too, what Mr Robinson stood for. Just one simple word described it. Mr Robinson represented Money with a capital M. Money in its every aspect. International money, world-wide money, private home finances, banking, money not in the way that the average person looked at it. You never thought of him as a very rich man. Undoubtedly he was a very rich man but that wasn't the important thing. He was one of the arrangers of money, the great clan of bankers. His personal tastes might even have been simple, but Sir Stafford Nye doubted if they were. A reasonable standard of comfort, even luxury, would be Mr Robinson's way of life. But not more than that. So behind all this mysterious business there was the power of money.

'I heard of you just a day or two ago,' said Mr Robinson, as he shook hands, 'from our friend Pikeaway, you know.'

That fitted in, thought Stafford Nye, because now he remembered that on the solitary occasion before that he had met Mr Robinson, Colonel Pikeaway had been present. Horsham, he remembered, had spoken of Mr Robinson. So now there was Mary Ann (or the Countess Zerkowski?) and Colonel Pikeaway sitting in his own smoke-filled room with his eyes half closed either going to sleep or just waking up, and there was Mr Robinson with his large, yellow face, and so there

84

was money at stake somewhere, and his glance shifted to the three other people in the room because he wanted to see if he knew who they were and what they represented, of if he could guess.

In two cases at least he didn't need to guess. The man who sat in the tall porter's chair by the fireplace, an elderly figure framed by the chair as a picture frame might have framed him, was a face that had been well known all over England. Indeed, it still *was* well known, although it was very seldom seen nowadays. A sick man, an invalid, a man who made very brief appearances, and then it was said, at physical cost to himself in pain and difficulty. Lord Altamount. A thin emaciated face, outstanding nose, grey hair which receded just a little from the forehead, and then flowed back in a thick grey mane; somewhat prominent ears that cartoonists had used in their time, and a deep piercing glance that not so much observed as probed. Probed deeply into what it was looking at. At the moment it was looking at Sir Stafford Nye. He stretched out a hand as Stafford Nye went towards him.

'I don't get up,' said Lord Altamount. His voice was faint, an old man's voice, a far-away voice. 'My back doesn't allow me. Just come back from Malaya, haven't you, Stafford Nye?'

'Yes.'

'Was it worth your going? I expect you think it wasn't. You're probably right, too. Still, we have to have these excrescences in life, these ornamental trimmings to adorn the better kind of diplomatic lies. I'm glad you could come here or were brought here tonight. Mary Ann's doing, I suppose?'

So that's what he calls her and thinks of her as, thought Stafford Nye to himself. It was what Horsham had called her. She was in with them then, without a doubt. As for Altamount, he stood for – what did he stand for nowadays? Stafford Nye thought to himself. He stands for England. He still stands for England until he's buried in Westminster Abbey or a country mausoleum, whatever he chooses. He has *been* England, and he knows England, and I should say he knows the value of every

85

politician and government official in England pretty well, even if he's never spoken to them.

Lord Altamount said:

'This is our colleague, Sir James Kleek.'

Stafford Nye didn't know Kleek. He didn't think he'd even heard of him. A restless, fidgety type. Sharp, suspicious glances that never rested anywhere for long. He had the contained eagerness of a sporting dog awaiting the word of command. Ready to start off at a glance from his master's eye.

But who was his master? Altamount or Robinson?

Stafford's eye went round to the fourth man. He had risen to his feet from the chair where he had been sitting close to the door. Bushy moustache, raised eyebrows, watchful, withdrawn, managing in some way to remain familiar yet almost unrecognizable.

'So it's you,' said Sir Stafford Nye, 'how are you, Horsham?'

'Very pleased to see you here, Sir Stafford.'

Quite a representative gathering, Stafford Nye thought, with a swift glance round.

They had set a chair for Renata not far from the fire and Lord Altamount. She had streched out a hand – her left hand, he noticed – and he had taken it between his two hands, holding it for a minute, then dropping it. He said:

'You took risks, child, you take too many risks.'

Looking at him, she said, 'It was you who taught me that, and it's the only way of life.'

Lord Altamount turned his head towards Sir Stafford Nye.

'It wasn't I who taught you to choose your man. You've got a natural genius for that.' Looking at Stafford Nye, he said, 'I know your great-aunt, or your great-great-aunt, is she?'

'Great-Aunt Matilda,' said Stafford Nye immediately.

'Yes. That's the one. One of the Victorian *tours-de-force* of the 'nineties. She must be nearly ninety herself now.'

He went on:

'I don't see her very often. Once or twice a year perhaps. But it strikes me every time – that sheer vitality of hers that outlives

86

her bodily strength. They have the secret of that, those indomitable Victorians and some of the Edwardians as well.'

Sir James Kleek said, 'Let me get you a drink, Nye? What will you have?'

'Gin and tonic, if I may.'

The Countess refused with a small shake of the head.

James Kleek brought Nye his drink and set it on the table near Mr Robinson. Stafford Nye was not going to speak first. The dark eyes behind the desk lost their melancholy for a moment. They had quite suddenly a twinkle in them.

'Any questions?' he said.

'Too many,' said Sir Stafford Nye. 'Wouldn't it be better to have explanations first, questions later?'

'Is that what you'd like?'

'It might simplify matters.'

'Well, we start with a few plain statements of facts. You may or you may not have been asked to come here. If not, that fact may rankle slightly.'

'He prefers to be asked always,' said the Countess. 'He said as much to me.'

'Naturally,' said Mr Robinson.

'I was hi-jacked,' said Stafford Nye. 'Very fashionable, I know. One of our more modern methods.'

He kept his tone one of light amusement.

'Which invites, surely, a question from you,' said Mr Robinson.

'Just one small word of three letters. Why?'

'Quite so. Why? I admire your economy of speech. This is a private committee – a committee of inquiry. An inquiry of world-wide significance.'

'Sounds interesting,' said Sir Stafford Nye.

'It is more than interesting. It is poignant and immediate. Four different ways of life are represented in this room tonight,' said Lord Altamount. 'We represent different branches. I have retired from active participation in the affairs of this country, but I am still a consulting authority. I have been consulted and asked to preside over this particular inquiry as to what is going on in the world in this particular year of our Lord, because something *is* going on. James, here, has his own special task. He is my right-hand man. He is also our spokesman. Explain the general set-out, if you will, Jamie, to Sir Stafford here.'

It seemed to Stafford Nye that the gun dog quivered. At last! At last I can speak and get on with it! He leaned forward a little in his chair.

'If things happen in the world, you have to look for a cause for them. The outward signs are always easy to see but they're not, or so the Chairman –' he bowed to Lord Altamount – ' and Mr Robinson and Mr Horsham believe, important. It's always been the same way. You take a natural force, a great fall of water that will give you turbine power. You take the discovery of uranium from pitchblende, and that will give you in due course nuclear power that had not been dreamt of or known. When you found coal and minerals, they gave you transport, power, energy. There are forces at work always that give you certain things. But behind each of them there is *someone who controls it*. You've got to find who's controlling the powers that are slowly gaining ascendancy in practically every country in Europe, further afield still in parts of Asia. Less, possibly, in Africa, but again in the American continents both north and south. You've got to get behind the things that are happening and find out the motive force that's making them happen. One thing that makes things happen is *money*.'

He nodded towards Mr Robinson.

'Mr Robinson, there, knows as much about money as anybody in the world, I suppose.'

'It's quite simple,' said Mr Robinson. 'There are big movements afoot. There has to be money behind them. We've got to find out where that money's coming from. Who's operating with it? Where do they get it from? Where are they sending it to? Why? It's quite true what James says: I know a lot about money! As much as any man alive knows today. Then there are what you might call trends. It's a word we use a good deal nowadays! Trends or tendencies – there are innumerable words one uses. They mean not quite the same thing, but they're in relationship with each other. A tendency, shall we say, to rebellion shows up. Look back through history. You'll find it coming again and again, repeating itself like a periodic table, repeating a pattern. A desire for rebellion, the means of rebellion, the form the rebellion takes. It's not a thing particular to any particular country. If it arises in one country, it will arise in other countries in less or more degrees. That's what you mean, sir, isn't it?' He half turned towards Lord Altamount. 'That's the way you more or less put it to me.'

'Yes, you're expressing things very well, James.'

'It's a pattern, a pattern that arises and seems inevitable. You can recognize it where you find it. There was a period when a yearning towards crusades swept countries. All over Europe people embarked in ships, they went off to deliver the Holy Land. All quite clear, a perfectly good pattern of determined behaviour. But *why* did they go? That's the interest of history, you know. Seeing why these desires and patterns arise. It's not always a materialistic answer either. All sorts of things can cause rebellion, a desire for freedom, freedom of speech, freedom of religious worship, again a series of closely related patterns. It led people to embrace emigration to other countries, to formation of new religions very often as full of tyranny as the forms of religion they had left behind. But in all this, if you look hard enough, if you make enough investigations, you can see what started the onset of these and many other – I'll use the same word – patterns. In some ways it's like a virus disease. The virus can be carried – round the world, across seas, up mountains. It can go and infect. It goes apparently without being set in motion. But one can't be sure, even now, that that was always really true. There could have been causes. Causes that made things happen. One can go a few steps further. There are *people*. One person – ten persons – a few hundred persons who are capable of being and setting in motion a cause. So it is not the *end process* that one has to look at. It is the first people who set the cause in motion. You have your crusaders, you have your religious enthusiasts, you have

89

your desires for liberty, you have all the other patterns but you've got to go further back still. Further back to a hinterland. Visions, dreams. The prophet Joel knew it when he wrote "Your old men shall dream dreams, your young men shall see visions." And of those two, which are the more powerful? Dreams are not destructive. But visions can open new worlds to you – and visions can also destroy the worlds that already exist ...'

James Kleek turned suddenly towards Lord Altamount. 'I don't know if it connects up, sir,' he said, 'but you told me a story once of somebody in the Embassy at Berlin. A woman.'

'Oh that? Yes, I found it interesting at the time. Yes, it has a bearing on what we are talking about now. One of the Embassy wives, clever, intelligent woman, well educated. She was very anxious to go personally and hear the Führer speak. I am talking, of course, of a time immediately preceding the 1939 war. She was curious to know what oratory could do. Why was everyone so impressed? And so she went. She came back and said, "It's extraordinary. I wouldn't have believed it. Of course I don't understand German very well but I was carried away, too. And I see now why everyone is. I mean, his ideas were wonderful ... They inflamed you. The things he said. I mean, you just felt there *was* no other way of thinking, that a whole new world would happen if only one followed him. Oh, I can't explain properly. I'm going to write down as much as I can remember, and then if I bring it to you to see, you'll see better than my just trying to tell you the effect it had."

'I told her that was a very good idea. She came to me the next day and she said, "I don't know if you'll believe this. I started to write down the things I'd heard, the things Hitler had said. What they'd *meant* – but – it was frightening – *there wasn't anything to write down at all, I didn't seem able to remember a single stimulating or exciting sentence.* I have some of the words, but it doesn't seem to mean the same things as when I wrote them down. They are just – oh, they are just *meaningless.* I don't understand."

'That shows you one of the great dangers one doesn't always

90

remember, *but it exists*. There are people capable of communicating to others a wild enthusiasm, a kind of vision of life and of happening. They can do that though it is not really by what they *say*, it is not the *words you hear*, it is not even the idea described. It's something else. It's the magnetic power that a very few men have of starting something, of producing and creating a vision. By their personal magnetism perhaps, a tone of voice, perhaps some emanation that comes forth straight from the *flesh*. I don't know, *but it exists*.

'Such people have power. The great religious teachers had this power, and so has an evil spirit power also. Belief can be created in a certain movement, in certain things to be done, things that will result in a new heaven and a new earth, and people will believe it and work for it and fight for it and even die for it.'

He lowered his voice as he said: 'Jan Smuts puts it in a phrase. He said Leadership, besides being a great creative force, can be *diabolical*.'

Stafford Nye moved in his chair.

'I understand what you mean. It is interesting what you say. I can see perhaps that it might be true.'

'But you think it's exaggerated, of course.'

'I don't know that I do,' said Stafford Nye. 'Things that sound exaggerated are very often not exaggerated at all. They are only things that you haven't heard said before or thought about before. And therefore they come to you as so unfamiliar that you can hardly do anything about them except accept them. By the way, may I ask a simple question? What *does* one do about them?'

'If you come across the suspicion that this sort of thing is going on, you must find out about them,' said Lord Altamount. 'You've got to go like Kipling's mongoose: Go and find out. Find out where the money comes from and where the ideas are coming from, and where, if I may say so, the *machinery* comes from. Who is directing the machinery? There's a chief of staff, you know, as well as a commander-in-chief. That's what we're trying to do. We'd like you to come and help us.'

It was one of the rare occasions in his life when Sir Stafford Nye was taken aback. Whatever he may have felt on some former occasions, he had always managed to conceal the fact. But this time it was different. He looked from one to the other of the men in the room. At Mr Robinson, impassively yellow-faced with his mouthful of teeth displayed; to Sir James Kleek, a somewhat brash talker, Sir Stafford Nye had considered him, but nevertheless he had obviously his uses; Master's dog, he called him in his own mind. He looked at Lord Altamount, the hood of the porter's chair framed round his head. The lighting was not strong in the room. It gave him the look of a saint in a niche in a cathedral somewhere. Ascetic. Fourteenth-century. A great man. Yes, Altamount had been one of the great men of the past. Stafford Nye had no doubt of that, but he was now a very old man. Hence, he supposed, the necessity for Sir James Kleek, and Lord Altamount's reliance on him. He looked past them to the enigmatic, cool creature who had brought him here, the Countess Renata Zerkowski alias Mary Ann, alias Daphne Theodofanous. Her face told him nothing. She was not even looking at him. His eyes came round last to Mr Henry Horsham of Security.

With faint surprise he observed that Henry Horsham was grinning at him.

'But look here,' said Stafford Nye, dropping all formal language, and speaking rather like the schoolboy of eighteen he had once been. 'Where on earth do I come in? What do *I* know? Quite frankly, I'm not distinguished in any way in my own profession, you know. They don't think very much of me at the FO. Never have.'

'We know that,' said Lord Altamount.

It was Sir James Kleek's turn to grin and he did so.

'All the better perhaps,' he remarked, and added apologetically as Lord Altamount frowned at him, 'Sorry, sir.'

'This is a committee of investigation,' said Mr Robinson. 'It is not a question of what you have done in the past, of what other people's opinion of you may be. What we are doing is to recruit a committee to investigate. There are not very many of

92

us at the moment forming this committee. We ask you to join it because we think that you have certain qualities which may help in an investigation.'

Stafford Nye turned his head towards the Security man. 'What about it, Horsham?' he said. 'I can't believe you'd agree with that?'

'Why not?' said Henry Horsham.

'Indeed? What are my "qualities", as you call them? I can't, quite frankly, believe in them myself.'

'You're not a hero-worshipper,' said Horsham. 'That's why. You're the kind who sees through humbug. You don't take anyone at their own or the world's valuation. You take them at your own valuation.'

Ce n'est pas un garçon sérieux. The words floated through Sir Stafford Nye's mind. A curious reason for which to be chosen for a difficult and exacting job.

'I've got to warn you,' he said, 'that my principal fault, and one that's been frequently noticed about me and which has cost me several good jobs is, I think, fairly well known. I'm not, I should say, a sufficiently serious sort of chap for an important job like this.'

'Believe it or not,' said Mr Horsham, 'that's one of the reasons why they want you. I'm right, my lord, aren't I?' He looked towards Lord Altamount.

'Public service!' said Lord Altamount. 'Let me tell you that very often one of the most serious disadvantages in public life is when people in a public position take themselves too seriously. We feel that you won't. Anyway,' he said, 'Mary Ann thinks so.'

Sir Stafford Nye turned his head. So here she was, no longer a countess. She had become Mary Ann again.

'You don't mind my asking,' he said, 'but who are you really? I mean, are you a real countess.'

'Absolutely. *Geboren*, as the Germans say. My father was a man of pedigree, a good sportsman, a splendid shot, and had a very romantic but somewhat dilapidated castle in Bavaria. It's still there, the castle. As far as that goes, I have connections

93

with that large portion of the European world which is still heavily snobbish as far as birth is concerned. A poor and shabby countess sits down first at the table whilst a rich American with a fabulous fortune in dollars in the bank is kept waiting.'

'What about Daphne Theodofanous? Where does she come in?'

'A useful name for a passport. My mother was Greek.'

'And Mary Ann?'

It was almost the first smile Stafford Nye had seen on her face. Her eyes went to Lord Altamount and from him to Mr Robinson.

'Perhaps,' she said, 'because I'm a kind of maid-of-all-work, going places, looking for things, taking things from one country to another, sweeping under the mat, do anything, go anywhere, clear up the mess.' She looked towards Lord Altamount again. 'Am I right, Uncle Ned?'

'Quite right, my dear. Mary Ann you are and always will be to us.'

'Were you taking something on that plane? I mean taking something important from one country to another?'

'Yes. It was known I was carrying it. If you hadn't come to my rescue, if you hadn't drunk possibly poisoned beer and handed over your bandit cloak of bright colours as a disguise, well, accidents happen sometimes. I shouldn't have got here.'

'What were you carrying – or mustn't I ask? Are there things I shall never know?'

'There are a lot of things you will never know. There are a lot of things you won't be allowed to ask. I think that question of yours I shall answer. A bare answer of fact. If I am allowed to do so.'

Again she looked at Lord Altamount.

'I trust your judgment,' said Lord Altamount. 'Go ahead.'

'Give him the dope,' said the irreverent James Kleek.

Mr Horsham said, 'I suppose you've got to know. *I* wouldn't tell you, but then I'm Security. Go ahead, Mary Ann.'

'One sentence. *I was bringing a birth certificate. That's all.* I

94

don't tell you any more and it won't be any use your asking any more questions.'

Stafford Nye looked round the assembly.

'All right. I'll join. I'm flattered at your asking me. Where do we go from here?'

'You and I,' said Renata, 'leave here tomorrow. We go to the Continent. You may have read, or know, that there's a Musical Festival taking place in Bavaria. It is something quite new which has only come into being in the last two years. It has a rather formidable German name meaning "The Company of Youthful Singers" and is supported by the Governments of several different countries. It is in opposition to the traditional festivals and productions of Bayreuth. Much of the music given is modern – new young composers are given the chance of their compositions being heard. Whilst thought of highly by some, it is utterly repudiated and held in contempt by others.'

'Yes,' said Sir Stafford, 'I have read about it. Are we going to attend it?'

'We have seats booked for two of the performances.'

'Has this festival any special significance in our investigation?'

'No,' said Renata. 'It is more in the nature of what you might call an exit and entry convenience. We go there for an ostensible and true reason, and we leave it for our next step in due course.'

He looked round. 'Instructions? Do I get any marching orders? Am I to be briefed?'

'Not in your meaning of those terms. You are going on a voyage of exploration. You will learn things as you go along. You will go as yourself, knowing only what you know at present. You go as a lover of music, as a slightly disappointed diplomat who had perhaps hoped for some post in his own country which he has not been given. Otherwise, you will know nothing. It is safer so.'

'But that is the sum of activities at present? Germany, Bavaria, Austria, the Tyrol – that part of the world?'

'It is one of the centres of interest.'

'It is not the only one?'

'Indeed, not even the principal one. There are other spots on the globe, all of varying importance and interest. How much importance each one holds is what we have to find out.'

'And I don't know, or am not to be told, anything about these other centres?'

'Only in cursory fashion. One of them, we think the most important one, has its headquarters in South America, there are two with headquarters in the United States of America, one in California, the other in Baltimore. There is one in Sweden, there is one in Italy. Things have become very active in the latter in the last six months. Portugal and Spain also have smaller centres. Paris, of course. There are further interesting spots just "coming into production", you might say. As yet not fully developed.'

'You mean Malaya, or Vietnam?'

'No. No, all that lies rather in the past. It was a good rallying cry for violence and student indignation and for many other things.

'What is being promoted, you must understand, is the growing organization of youth everywhere against their mode of government; against their parental customs, against very often the religions in which they have been brought up. There is the insidious cult of permissiveness, there is the increasing cult of violence. Violence not as a means of gaining money, but violence for the love of violence. That particularly is stressed, and the reasons for it are to the people concerned one of the most important things and of the utmost significance.'

'Permissiveness, is that important?'

'It is a way of life, no more. It lends itself to certain abuses but not unduly.'

'What about drugs?'

'The cult of drugs has been deliberately advanced and fomented. Vast sums of money have been made that way, but it is not, or so we think, entirely activated for the money motive.'

All of them looked at Mr Robinson, who slowly shook his head.

'No,' he said, 'it *looks* that way. There are people who are being apprehended and brought to justice. Pushers of drugs will be followed up. But there is more than just the drug racket behind all this. The drug racket is a means, and an evil means, of making money. But there is more to it than that.'

'But who –' Stafford Nye stopped.

'Who and what and why and where? The four W's. That is your mission, Sir Stafford,' said Mr Robinson. 'That's what you've got to find out. You and Mary Ann. It won't be easy, and one of the hardest things in the world, remember, is to keep one's secrets.'

Stafford Nye looked with interest at the fat yellow face of Mr Robinson. Perhaps the secret of Mr Robinson's domination in the financial world was just that. His secret was that he kept his secret. Mr Robinson's mouth showed its smile again. The large teeth gleamed.

'If you know a thing,' he said, 'it is always a great temptation to show that you know it; to talk about it, in other words. It is not that you want to give information, it is not that you have been offered payment to give information. It is that you want to show how important you are. Yes, it's just as simple as that. In fact,' said Mr Robinson, and he half closed his eyes, 'everything in this world is so very, *very* simple. That's what people don't understand.'

The Countess got to her feet and Stafford Nye followed her example.

'I hope you will sleep well and be comfortable,' said Mr Robinson. 'This house is, I think, moderately comfortable.'

Stafford Nye murmured that he was quite sure of that, and on that point he was shortly to be proved to have been quite right. He laid his head on the pillow and went to sleep immediately.

BOOK 2

Journey To Siegfried

CHAPTER 10

The Woman In The Schloss

They came out of the Festival Youth Theatre to the refreshing night air. Below them in a sweep of the ground, was a lighted restaurant. On the side of the hill was another, smaller one. The restaurants varied slightly in price though neither of them was inexpensive. Renata was in evening dress of black velvet, Sir Stafford Nye was in white tie and full evening dress.

'A very distinguished audience,' murmured Stafford Nye to his companion. 'Plenty of money there. A young audience on the whole. You wouldn't think they could afford it.'

'Oh! that can be seen to - it *is* seen to.'

'A subsidy for the élite of youth? That kind of thing?'

'Yes.'

They walked towards the restaurant on the high side of the hill.

'They give you an hour for the meal. Is that right?'

'Technically an hour. Actually an hour and a quarter.'

'That audience,' said Sir Stafford Nye, 'most of them, nearly all of them, I should say, are real lovers of music.'

'Most of them, yes. It's important, you know.'

'What do you mean - important?'

'That the enthusiasm should be genuine. At both ends of the scale,' she added.

'What did you mean, exactly, by that?'

'Those who practise and organize violence must love violence, must want it, must yearn for it. The seal of ecstasy in every movement, of slashing, hurting, destroying. And the same thing with the music. The ears must appreciate every moment of the harmonies and beauties. There can be no pretending in this game.'

'Can you double the rôles - do you mean you can combine violence *and* a love of music or a love of art?'

'It is not always easy, I think, but yes. There are many who can. It is safer really, if they don't have to combine rôles.'

'It's better to keep it simple, as our fat friend Mr Robinson would say? Let the lovers of music love music, let the violent practitioners love violence. Is that what you mean?'

'I think so.'

'I am enjoying this very much. The two days that we have stayed here, the two nights of music that we have enjoyed. I have not enjoyed all the music because I am not perhaps sufficiently modern in my taste. I find the clothes very interesting.'

'Are you talking of the stage production?'

'No, no, I was talking of the audience, really. You and I, the squares, the old-fashioned. You, Countess, in your society gown, I in my white tie and tails. Not a comfortable get-up, it never has been. And then the others, the silks and the velvets, the ruffled shirts of the men, real lace, I noticed, several times – and the plush and the hair and the luxury of *avant garde*, the luxury of the eighteen-hundreds or you might almost say of the Elizabethan age or of Van Dyck pictures.'

'Yes, you are right.'

'I'm no nearer, though, to what it all *means*. I haven't *learnt* anything. I haven't found out anything.'

'You mustn't be impatient. This is a rich show, supported, asked for, demanded perhaps by youth and provided by –'

'By whom?'

'We don't know yet. We shall know.'

'I'm so glad you are sure of it.'

They went into the restaurant and sat down. The food was good though not in any way ornate or luxurious. Once or twice they were spoken to by an acquaintance or a friend. Two people who recognized Sir Stafford Nye expressed pleasure and surprise at seeing him. Renata had a bigger circle of acquaintances since she knew more foreigners – well-dressed women, a man or two, mostly German or Austrian, Stafford Nye thought, one or two Americans. Just a few desultory words. Where people had come from or were going to, criticism or appreciation of the musical fare. Nobody wasted much time since the interval for eating had not been very long.

They returned to their seats for the two final musical offerings. A Symphonic Poem, 'Disintegration in Joy', by a new young composer, Solukonov, and then the solemn grandeur of the March of the Meistersingers.

They came out again into the night. The car which was at their disposal every day was waiting there to take them back to the small but exclusive hotel in the village street. Stafford Nye said good-night to Renata. She spoke to him in a lowered voice.

'Four a.m.,' she said. 'Be ready.'

She went straight into her room and shut the door and he went to his.

The faint scrape of fingers on his door came precisely at three minutes to four the next morning. He opened the door and stood ready.

'The car is waiting,' she said. 'Come.'

They lunched at a small mountain inn. The weather was good, the mountains beautiful. Occasionally Stafford Nye wondered what on earth he was doing here. He understood less and less of his travelling companion. She spoke little. He found himself watching her profile. Where was she taking him? What was her real reason? At last, as the sun was almost setting, he said:

'Where are we going? Can I ask?'

'You can ask, yes.'

'But you do not reply?'

'I could reply. I could tell you things, but would they mean anything? It seems to me that if you come to where we are going without my preparing you with explanations (which cannot in the nature of things mean anything), your first impressions will have more force and significance.'

He looked at her again thoughtfully. She was wearing a tweed coat trimmed with fur, smart travelling clothes, foreign in make and cut.

'Mary Ann,' he said thoughtfully.

There was a faint question in it.

'No,' she said, 'not at the moment.'

'Ah. You are still the Countess Zerkowski.'

'At the moment I am still the Countess Zerkowski.'

'Are you in your own part of the world?'

'More or less. I grew up as a child in this part of the world. For a good portion of each year we used to come here in the autumn to a Schloss not very miles from here.'

He smiled and said thoughtfully, 'What a nice word it is. A Schlos. So solid-sounding.'

'Schlösser are not standing very solidly nowadays. They are mostly disintegrated.'

'This is Hitler's country, isn't it? We're not far, are we, from Berchtesgaden?'

'It lies over there to the north-east.'

'Did your relations, your friends – did they accept Hitler, believe in him? Perhaps I ought not to ask things like that.'

'They disliked him and all he stood for. But they said "Heil Hitler". They acquiesced in what had happened to their country. What else could they do? What else could anybody do at that date?'

'We are going towards the Dolomites, are we not?'

'Does it matter where we are, or which way we are going?'

'Well, this is a voyage of exploration, is it not?'

'Yes, but the exploration is not geographical. We are going to see a personality.'

'You make me feel –' Stafford Nye looked up at the landscape of swelling mountains reaching up to the sky – 'as though we were going to visit the famous Old Man of the Mountain.'

'The Master of the Assassins, you mean, who kept his followers under drugs so that they died for him wholeheartedly, so that they killed, knowing that they themselves would also be killed, but believing, too, that that would transfer them immediately to the Moslem Paradise – beautiful women, hashish and erotic dreams – perfect and unending happiness.'

She paused a minute and then said:

'Spell-binders! I suppose they've always been there

throughout the ages. People who make you believe in them so that you are ready to die for them. Not only Assassins. The Christians died also.'

'The holy Martyrs? Lord Altamount?'

'Why do you say Lord Altamount?'

'I saw him that way – suddenly – that evening. Carved in stone – in a thirteenth-century cathedral, perhaps.'

'One of us may have to die. Perhaps more.'

She stopped what he was about to say.

'There is another thing I think of sometimes. A verse in the New Testament – Luke, I think. Christ at the Last Supper saying to his followers: "You are my companions and my friends, *yet one of you is a devil.*" So in all probability one of *us* is a devil.'

'You think it possible?'

'Almost certain. Someone we trust and know, but who goes to sleep at night, not dreaming of martyrdom but of thirty pieces of silver, and who wakes with the feel of them in the palm of his hand.'

'The love of money?'

'Ambition covers it better. How does one recognize a devil? How would one *know*? A devil would stand out in a crowd, would be exciting – would advertise himself – would exercise leadership.'

She was silent a moment and then said in a thoughtful voice:

'I had a friend once in the Diplomatic Service who told me how she had said to a German woman how moved she herself had been at the performance of the Passion Play at Oberammergau. But the German woman said scornfully: "You do not understand. *We* Germans have no need of a Jesus Christ! We have our Adolf Hitler here with us. He is greater than any Jesus that ever lived." She was quite a nice ordinary woman. But that is how she felt. Masses of people felt it. Hitler was a spell-binder. He spoke and they listened – and accepted the sadism, the gas chambers, the tortures of the Gestapo.'

She shrugged her shoulders and then said in her normal

voice, 'All the same, it's odd that you should have said what you did just now.'

'What was that?'

'About the Old Man of the Mountain. The head of the Assassins.'

'Are you telling me there *is* an Old Man of the Mountain here?'

'No. Not an Old Man of the Mountain, but there might be an Old Woman of the Mountain.'

'An Old Woman of the Mountain. What's she like?'

'You'll see this evening.'

'What are we doing this evening?'

'Going into society,' said Renata.

'It seems a long time since you've been Mary Ann.'

'You'll have to wait till we're doing some air travel again.'

'I suppose it's very bad for one's morale,' Stafford Nye said thoughtfully, 'living high up in the world.'

'Are you talking socially?'

'No. Geographically. If you live in a castle on a mountain peak overlooking the world below you, well, it makes you despise the ordinary folk, doesn't it? You're the top one, you're the grand one. That's what Hitler felt in Berchtesgaden, that's what many people feel perhaps who climb mountains and look down on their fellow creatures in valleys below.'

'You must be careful tonight,' Renata warned him. 'It's going to be ticklish.'

'Any instructions?'

'You're a disgruntled man. You're one that's against the Establishment, against the conventional world. You're a rebel, but a secret rebel. Can you do it?'

'I can try.'

The scenery had grown wilder. The big car twisted and turned up the roads, passing through mountain villages, sometimes looking down on a bewilderingly distant view where lights shone on a river, where the steeples of churches showed in the distance.

'Where are we going, Mary Ann?'

'To an Eagle's nest.'

The road took a final turn. It wound through a forest. Stafford Nye thought he caught glimpses now and again of deer or of animals of some kind. Occasionally, too, there were leather-jacketed men with guns. Keepers, he thought. And then they came finally to a view of an enormous Schloss standing on a crag. Some of it, he thought, was partially ruined, though most of it had been restored and rebuilt. It was both massive and magnificent but there was nothing new about it or in the message it held. It was representative of past power, power held through bygone ages.

'This was originally the Grand Duchy of Liechtenstolz. The Schloss was built by the Grand Duke Ludwig in 1790,' said Renata.

'Who lives there now? The present Grand Duke?'

'No. They're all gone and done with. Swept away.'

'And who lives here now then?'

'Someone who has present-day power,' said Renata.

'Money?'

'Yes. Very much so.'

'Shall we meet Mr Robinson, flown on ahead by air to greet us?'

'The last person you'll meet here will be Mr Robinson, I can assure you.'

'A pity,' said Stafford Nye. 'I like Mr Robinson. He's quite something, isn't he? Who is he really – what nationality is he?'

'I don't think anybody has ever known. Everyone tells one something different. Some people say he's a Turk, some that he's an Armenian, some that he's Dutch, some that he's just plain English. Some say that his mother was a Circassian slave, a Russian Grand-Duchess, an Indian Begum and so on. Nobody knows. One person told me that his mother was a Miss McLellan from Scotland. I think that's as likely as anything.'

They had drawn up beneath a large portico. Two menservants in livery came down the steps. Their bows were ostentatious as they welcomed the guests. The luggage was removed; they had a good deal of luggage with them. Stafford

Nye had wondered to begin with why he had been told to bring so much, but he was beginning to understand now that from time to time there was need for it. There would, he thought, be need for it this evening. A few questioning remarks and his companion told him that this was so.

They met before dinner, summoned by the sound of a great resounding gong. As he paused in the hall, he waited for her to join him coming down the stairs. She was in full elaborate evening dress tonight, wearing a dark red velvet gown, rubies round her neck and a ruby tiara on her head. A manservant stepped forward and conducted them. Flinging open the door, he announced:

'The Gräfin Zerkowski, Sir Stafford Nye.'

'Here we come, and I hope we look the part,' said Sir Stafford Nye to himself.

He looked down in a satisfied manner at the sapphire and diamond studs in the front of his shirt. A moment later he had drawn his breath in an astonished gasp. Whatever he had expected to see it had not been this. It was an enormous room, rococo in style, chairs and sofas and hangings of the finest brocades and velvets. On the walls there were pictures that he could not recognize all at once, but where he noted almost immediately – for he was fond of pictures – what was certainly a Cézanne, a Matisse, possibly a Renoir. Pictures of inestimable value.

Sitting on a vast chair, throne-like in its suggestion, was an enormous woman. A whale of a woman, Stafford Nye thought, there really was no other word to describe her. A great, big, cheesy-looking woman, wallowing in fat. Double, treble, almost quadruple chins. She wore a dress of stiff orange satin. On her head was an elaborate crown-like tiara of precious stones. Her hands, which rested on the brocaded arms of her seat, were also enormous. Great, big, fat hands with great, big, fat, shapeless fingers. On each finger, he noticed, was a solitaire ring. And in each ring, he thought, was a genuine solitaire stone. A ruby, an emerald, a sapphire, a diamond, a pale green stone which he did not know, a chrysoprase, perhaps, a yellow stone which, if not a topaz, was a yellow diamond. She was horrible, he thought. She wallowed in her fat. A great, white, creased, slobbering mass of fat was her face. And set in it, rather like currants in a vast currant bun, were two small black eyes. Very shrewd eyes, looking on the world, appraising it, appraising him, not appraising Renata, he thought. Renata she knew. Renata was here by command, by appointment. However you liked to put it. Renata had been told to bring *him* here. He wondered why. He couldn't really think why, but he was quite sure of it. It was at him she was looking. She was appraising *him*, summing *him* up. Was he what she wanted? Was he, yes, he'd rather put it this way, was he what the customer had ordered?

I'll have to make quite sure that I know what it is she does want, he thought. I'll have to do my best, otherwise ... Otherwise he could quite imagine that she might raise a fat ringed hand and say to one of the tall, muscular footmen: 'Take him and throw him over the battlements.' It's ridiculous, thought Stafford Nye. Such things can't happen nowadays. Where am I? What kind of a parade, a masquerade or a theatrical performance am I taking part in?

'You have come very punctual to time, child.'

It was a hoarse, asthmatic voice which had once had an undertone, he thought, of strength, possibly even of beauty. That was over now. Renata came forward, made a slight curtsy. She picked up the fat hand and dropped a courtesy kiss upon it.

'Let me present to you Sir Stafford Nye. The Gräfin Charlotte von Waldsausen.'

The fat hand was extended towards him. He bent over it in the foreign style. Then she said something that surprised him.

'I know your great-aunt,' she said.

He looked astounded, and he saw immediately that she was amused by that, but he saw too, that she had expected him to be surprised by it. She laughed, a rather queer, grating laugh. Not attractive.

'Shall we say, I used to know her. It is many, many years

since I have seen her. We were in Switzerland together, at Lausanne, as girls. Matilda. Lady Matilda Baldwen-White.'

'What a wonderful piece of news to take home with me,' said Stafford Nye.

'She is older than I am. She is in good health?'

'For her age, in very good health. She lives in the country quietly. She has arthritis, rheumatism.'

'Ah yes, all the ills of old age. She should have injections of procaine. That is what the doctors do here in this altitude. It is very satisfactory. Does she know that you are visiting me?'

'I imagine that she has not the least idea of it,' said Sir Stafford Nye. 'She knew only that I was going to this festival of modern music.'

'Which you enjoyed, I hope?'

'Oh, enormously. It is a fine Festival Opera Hall, is it not?'

'One of the finest. Pah! It makes the old Bayreuth Festival Hall look like a comprehensive school! Do you know what it cost to build, that Opera House?'

She mentioned a sum in millions of marks. It quite took Stafford Nye's breath away, but he was under no necessity to conceal that. She was pleased with the effect it made upon him.

'With money,' she said, 'if one knows, if one has the ability, if one has the discrimination, what is there that money cannot do? It can give one the best.'

She said the last two words with a rich enjoyment, a kind of smacking of the lips which he found both unpleasant and at the same time slightly sinister.

'I see that here,' he said, as he looked round the walls.

'You are fond of art? Yes, I see you are. There, on the east wall is the finest Cézanne in the world today. Some say that the – ah, I forget the name of it at the moment, the one in the Metropolitan in New York – is finer. That is not true. The best Matisse, the best Cézanne, the best of all that great school of art are here. Here in my mountain eyrie.'

'It is wonderful,' said Sir Stafford. 'Quite wonderful.'

Drinks were being handed round. The Old Woman of the Mountain, Sir Stafford Nye noticed, did not drink anything. It was possible, he thought, that she feared to take any risks over her blood pressure with that vast weight.

'And where did you meet this child?' asked the mountainous Dragon.

Was it a trap? He did not know, but he made his decision.

'At the American Embassy, in London.'

'Ah yes, so I heard. And how is – ah, I forget her name now – ah yes, Milly Jean, our southern heiress? Attractive, did you think?'

'Most charming. She has a great success in London.'

'And poor dull Sam Cortman, the United States Ambassador?'

'A very sound man, I'm sure,' said Stafford Nye politely.

She chuckled.

'Aha, you're tactful, are you not? Ah well, he does well enough. He does what he is told as a good politician should. And it is enjoyable to be Ambassador in London. She could do that for him, Milly Jean. Ah, she could get him an Embassy anywhere in the world, with that well-stuffed purse of hers. Her father owns half the oil in Texas, he owns land, goldfields, everything. A coarse, singularly ugly man – But what does she look like? A gentle little aristocrat. Not blatant, not rich. That is very clever of her, is it not?'

'Sometimes it presents no difficulties,' said Sir Stafford Nye.

'And you? You are not rich?'

'I wish I was.'

'The Foreign Office nowadays, it is not, shall we say, very rewarding?'

'Oh well, I would not put it like that ... After all, one goes places, one meets amusing people, one sees the world, one sees something of what goes on.'

'Something, yes. But not everything.'

'That would be very difficult.'

'Have you ever wished to see what – how shall I put it – what goes on behind the scenes in life?'

'One has an idea sometimes.' He made his voice non-committal.

'I have heard it said that that is true of you, that you have sometimes ideas about things. Not perhaps the conventional ideas?'

'There have been times when I've been made to feel the bad boy of the family,' said Stafford Nye and laughed.

Old Charlotte chuckled.

'You don't mind admitting things now and again, do you?'

'Why pretend? People always know what you're concealing.'

She looked at him.

'What do you want out of life, young man?'

He shrugged his shoulders. Here again, he had to play things by ear.

'Nothing,' he said.

'Come now, come now, am I to believe that?'

'Yes, you can believe it. I am not ambitious. Do I look ambitious?'

'No, I will admit that.'

'I ask only to be amused, to live comfortably, to eat, to drink in moderation, to have friends who amuse me.'

The old woman leant forward. Her eyes snapped open and shut three or four times. Then she spoke in a rather different voice. It was like a whistling note.

'Can you hate? Are you capable of hating?'

'To hate is a waste of time.'

'I see. I see. There are no lines of discontent in your face. That is true enough. All the same, I think you are ready to take a certain path which will lead you to a certain place, and you will go along it smiling, as though you did not care, but all the same, in the end, if you find the right advisers, the right helpers, you might attain what you want, if you are capable of wanting.'

'As to that,' said Stafford Nye, 'who isn't?' He shook his head at her very gently. 'You see too much,' he said. 'Much too much.'

Footmen threw open a door.

'Dinner is served.'

The proceedings were properly formal. They had indeed almost a royal tinge about them. The big doors at the far end of the room were flung open, showing through to a brightly lighted ceremonial dining-room, with a painted ceiling and three enormous chandeliers. Two middle-aged women approached the Gräfin, one on either side. They wore evening dress, their grey hair was carefully piled on their heads, each wore a diamond brooch. To Sir Stafford Nye, all the same, they brought a faint flavour of wardresses. They were, he thought, not so much security guards as perhaps high-class nursing attendants in charge of the health, the toilet and other intimate details of the Gräfin Charlotte's existence. After respectful bows, each one of them slipped an arm below the shoulder and elbow of the sitting woman. With the ease of long practice aided by the effort which was obviously as much as she could make, they raised her to her feet in a dignified fashion.

'We will go in to dinner now,' said Charlotte.

With her two female attendants, she led the way. On her feet she looked even more a mass of wobbling jelly, yet she was still formidable. You could not dispose of her in your mind as just a fat old woman. She was somebody, knew she was somebody, intended to be somebody. Behind the three of them he and Renata followed.

As they entered through the portals of the dining-room, he felt it was almost more a banquet hall than a dining-room. There was a bodyguard here. Tall, fair-haired, handsome young men. They wore some kind of uniform. As Charlotte entered there was a clash as one and all drew their swords. They cross them overhead to make a passageway, and Charlotte, steadying herself, passed along that passageway, released by her attendants and making her progress solo to a vast carved chair with gold fittings and upholstered in golden brocade at the head of the long table. It was rather like a wedding procession, Stafford Nye thought. A naval or military one. In this case surely, military, strictly military – but lacking a bridegroom.

113

They were all young men of super physique. None of them, he thought, was older than thirty. They had good looks, their health was evident. They did not smile, they were entirely serious, they were – he thought of a word for it – yes, dedicated. Perhaps not so much a military procession as a religious one. The servitors appeared, old-fashioned servitors belonging, he thought, to the Schloss's past, to a time before the 1939 war. It was like a super production of a period historic play. And queening over it, sitting in the chair or the throne or whatever you liked to call it, at the head of the table, was not a queen or an empress but an old woman noticeable mainly for her avoirdupois weight and her extraordinary and intense ugliness. Who was she? What was she doing here? Why?

Why all this masquerade, why this bodyguard, a security bodyguard perhaps? Other diners came to the table. They bowed to the monstrosity on the presiding throne and took their places. They wore ordinary evening dress. No introductions were made.

Stafford Nye, after long years of sizing up people, assessed them. Different types. A great many different types. Lawyers, he was certain. Several lawyers. Possibly accountants or financiers; one or two army officers in plain clothes. They were of the Household, he thought, but they were also in the old-fashioned feudal sense of the term those who 'sat below the salt'.

Food came. A vast boar's head pickled in aspic, venison, a cool refreshing lemon sorbet, a magnificent edifice of pastry – a super millefeuille that seemed of unbelievable confectionary richness.

The vast woman ate, ate greedily, hungrily, enjoying her food. From outside came a new sound. The sound of the powerful engine of a super sports car. It passed the windows in a white flash. There came a cry inside the room from the bodyguard. A great cry of 'Heil! Heil! Heil Franz!'

The bodyguard of young men moved with the ease of a military manoeuvre known by heart. Everyone had risen to their feet. Only the old woman sat without moving, her head lifted high, on her dais. And, so Stafford Nye thought, a new excitement now permeated the room.

The other guests, or the other members of the household, whatever they were, disappeared in a way that somehow reminded Stafford of lizards disappearing into the cracks of a wall. The golden-haired boys formed a new figure, their swords flew out, they saluted their patroness, she bowed her head in acknowledgment, their swords were sheathed and they turned, permission given, to march out through the door of the room. Her eyes followed them, then went first to Renata, and then to Stafford Nye.

'What do you think of them?' she said. 'My boys, my youth corps, my children. Yes, my children. Have you a word that can describe them?'

'I think so,' said Stafford Nye. 'Magnificent.' He spoke to her as to Royalty. 'Magnificent, ma'am.'

'Ah!' She bowed her head. She smiled, the wrinkles multiplying all over her face. It made her look exactly like a crocodile.

A terrible woman, he thought, a terrible woman, impossible, dramatic. Was any of this happening? He couldn't believe it was. What could this be but yet another festival hall in which a production was being given.

The doors clashed open again. The yellow-haired band of the young supermen marched as before through it. This time they did not wield swords, instead they sang. Sang with unusual beauty of tone and voice.

After a good many years of pop music Stafford Nye felt an incredulous pleasure. Trained voices, these. Not raucous shouting. Trained by masters of the singing art. Not allowed to strain their vocal cords, to be off key. They might be the new Heroes of a New World, but what they sang was not new music. It was music he had heard before. An arrangement of the Preislied, there must be a concealed orchestra somewhere, he thought, in a gallery round the top of the room. It was an arrangement or adaptation of various Wagnerian themes. It

115

passed from the Preislied to the distant echoes of the Rhine music.

The Elite Corps made once more a double lane where somebody was expected to make an entrance. It was not the old Empress this time. She sat on her dais awaiting whoever was coming.

And at last he came. The music changed as he came. It gave out that motif which by now Stafford Nye had got by heart. The melody of the Young Siegfried. Siegfried's horn call, rising up in its youth and its triumph, its mastery of a new world which the young Siegfried came to conquer.

Through the doorway, marching up between the lines of what were clearly his followers, came one of the handsomest young men Stafford Nye had ever seen. Golden-haired, blue-eyed, perfectly proportioned, conjured up as it were by the wave of a magician's wand, he came forth out of the world of myth. Myth, heroes, resurrection, rebirth, it was all there. His beauty, his strength, his incredible assurance and arrogance.

He strode through the double lines of his bodyguard, until he stood before the hideous mountain of womanhood that sat there on her throne; he knelt on one knee, raised her hand to his lips, and then rising to his feet, he threw up one arm in salutation and uttered the cry that Stafford Nye had heard from the others. 'Heil!' His German was not very clear, but Stafford Nye thought he distinguished the syllables 'Heil to the great mother!'

Then the handsome young hero looked from one side to the other. There was some faint recognition, though an uninterested one, of Renata, but when his gaze turned to Stafford Nye, there was definite interest and appraisal. Caution, thought Stafford Nye. Caution! He must play his part right now. Play the part that was expected of him. Only – what the hell was that part? What was he doing here? What were he or the girl supposed to be doing here? Why had they come?

The hero spoke.

'So,' he said, 'we have guests!' And he added, smiling with the arrogance of a young man who knows that he is vastly superior to any other person in the world. 'Welcome, guests, welcome to you both.'

Somewhere in the depths of the Schloss a great bell began tolling. It had no funereal sound about it, but it had a disciplinary air. The feeling of a monastery summoned to some holy office.

'We must sleep now,' said old Charlotte. 'Sleep. We will meet again tomorrow morning at eleven o'clock.'

She looked towards Renata and Sir Stafford Nye.

'You will be shown to your rooms. I hope you will sleep well.'

It was the Royal dismissal.

Stafford Nye saw Renata's arm fly up in the Fascist salute, but it was addressed not to Charlotte, but to the golden-haired boy. He thought she said: 'Heil Franz Joseph.' He copied her gesture and he, too, said 'Heil!'

Charlotte spoke to them.

'Would it please you tomorrow morning to start the day with a ride through the forest?'

'I should like it of all things,' said Stafford Nye.

'And you, child?'

'Yes, I too.'

'Very good then. It shall be arranged. Good night to you both. I am glad to welcome you here. Franz Joseph – give me your arm. We will go into the Chinese Boudoir. We have much to discuss, and you will have to leave in good time tomorrow morning.'

The menservants escorted Renata and Stafford Nye to their apartments. Nye hesitated for a moment on the threshold. Would it be possible for them to have a word or two now? He decided against it. As long as the castle walls surrounded them it was well to be careful. One never knew – each room might be wired with microphones.

Sooner or later, though, he *had* to ask questions. Certain things aroused a new and sinister apprehension in his mind. He was being persuaded, inveigled into something. But what? And whose doing was it?

117

The bedrooms were handsome, yet oppressive. The rich hangings of satin and velvets, some of them antique, gave out a faint perfume of decay, tempered by spices. He wondered how often Renata had stayed here before.

CHAPTER 11

The Young And The Lovely

After breakfasting on the following morning in a small breakfast-room downstairs, he found Renata waiting for him. The horses were at the door.

Both of them had brought riding clothes with them. Everything they could possibly require seemed to have been intelligently anticipated.

They mounted and rode away down the castle drive. Renata spoke with the groom at some length.

'He asked if we would like him to accompany us but I said no. I know the tracks round here fairly well.'

'I see. You have been here before?'

'Not very often of late years. Early in the my life I knew this place very well.'

He gave her a sharp look. She did not return it. As she rode beside him, he watched her profile – the thin, aquiline nose, the head carried so proudly on the slender neck. She rode a horse well, he saw that.

All the same, there was a sense of ill ease in his mind this morning. He wasn't sure why ...

His mind went back to the Airport Lounge. The woman who had come to stand beside him. The glass of Pilsner on the table ... Nothing in it that there shouldn't have been – neither then, nor later. A risk he had accepted. Why, when all that was long over, should it rouse uneasiness in him now?

They had a brief canter following a ride through the trees. A beautiful property, beautiful woods. In the distance he saw horned animals. A paradise for a sportsman, a paradise for the old way of living, a paradise that contained – what? A serpent? As it was in the beginning – with Paradise went a serpent. He drew rain and the horses fell to a walk. He and Renata were alone – no microphones, no listening walls – The time had come for his questions.

'Who is she?' he said urgently. 'What is she?'

'It's easy to answer. So easy that it's hardly believable.'

'Well?' he said.

'She's oil. Copper. Goldmines in South Africa. Armaments in Sweden. Uranium deposits in the north. Nuclear development, vast stretches of cobalt. She's all those things.'

'And yet, I hadn't heard about her, I didn't know her name, I didn't know –'

'She has not wanted people to know.'

'Can one keep such things quiet?'

'Easily, if you have enough copper and oil and nuclear deposits and armaments and all the rest of it. Money can advertise, or money can keep secrets, can hush things up.'

'But who *actually* is she?'

'Her grandfather was American. He was mainly railways, I think. Possibly Chicago hogs in those times. It's like going back into history, finding out. He married a German woman. You've heard of her, I expect. Big Belinda, they used to christen her. Armaments, shipping, the whole industrial wealth of Europe. She was her father's heiress.'

'Between those two, unbelievable wealth,' said Sir Stafford Nye. 'And so – power. Is that what you're telling me?'

'Yes. She didn't just inherit things, you know. She made money as well. She'd inherited brains, she was a big financier in her own right. Everything she touched multiplied itself. Turned to incredible sums of money, and she invested them. Taking advice, taking other people's judgment, but in the end always using her own. And always prospering. Always adding

119

to her wealth so that it was too fabulous to be believed. Money creates money.'

'Yes, I can understand that. Wealth *has* to increase if there's a superfluity of it. But – what did *she* want? What has *she* got?'

'You said it just now. Power.'

'And she lives here? Or does she –?'

'She visits America and Sweden. Oh yes, she visits places, but not often. This is where she prefers to be, in the centre of a web like a vast spider controlling all the threads. The threads of finance. Other threads too.'

'When you say, other threads –'

'The arts. Music, pictures, writers. Human beings – young human beings.'

'Yes. One might know that. Those pictures, a wonderful collection.'

'There are galleries of them upstairs in the Schloss. There are Rembrandts and Giottos and Raphaels and there are cases of jewels – some of the most wonderful jewels in the world.'

'All belonging to one ugly, gross old woman. Is she satisfied?'

'Not yet, but well on the way to being.'

'Where is she going, what does she want?'

'She loves youth. That is her mode of power. To control youth. The world is full of rebellious youth at this moment. That's been helped on. Modern philosophy, modern thought, writers and others whom she finances and controls.'

'But how can –?' He stopped.

'I can't tell you because I don't know. It's an enormous ramification. She's behind it in one sense, supports rather curious charities, earnest philanthropists and idealists, raises innumerable grants for students and artists and writers.'

'And yet you say it's not –'

'No, it's not yet complete. It's a great upheaval that's being planned. It's believed in, it's the new heaven and the new earth. That's what's been promised by leaders for thousands of years. Promised by religions, promised by those who support Messiahs, promised by those who come back to teach the law, like the Buddha. Promised by politicians. The crude heaven of an easy attainment such as the Assassins believed in, and the Old Man of the Assassins promised his followers and, from their point of view, gave to them.'

'Is she behind drugs as well?'

'Yes. Without conviction, of course. Only a means of having people bent to her will. It's one way, too, of destroying people. The weak ones. The ones she thinks are no good, although they had once shown promise. She'd never take drugs herself – she's strong. But drugs destroy weak people more easily and naturally than anything else.'

'And force? What about force? You can't do everything by propaganda.'

'No, of course not. Propaganda is the first stage and behind it there are vast armaments piling up. Arms that go to deprived countries and then on elsewhere. Tanks and guns and nuclear weapons that go to Africa and the South Seas and South America. In South America there's a lot building up. Forces of young men and women drilling and training. Enormous arms dumps – means of chemical warfare –'

'It's a nightmare! How do you know all this, Renata?'

'Partly because I've been told it; from information received, partly because I have been instrumental in proving some of it.'

'But *you*. You and *she*?'

'There's always something idiotic behind all great and vast projects.' She laughed suddenly. 'Once, you see, she was in love with my grandfather. A foolish story. He lived in this part of the world. He had a castle a mile or two from here.'

'Was he a man of genius?'

'Not at all. He was just a very good sportsman. Handsome, dissolute and attractive to women. And so, because of that, she is in a sense my protectress. And I am one of her converts or slaves! I work for her. I find people for her. I carry out her commands in different parts of the world.'

'Do you?'

'What do you mean by that?'

'I wondered,' said Sir Stafford Nye.

121

He did wonder. He looked at Renata and he thought again of the airport. He was working *for* Renata, he was working *with* Renata. She had brought him to this Schloss. Who had told her to bring him here? Big, gross Charlotte in the middle of her spider's web? He had had a reputation, a reputation of being unsound in certain diplomatic quarters. He could be useful to these people perhaps, but useful in a small and rather humiliating way. And he thought suddenly, in a kind of fog of question marks: Renata??? I took a risk with her at Frankfurt airport. But I was right. It came off. Nothing happened to me. But all the same, he thought, who is she? *What* is she? I don't know. I can't be *sure*. One can't in the world today be sure of *anyone*. Anyone at all. She was told perhaps to get me. To get me into the hollow of her hand, so that business at Frankfurt might have been cleverly thought out. It fitted in with my sense of risk, and it would make me sure of her. It would make me trust her.

'Let's canter again,' she said. 'We've walked the horses too long.'

'I haven't asked you what *you* are in all this?'

'I take orders.'

'From whom?'

'There's an opposition. There's always an opposition. There are people who have a suspicion of what's going on, of how the world is going to be made to change, of how with money, wealth, armaments, idealism, great trumpeting words of power that's going to happen. There are people who say it shall *not* happen.'

'And you are with them?'

'I say so.'

'What do you mean by that, Renata?'

She said, '*I say so.*'

He said: 'That young man last night –'

'Franz Joseph?'

'Is that his name?'

'It is the name he is known by.'

'But he has another name, hasn't he?'

'Do you think so?'

'He is, isn't he, the young Siegfried?'

'You saw him like that? You realized that's what he was, what he stands for?'

'I think so. Youth. Heroic youth. Aryan youth, it has to be Aryan youth in this part of the world. There is still that point of view. A super race, the supermen. They must be of Aryan descent.'

'Oh yes, it's lasted on from the time of Hitler. It doesn't always come out into the open much and, in other places all over the world, it isn't stressed so much. South America, as I say, is one of the strongholds. And Peru and South Africa also.'

'What does the young Siegfried do? What does he do besides look handsome and kiss the hand of his protectress?'

'Oh, he's quite an orator. He speaks and his following would follow him to death.'

'Is that true?'

'He believes it.'

'And you?'

'I think I might believe it.' She added: 'Oratory is very frightening, you know. What a voice can do, what words can do, and not particularly convincing words at that. The *way* they are said. His voice rings like a bell, and women cry and scream and faint away when he addresses them – you'll see that for yourself.

'You saw Charlotte's Bodyguard last night all dressed up – people do love dressing up nowadays. You'll see them all over the world in their own chosen get-up, different in different places, some with their long hair and their beards, and girls in their streaming white nightgowns, talking of peace and beauty, and the wonderful world that is the world of the young which is to be theirs when they've destroyed enough of the old world. The original Country of the Young was west of the Irish Sea, wasn't it? A very simple place, a different Country of the Young from what we're planning now – It was silver sands, and sunshine and singing in the waves ...

'But now we want Anarchy, and breaking down and

123

destroying. Only Anarchy can benefit those who march behind it. It's frightening, it's also wonderful – because of its violence, because it's bought with pain and suffering –'

'So that is how you see the world today?'

'Sometimes.'

'And what am *I* to do next?'

'Come with your guide. I'm your guide. Like Virgil with Dante, I'll take you down into hell, I'll show you the sadistic films partly copied from the old SS, show you cruelty and pain and violence worshipped. And I'll show you the great dreams of paradise in peace and beauty. You won't know which is which and what is what. But you'll have to make up your mind.'

'Do I trust you, Renata?'

'That will be your choice. You can run away from me if you like, or you can stay with me and see the new world. The new world that's in the making.'

'Pasteboard,' said Sir Stafford Nye violently.

She looked at him inquiringly.

'Like Alice in Wonderland. The cards, the pasteboard cards all rising up in the air. Flying about. Kings and Queens and Knaves. All sorts of things.'

'You mean – what do you mean exactly?'

'I mean it isn't real. It's make-believe. The whole damn thing is make-believe.'

'In one sense, yes.'

'All dressed up playing parts, putting on a show. I'm getting nearer, aren't I, to the meaning of things?'

'In a way, yes, and in a way, no –'

'There's one thing I'd like to ask you because it puzzles me. Big Charlotte ordered you to bring me to see her – why? What did she know about me? What use did she think she could make of me?'

'I don't quite know – possibly a kind of *Eminence Grise* – working behind a façade. That would suit you rather well.'

'But she knows nothing whatever about me!'

'Oh, *that*!' Suddenly Renata went into peals of laughter. 'It's so ridiculous, really – the same old nonsense all over again.'

'I don't understand you, Renata.'

'No – because it's so simple. Mr Robinson would understand.'

'Would you kindly explain what you are talking about?'

'It's the same old business – "*It's not what you are. It's who you know*". Your Great-Aunt Matilda and Big Charlotte were at school together –'

'You actually mean –'

'Girls together.'

He stared at her. Then he threw his head back and roared with laughter.

CHAPTER 12

Court Jester

They left the Schloss at midday, saying goodbye to their hostess. Then they had driven down the winding road, leaving the Schloss high above them and they had come at last, after many hours of driving, to a stronghold in the Dolomites – an amphitheatre in the mountains where meetings, concerts and reunions of the various Youth Groups were held.

Renata had brought him there, his guide, and from his seat on the bare rock he had watched what went on and had listened. He understood a little more what she had been talking about earlier that day. This great mass gathering, animated as all mass gatherings can be whether they are called by an evangelistic religious leader in Madison Square, New York, or in the shadow of a Welsh church or in a football crowd or in the super demonstrations which marched to attack embassies and police and universities and all the rest of it.

She had brought him there to show him the meaning of that one phrase: 'The Young Siegfried'.

Franz Joseph, if that was really his name, had addressed the crowd. His voice, rising, falling, with its curious exciting quality, its emotional appeal, had held sway over that groaning, almost moaning crowd of young women and young men. Every word that he had uttered had seemed pregnant with meaning, had held incredible appeal. The crowd had responded like an orchestra. His voice had been the baton of the conductor. And yet, what had the boy said? What had been the young Siegfried's message? There were no words that he could remember when it came to an end, but he knew that he had been moved, promised things, roused to enthusiasm. And now it was over. The crowd had surged round the rocky platform, calling, crying out. Some of the girls had been screaming with enthusiasm. Some of them had fainted. What a world it was nowadays, he thought. Everything used the whole time to arouse emotion. Discipline? Restraint? None of those things counted for anything any more. Nothing mattered but to *feel*.

What sort of a world, thought Stafford Nye, could that make?

His guide had touched him on the arm and they had disentangled themselves from the crowd. They had found their car and the driver had taken them by roads with which he was evidently well acquainted, to a town and an inn on a mountain side where rooms had been reserved for them.

They walked out of the inn presently and up the side of a mountain by a well-trodden path until they came to a seat. They sat there for some moments in silence. It was then that Stafford Nye had said again, 'Pasteboard.'

For some five minutes or so they sat looking down the valley, then Renata said, 'Well?'

'What are you asking me?'

'What you think so far of what I have shown you?'

'I'm not convinced,' said Stafford Nye.

She gave a sigh, a deep, unexpected sigh.

'That's what I hoped you would say.'

'It's none of it true, is it? It's a gigantic show. A show put on by a producer – a complete group of producers, perhaps.

'That monstrous woman pays the producer, hires the producer. We've not seen the producer. What we've seen today is the star performer.'

'What do you think of him?'

'He's not real either,' said Stafford Nye. 'He's just an actor. A first-class actor, superbly produced.'

A sound surprised him. It was Renata laughing. She got up from her seat. She looked suddenly excited, happy, and at the same time faintly ironical.

'I knew it,' she said. 'I knew you'd see. I knew you'd have your feet on the ground. You've always known, haven't you, about everything you've met in life? You've known humbug, you've known everything and everyone for what they really are.

'No need to go to Stratford and see Shakespearian plays to know what part you are cast for – The Kings and the great men have to have a Jester – The King's Jester who tells the King the truth, and talks common sense, and makes fun of all the things that are taking in other people.'

'So that's what I am, is it? A Court Jester?'

'Can't you feel it yourself? That's what we want – That's what we need. "Pasteboard," you said. "Cardboard". A vast, well-produced, splendid *show*! And how right you are. But people are taken in. They think something's wonderful, or they think something's devilish, or they think it's something terribly important. Of course it isn't – only – only one's got to find out just how to *show* people – that the whole thing, all of it, is just *silly*. Just damn *silly*. That's what you and I are going to do.'

'Is it your idea that in the end we debunk all this?'

'It seems wildly unlikely, I agree. But you know once people are shown that something isn't real, that it's just one enormous leg-pull, well –'

'Are you proposing to preach a gospel of common sense?'

'Of course not,' said Renata. 'Nobody'd listen to that, would they?'

'Not just at present.'

'No. We'll have to give them evidence – facts – truth –'

'Have we got such things?'

'Yes. What I brought back with me via Frankfurt – what you helped to bring safely into England –'

'I don't understand –'

'Not yet – You will know later. For now we've got a part to play. We're ready and willing, fairly panting to be indoctrinated. We worship youth. We're followers and believers in the young Siegfried.'

'*You* can put that over, no doubt. I'm not so sure about myself. I've never been very successful as a worshipper of anything. The King's Jester isn't. He's the great debunker. Nobody's going to appreciate that very much just now, are they?'

'Of course they're not. No. You don't let that side of yourself show. Except, of course, when talking about your masters and betters, politicians and diplomats, Foreign Office, the Establishment, all the other things. Then you can be embittered, malicious, witty, slightly cruel.'

'I still don't see my rôle in the world crusade.'

'That's a very ancient one, the one that everybody understands and appreciates. Something in it for you. That's your line. You haven't been appreciated in the past, but the young Siegfried and all he stands for will hold out the hope of reward to you. Because you give him all the inside dope he wants about your own country, he will promise you places of power in that country in the good times to come.'

'You insinuate that this is a world movement. Is that true?'

'Of course it is. Rather like one of those hurricanes, you know, that have names. Flora or Little Annie. They come up out of the south or the north or the east or the west, but they come up from nowhere and destroy everything. That's what everyone wants. In Europe and Asia and America. Perhaps Africa, though there won't be so much enthusiasm there. They're fairly new to power and graft and things. Oh yes, it's a world movement all right. Run by youth and all the intense vitality of youth. They haven't got knowledge and they haven't got experience, but they've got vision and vitality, and they're backed by money. Rivers and rivers of money pouring in. There's been too much materialism, so we've asked for something else, and we've got it. But as it's based on hate, it can't get anywhere. It can't move off the ground. Don't you remember in 1919 everyone going about with a rapt face saying Communism was the answer to everything. That Marxist doctrine would produce a new heaven brought down to a new earth. So many noble ideas flowing about. But then, you see, whom have you got to work out the ideas with? After all, only the same human beings you've always had. You can create a third world now, or so everyone thinks, but the third world will have the same people in it as the first world or the second world or whatever names you like to call things. And when you have the same human beings running things, they'll run them the same way. You've only got to look at history.'

'Does anybody care to look at history nowadays?'

'No. They'd much rather look forward to an unforeseeable future. Science was once going to be the answer to everything. Freudian beliefs and unrepressed sex would be the next answer to human misery. There'd be no more people with mental troubles. If anyone had said that mental homes would be even fuller as the result of shutting out repressions nobody would have believed him.'

Stafford Nye interrupted her:

'I want to know something,' said Sir Stafford Nye.

'What is it?'

'Where are we going next?'

'South America. Possibly Pakistan or India on the way. And we must certainly go to the USA. There's a lot going on there that's very interesting indeed. Especially in California –'

'Universities?' Sir Stafford sighed. 'One gets very tired of universities. They repeat themselves so much.'

They sat silent for some minutes. The light was failing, but a mountain peak showed softly red.

Stafford Nye said in a nostalgic tone:

'If we had some more music *now* – this moment – do you know what I'd order?'

'More Wagner? Or have you torn yourself free from Wagner?'

'No – you're quite right – more Wagner. I'd have Hans Sachs sitting under his elder tree, saying of the world: "Mad, mad, all mad" –'

'Yes – that expresses it. It's lovely music, too. But *we're* not mad. We're sane.'

'Eminently sane,' said Stafford Nye. 'That is going to be the difficulty. There's one more thing I want to know.'

'Well?'

'Perhaps you won't tell me. But I've *got* to know. Is there going to be any fun to be got out of this mad business that we're attempting?'

'Of course there is. Why not?'

'Mad, mad, all mad – but we'll enjoy it all very much. Will our lives be long, Mary Ann?'

'Probably not,' said Renata.

'That's the spirit. I'm with you, my comrade, and my guide. Shall we get a better world as a result of our efforts?'

'I shouldn't think so, but it might be a kinder one. It's full of beliefs without kindness at present.'

'Good enough,' said Stafford Nye. 'Onward!'

BOOK 3

At Home And Abroad

CHAPTER 13

Conference In Paris

In a room in Paris five men were sitting. It was a room that had seen historic meetings before. Quite a number of them. This meeting was in many ways a meeting of a different kind yet it promised to be no less historic.

Monsieur Grosjean was presiding. He was a worried man doing his best to slide over things with facility and a charm of manner that had often helped him in the past. He did not feel it was helping him so much today. Signor Vitelli had arrived from Italy by air an hour before. His gestures were feverish, his manner unbalanced.

'It is beyond anything,' he was saying, 'it is beyond anything one could have imagined.'

'These students,' said Monsieur Grosjean, 'do we not all suffer?'

'This is more than students. It is beyond students. What can one compare this to? A swarm of bees. A disaster of nature intensified. Intensified beyond anything one could have imagined. They march. They have machine-guns. Somewhere they have acquired planes. They propose to take over the whole of North Italy. But it is madness, that! They are children – nothing more. And yet they have bombs, explosives. In the city of Milan alone they outnumber the police. What can we do, I ask you? The military? The army too – it is in revolt. They say they are with *les jeunes*. They say there is no hope for the world except in anarchy. They talk of something they call the Third World, but this cannot just happen.'

Monsieur Grosjean sighed. 'It is very popular among the young,' he said, 'the anarchy. A belief in anarchy. We know that from the days of Algeria, from all the troubles from which our country and our colonial empire has suffered. And what can we do? The military? In the end they back the students.'

'The students, ah, the students,' said Monsieur Poissonier. He was a member of the French government to whom the word 'student' was anathema. If he had been asked he would have admitted to a preference for Asian 'flu or even an outbreak of bubonic plague. Either was preferable in his mind to the activities of students. A world with no students in it! That was what Monsieur Poissonier sometimes dreamt about. They were good dreams, those. They did not occur often enough.

'As for magistrates,' said Monsieur Grosjean, 'what has happened to our judicial authorities? The police – yes, they are loyal still, but the judiciary, they will not impose sentences, not on young men who are brought before them, young men who have destroyed property, government property, private property – every kind of property. And why not, one would like to know? I have been making inquiries lately. The Préfecture have suggested certain things to me. An increase is needed, they say, in the standard of living among judiciary authorities, especially in the provincial areas.'

'Come, come,' said Monsieur Poissonier, 'you must be careful what you suggest.'

'*Ma foi*, why should I be careful? Things need bringing into the open. We have had frauds before, gigantic frauds and there is money now circulating around. Money, and we do not know where it comes from, but the Préfecture have said to me – and I believe it – that they begin to get an idea of where it is *going*. Do we contemplate, can we contemplate a corrupt state subsidized from some outside source?'

'In Italy too,' said Signor Vitelli, 'in Italy, ah, I could tell you things. Yes, I could tell you of what we suspect. But who, who is corrupting our world? A group of industrialists, a group of tycoons? How could such a thing be so.'

'This business has got to stop,' said Monsieur Grosjean. 'Action must be taken. Military action. Action from the Air

Force. These anarchists, these marauders, they come from every class. It must be put down.'

'Control by tear gas has been fairly successful,' said Poissonier dubiously.

'Tear gas is not enough,' said Monsieur Grosjean. 'The same result could be got by setting students to peel bunches of onions. Tears would flow from their eyes. It needs more than that.'

Monsieur Poissonier said in a shocked voice:

'You are not suggesting the use of nuclear weapons?'

'Nuclear weapons? *Quelle blague!* What can we do with nuclear weapons. What would become of the soil of France, of the air of France if we use nuclear weapons? We can destroy Russia, we know that. We also know that Russia can destroy us.'

'You're not suggesting that groups of marching and demonstrating students could destroy our authoritarian forces?'

'That is exactly what I am suggesting. I have had a warning of such things. Of stock-piling of arms, and various forms of chemical warfare and of other things. I have had reports from some of our eminent scientists. Secrets are known. Stores – held in secret – weapons of warfare have been stolen. What is to happen next, I ask you. What is to happen next?'

The question was answered unexpectedly and with more rapidity than Monsieur Grosjean could possibly have calculated. The door opened and his principal secretary approached his master, his face showing urgent concern. Monsieur Grosjean looked at him with displeasure.

'Did I not say I wanted no interruptions?'

'Yes indeed, Monsieur le Président, but this is somewhat unusual –' He bent towards his master's ear. 'The Marshal is here. He demands entrance.'

'The Marshal? You mean –'

The secretary nodded his head vigorously several times to show that he did mean. Monsieur Poissonier looked at his colleague in perplexity.

'He demands admission. He will not take refusal.'

135

The two other men in the room looked first at Grosjean and then at the agitated Italian.

'Would it not be better,' said Monsieur Coin, the Minister for Home Affairs, 'if –'

He paused at the 'if' as the door was once more flung open and a man strode in. A very well-known man. A man whose word had been not only law, but above law in the country of France for many past years. To see him at this moment was an unwelcome surprise for those sitting there.

'Ah, I welcome you, dear colleagues,' said the Marshal. 'I come to help you. Our country is in danger. Action must be taken, immediate action! I come to put myself at your service. I take over all responsibility for acting in this crisis. There may be danger. I know there is, but honour is above danger. The salvation of France is above danger. They march this way now. A vast herd of students, of criminals who have been released from jails, some of them who have committed the crime of homicide. Men who have committed incendiarism. They shout names. They sing songs. They call on the names of their teachers, of their philosophers, of those who have led them on this path of insurrection. Those who will bring about the doom of France unless something is done. You sit here, you talk, you deplore things. More than that must be done. I have sent for two regiments. I have alerted the air force, special coded wires have gone out to our neighbouring ally, to my friends in Germany, for she is our ally now in this crisis!

'Riot must be put down. Rebellion! Insurrection! The danger to men, women and children, to property. I go forth now to quell the insurrection, to speak to them as their father, their leader. These students, these criminals even, they are my children. They are the youth of France. I go to speak to them of that. They shall listen to me, governments will be revised, their studies can be resumed under their own auspices. Their grants have been insufficient, their lives have been deprived of beauty, of leadership. I come to promise all this. I speak in my own name. I shall speak also in your name, the name of the Government, you have done your best, you have acted as well as you know how. But it needs higher leadership. It needs *my* leadership. I go now. I have lists of further coded wires to be sent. Such nuclear deterrents as can be used in unfrequented spots can be put into action in such a modified form that though they may bring terror to the mob, we ourselves shall know that there is no real danger in them. I have thought out everything. My plan will go. Come, my loyal friends, accompany me.'

'Marshal, we cannot allow – you cannot imperil yourself. We must ...'

'I listen to nothing you say. I embrace my doom, my destiny.'

The Marshal strode to the door.

'My staff is outside. My chosen bodyguard. I go now to speak to these young rebels, this young flower of beauty and terror, to tell them where their duty lies.'

He disappeared through the door with the grandeur of a leading actor playing his favourite part.

'*Bon Dieu*, he means it!' said Monsieur Poissonier.

'He will risk his life,' said Signor Vitelli. 'Who knows? It is brave, he is a brave man. It is gallant, yes, but what will happen to him? In the mood *les jeunes* are in now, they might kill him.'

A pleasurable sigh fell from Monsieur Poissonier's lips. It might be true, he thought. Yes, it might be true.

'It is possible,' he said. 'Yes, they might kill him.'

'One cannot wish that, of course,' said Monsieur Grosjean carefully.

Monsieur Grosjean did wish it. He hoped for it, though a natural pessimism led him to have the second thought that things seldom fell out in the way you wanted them to. Indeed, a much more awful prospect confronted him. It was quite possible, it was within the traditions of the Marshal's past, that somehow or other he might induce a large pack of exhilarated and bloodthirsty students to listen to what he said, trust in his promises, and insist on restoring him to the power that he had once held. It was the sort of thing that had happened once or twice in the career of the Marshal. His personal magnetism was such that politicians had before now met their defeat when they least expected it.

'We must restrain him,' he cried.

'Yes, yes,' said Signor Vitelli, 'he cannot be lost to the world.'

'One fears,' said Monsieur Poissonier. 'He has too many friends in Germany, too many contacts, and you know they move very quickly in military matters in Germany. They might leap at the opportunity.'

'*Bon Dieu, Bon Dieu*,' said Monsieur Grosjean, wiping his brow. 'What shall we do? What can we do? What is that noise? I hear rifles, do I not?'

'No, no,' said Monsieur Poissonier consolingly. 'It is the canteen coffee trays you hear.'

'There is a quotation I could use,' said Monsieur Grosjean, who was a great lover of the drama, 'if I could only remember it. A quotation from Shakespeare. "Will nobody rid me of this –"'

'"turbulent priest,"' said Monsieur Poissonier. 'From the play, Becket.'

'A madman like the Marshal is worse than a priest. A priest should at least be harmless, though indeed even His Holiness the Pope received a delegation of students only yesterday. He *blessed* them. He called them his children.'

'A Christian gesture, though,' said Monsieur Coin dubiously.

'One can go too far even with Christian gestures,' said Monsieur Grosjean.

CHAPTER 14

Conference In London

In the Cabinet Room at 10 Downing Street, Mr Cedric Lazenby, the Prime Minister, sat at the head of the table and looked at his assembled Cabinet without any noticeable pleasure. The expression on his face was definitely gloomy, which in a way afforded him a certain relief. He was beginning to think that it was only in the privacy of his Cabinet Meetings that he could relax his face into an unhappy expression, and could abandon that look which he presented usually to the world, of a wise and contented optimism which had served him so well in the various crises of political life.

He looked round at Gordon Chetwynd, who was frowning, at Sir George Packham who was obviously worrying, thinking, and wondering as usual, at the military imperturbability of Colonel Munro, at Air Marshal Kenwood, a tight-lipped man who did not trouble to conceal his profound distrust of politicians. There was also Admiral Blunt, a large formidable man, who tapped his fingers on the table and bided his time until his moment should come.

'It is not too good,' the Air Marshal was saying. 'One has to admit it. Four of our planes hi-jacked within the last week. Flew 'em to Milan. Turned the passengers out, and flew them on somewhere else. Actually Africa. Had pilots waiting there. Black men.'

'Black Power,' said Colonel Munro thoughtfully.

'Or Red Power?' suggested Lazenby. 'I feel, you know, that all our difficulties might stem from Russian indoctrination. If one could get into touch with the Russians – I really think a personal visit at top level –'

'You stick where you are, Prime Minister,' said Admiral Blunt. 'Don't you start arseing around with the Russkies again. All *they* want at present is to keep out of all this mess. They haven't had as much trouble there with their students as most of us have. All they mind about is keeping an eye on the Chinese to see what they'll be up to next.'

'I do think that personal influence –'

'You stay here and look after your own country,' said Admiral Blunt. True to his name, and as was his wont, he said it bluntly.

'Hadn't we better hear – have a proper report of what's actually been happening?' Gordon Chetwynd looked towards Colonel Munro.

'Want facts? Quite right. They're all pretty unpalatable. I presume you want, not particulars of what's been happening here so much, as the general world situation?'

'Quite so.'

'Well, in France the Marshal's in hospital still. Two bullets in his arm. Hell's going on in political circles. Large tracts of the country are held by what they call the Youth Power troops.'

'You mean they've got arms?' said Gordon Chetwynd in a horrified voice.

'They've got a hell of a lot,' said the Colonel. 'I don't know really where they've got them from. There are certain ideas as to that. A large consignment was sent from Sweden to West Africa.'

'What's that got to do with it?' said Mr Lazenby. 'Who cares? Let them have all the arms they want in West Africa. They can go on shooting each other.'

'Well, there's something a little curious about it as far as our Intelligence reports go. Here is a list of the armaments that were sent to West Africa. The interesting thing is they were sent there, but they were sent out again. They were accepted, delivery was acknowledged, payment may or may not have been made, but they were sent out of the country again before five days had passed. They were sent out, re-routed elsewhere.'

'But what's the idea of that?'

'The idea seems to be,' said Munro, 'that they were never really intended for West Africa. Payments were made and they were sent on somewhere else. It seems possible that they went on from Africa to the Near East. To the Persian Gulf, to Greece and to Turkey. Also, a consignment of planes was sent to Egypt. From Egypt they were sent to India, from India they were sent to Russia.'

'I thought they were sent *from* Russia.'

'– And from Russia they went to Prague. The whole thing's mad.'

'I don't understand,' said Sir George, 'one wonders –'

'Somewhere there seems to be some central organization which is directing the supplies of various things. Planes, armaments, bombs, both explosive and those that are used in germ warfare. All these consignments are moving in unexpected directions. They are delivered by various cross-country routes to trouble-spots, and used by leaders and regiments – if you like to call them that – of the Youth Power. They mostly go to the leaders of young guerrilla movements, professed anarchists who preach anarchy, and accept – though one doubts if they ever pay for – some of the latest most up-to-date models.'

'Do you mean to say we're facing something like war on a world scale?' Cedric Lazenby was shocked.

The mild man with the Asiatic face who sat lower down at the table, and had not yet spoken, lifted up his face with the Mongolian smile, and said:

'That is what one is now forced to believe. Our observations tell us –'

Lazenby interrupted.

'You'll have to stop observing. UNO will have to take arms itself and put all this down.'

The quiet face remained unmoved.

'That would be against our principles,' he said.

Colonel Munro raised his voice and went on with his summing up.

'There's fighting in some parts of every country. South-East Asia claimed Independence long ago and there are four, five different divisions of power in South America, Cuba, Peru, Guatemala and so on. As for the United States, you know

Washington was practically burn out – the West is overrun with Youth Power Armed Forces – Chicago is under Martial Law. You know about Sam Cortman? Shot last night on the steps of the American Embassy here.'

'He was to attend here today,' said Lazenby. 'He was going to have given us his views of the situation.'

'I don't suppose that would have helped much,' said Colonel Munro. 'Quite a nice chap – but hardly a live wire.'

'But who's *behind* all this?' Lazenby's voice rose fretfully.

'It could be the Russians, of course –' He looked hopeful. He still envisaged himself flying to Moscow.

Colonel Munro shook his head. 'Doubt it,' he said.

'A personal appeal,' said Lazenby. His face brightened with hope. 'An entirely new sphere of influence. The Chinese ...?'

'Nor the Chinese,' said Colonel Munro. 'But you know there's been a big revival in Neo-Fascism in Germany.'

'You don't really think the Germans could possibly ...'

'I don't think they're behind all this necessarily, but when you say possibly – yes, I think possibly they easily could. They've done it before, you know. Prepared things years before, planned them, everything ready, waiting for the word GO. Good planners, very good planners. Staff work excellent. I admire them, you know. Can't help it.'

'But Germany seemed to be so peaceful and well run.'

'Yes, of course it is up to a point. But do you realize, South America is practically alive with Germans, with young Neo-Fascists, and they've got a big Youth Federation there. Call themselves the Super-Aryans, or something of that kind. You know, a bit of the old stuff still, swastikas and salutes, and someone who's running it, called the Young Wotan or the Young Siegfried or something like that. Lot of Aryan nonsense.'

There was a knock on the door and the secretary entered.

'Professor Eckstein is here, sir.'

'We'd better have him in,' said Cedric Lazenby. 'After all, if anyone can tell us what our latest research weapons are, he's the man. We may have something up our sleeve that can soon

142

put an end to all this nonsense.' Besides being a professional traveller to foreign parts in the rôle of peacemaker, Mr Lazenby had an incurable fund of optimism seldom justified by results.

'We could do with a good secret weapon,' said the Air Marshal hopefully.

Professor Eckstein, considered by many to be Britain's top scientist, when you first looked at him seemed supremely unimportant. He was a small man with old-fashioned mutton-chop whiskers and an asthmatic cough. He had the manner of one anxious to apologize for his existence. He made noises like 'ah', 'hrrumph', 'mrrh', blew his nose, coughed asthmatically again and shook hands in a shy manner, as he was introduced to those present. A good many of them he already knew and these he greeted with nervous nods of the head. He sat down on the chair indicated and looked round him vaguely. He raised a hand to his mouth and began to bite his nails.

'The heads of the Services are here,' said Sir George Packham. 'We are very anxious to have your opinion as to what can be done.'

'Oh,' said Professor Eckstein, 'done? Yes, yes, done?'

There was a silence.

'The world is fast passing into a state of anarchy,' said Sir George.

'Seems so, doesn't it? At least, from what I read in the paper. Not that I trust to that. Really, the things journalists think up. Never any accuracy in their statements.'

'I understand you've made some most important discoveries lately, Professor,' said Cedric Lazenby encouragingly.

'Ah yes, so we have. So we have.' Professor Eckstein cheered up a little. 'Got a lot of very nasty chemical warfare fixed up. If we ever wanted it. Germ warfare, you know, biological stuff, gas laid on through normal gas outlets, air pollution and poisoning of water supplies. Yes, if you wanted it, I suppose we could kill half the population of England given about three days to do it in.' He rubbed his hands. 'That what you want?'

'No, no indeed. Oh dear, of course not.' Mr Lazenby looked horrified.

'Well, that's what I mean, you know. It's not a question of not having enough lethal weapons. We've got too much. Everything we've got is *too* lethal. The difficulty would be in keeping anybody alive, even ourselves. Eh? All the people at the top, you know. Well – *us*, for instance.' He gave a wheezy, happy little chuckle.

'But that isn't what we *want*,' Mr Lazenby insisted.

'It's not a question of what you *want*, it's a question of what we've *got*. Everything we've got is terrifically lethal. If you want everybody under thirty wiped off the map, I expect you could do it. Mind you, you'd have to take a lot of the older ones as well. It's difficult to segregate one lot from the other, you know. Personally, I should be against that. We've got some very good young Research fellows. Bloody-minded, but clever.'

'What's gone wrong with the world?' asked Kenwood suddenly.

'That's the point,' said Professor Eckstein. 'We don't know. We don't know up at our place in spite of all we *do* know about this, that and the other. We know a bit more about the moon nowadays, we know a lot about biology, we can transplant hearts and livers; brains, too, soon, I expect, though I don't know how *that'll* work out. But we don't know who is doing *this*. Somebody is, you know. It's a sort of high-powered background stuff. Oh yes, we've got it cropping up in different ways. You know, crime rings, drug rings, all that sort of thing. A high-powered lot, directed by a few good, shrewd brains behind the scenes. We've had it going on in this country or that country, occasionally on a European scale. But it's going a bit further now, other side of the globe – Southern Hemisphere. Down to the Antarctic Circle before we've finished, I expect.' He appeared to be pleased with his diagnosis.

'People of ill-will –'

'Well, you could put it like that. Ill-will for ill-will's sake or ill-will for the sake of money or power. Difficult, you know, to

144

get at the *point* of it all. The poor dogsbodies themselves don't know. They want violence and they like violence. They don't like the world, they don't like our materialistic attitude. They don't like a lot of our nasty ways of making money, they don't like a lot of the fiddles we do. They don't like seeing poverty. They want a better world. Well, you *could* make a better world, perhaps, if you thought about it long enough. But the trouble is, if you insist on taking away something first, you've got to put something back in its place. Nature won't have a vacuum – an old saying, but true. Dash it all, it's like a heart transplant. You take one heart away but you've got to put another one there. One that works. And you've got to arrange about the heart you're going to put there *before* you take away the faulty heart that somebody's got at present. Matter of fact, I think a lot of those things are better left alone altogether, but nobody would listen to me, I suppose. And anyway it's not my subject.'

'A gas?' suggested Colonel Munro.

Professor Eckstein brightened.

'Oh, we've got all sorts of *gases* in stock. Mind you, some of them are reasonably harmless. Mild deterrents, shall we say. We've got all *those*.' He beamed like a complacent hardware dealer.

'Nuclear weapons?' suggested Mr Lazenby.

'Don't you monkey with *that*! You don't want a radio-active England, do you, or a radio-active continent, for that matter?'

'So you can't help us,' said Colonel Munro.

'Not until somebody's found out a bit more about all this,' said Professor Eckstein. 'Well, I'm sorry. But I must impress upon you that most of the things we're working on nowadays are *dangerous*.' He stressed the word. '*Really* dangerous.'

He looked at them anxiously, as a nervous uncle might look at a group of children left with a box of matches to play with, and who might quite easily set the house on fire.

'Well, thank you, Professor Eckstein,' said Mr Lazenby. He did not sound particularly thankful.

The Professor gathering correctly that he was released, smiled all round and trotted out of the room.

Mr Lazenby hardly waited for the door to close before venting his feelings.

'All alike, these scientists,' he said bitterly. 'Never any practical good. Never come up with anything sensible. All they can do is split the atom – and then tell *us* not to mess about with it!'

'Just as well if we never had,' said Admiral Blunt, again bluntly. 'What *we* want is something homely and domestic like a kind of selective weedkiller which would –' He paused abruptly. 'Now what the devil –?'

'Yes, Admiral?' said the Prime Minister politely.

'Nothing – just reminded me of something. Can't remember what –'

The Prime Minister sighed.

'Any more scientific experts waiting on the mat?' asked Gordon Chetwynd, glancing hopefully at his wristwatch.

'Old Pikeaway is here, I believe,' said Lazenby. 'Got a picture – or a drawing – or a map or something or other he wants us to look at –'

'What's it all about?'

'I don't know. It seems to be all bubbles,' said Mr Lazenby vaguely.

'Bubbles? Why bubbles?'

'I've no idea. Well,' he sighed, 'we'd better have a look at it.'

'Horsham's here, too –'

'He may have something new to tell us,' said Chetwynd.

Colonel Pikeaway stumped in. He was supporting a rolled-up burden which with Horsham's aid was unrolled and which with some difficulty was propped up so that those sitting round the table could look at it.

'Not exactly drawn to scale yet, but it gives you a rough idea,' said Colonel Pikeaway.

'What does it mean, if anything?'

'Bubbles?' murmured Sir George. An idea came to him. 'Is it a gas? A new gas?'

'You'd better deliver the lecture, Horsham,' said Pikeaway. 'You know the general idea.'

146

'I only know what I've been told. It's a rough diagram of an association of world control.'

'By whom?'

'By groups who own or control the sources of power – the raw materials of power.'

'And the letters of the alphabet?'

'Stand for a person or a code name for a special group. They are intersecting circles that by now cover the globe.

'That circle marked "A" stands for armaments. Someone, or some group is in control of armaments. All types of armaments. Explosives, guns, rifles. All over the world armaments are being produced according to plan, dispatched ostensibly to under-developed nations, backward nations, nations at war. But they don't remain where they are sent. They are re-routed almost immediately elsewhere. To guerrilla warfare in the South American Continent – to rioting and fighting in the USA – to Depots of Black Power – to various countries in Europe.

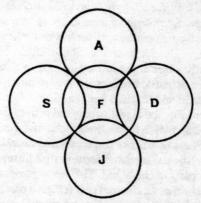

'"D" represents drugs – a network of suppliers run them from various depots and stockpiles. All kinds of drugs, from the more harmless varieties up to the true killers. The headquarters seem likely to be situated in the Levant, and to pass out through Turkey, Pakistan, India and Central Asia.'

'They make money out of it?'

'Enormous sums of money. But it's more than just an association of Pushers. It has a more sinister side to it. It's being used to finish off the weaklings amongst the young, shall we say, to make them complete slaves. Slaves so that they cannot live and exist or do jobs for their employers without a supply of drugs.'

Kenwood whistled.

'That's a bad show, isn't it? Don't you know at all who those Drug Pushers are?'

'Some of them, yes. But only the lesser fry. Not the real controllers. Drug headquarters are, so far as we can judge, in Central Asia and the Levant. They get delivered from there in the tyres of cars, in cement, in concrete, in all kinds of machinery and industrial goods. They're delivered all over the world and passed on as ordinary trade goods to where they are meant to go.

'"F" stands for finance. Money! A money spider's web in the centre of it all. You'll have to go to Mr Robinson to tell you about money. According to a memo here, money is coming very largely from America and there's also a headquarters in Bavaria. There's a vast reserve in South Africa, based on gold and diamonds. Most of the money is going to South America. One of the principal controllers, if I may so put it, of money, is a very powerful and talented woman. She's old now: must be near to death. But she is still strong and active. Her name was Charlotte Krapp. Her father owned the vast Krapp yards in Germany. She was a financial genius herself and operated in Wall Street. She accumulated fortune after fortune by investments in all parts of the world. She owns transport, she owns machinery, she owns industrial concerns. All these things. She lives in a vast castle in Bavaria – from there she directs a flow of money to different parts of the globe.

'"S" represents science – the new knowledge of chemical and biological warfare – Various young scientists have defected – There is a nucleus of them in the US, we believe, vowed and dedicated to the cause of anarchy.'

148

'Fighting for anarchy? A contradiction in terms. Can there be such a thing?'

'You believe in anarchy if you are young. You want a new world, and to begin with you must pull down the old one – just as you pull down a house before you build a new one to replace it. But if you don't know where you are going, if you don't know where you are being lured to go, or even pushed to go, what will the new world be like, and where will the believers be when they get it? Some of them slaves, some of them blinded by hate, some by violence and sadism, both preached and practised. Some of them – and God help those – still idealistic, still believing as people did in France at the time of the French Revolution that that revolution would bring prosperity, peace, happiness, contentment to its people.'

'And what are *we* doing about all this? What are we proposing to do about it?' It was Admiral Blunt who spoke.

'What are we doing about it? All that we can. I assure you, all you who are here, we are doing all that we can. We have people working for us in every country. We have agents, inquirers, those who gather information, and bring it back here –'

THE RING

F	Big Charlotte	—Bavaria
A	Eric Olafsson	—Sweden, Industrialist, Armaments
D	Said to go by the name of Demetrios	—Smyrna, Drugs
S	Dr Sarolensky	—Colorado, USA, Physicist-Chemist. Suspicion only
J		—A woman. Goes by Code name of Juanita. Said to be dangerous. Now knowledge of her real name. ·

149

'Which is very necessary,' said Colonel Pikeaway. 'First we've got to *know* – know who's who, who's with us and who's against us. And after that we've got to see what, if anything, can be done.'

'Our name for this diagram is The Ring. Here's a list of what we know about the Ring leaders. Those with a query mean that we know only the name they go by – or alternatively we only suspect that they are the ones we want.'

CHAPTER 15

Aunt Matilda Takes A Cure

I

'A cure of some kind, I thought?' Lady Matilda hazarded.

'A cure?' said Dr Donaldson. He looked faintly puzzled for a moment, losing his air of medical omniscience, which, of course, so Lady Matilda reflected, was one of the slight disadvantages attached to having a younger doctor attending one rather than the older specimen to whom one has been accustomed for several years.

'That's what we used to call them,' Lady Matilda explained. 'In my young days, you know, you went for the Cure. Marienbad, Carlsbad, Baden-Baden, all the rest of it. Just the other day I read about this new place in the paper. Quite new and up to date. Said to be all new ideas and things like that. Not that I'm really sold on new ideas, but I wouldn't really be afraid of them. I mean, they would probably be all the same things all over again. Water tasting of bad eggs and the latest sort of diet and walking to take the Cure, or the Waters, or whatever they call them now, at a rather inconvenient hour in the morning.

And I expect they give you massage or something. It used to be seaweed. But this place is somewhere in the mountains. Bavaria or Austria or somewhere like that. So I don't suppose it would be seaweed. Shaggy moss, perhaps – sounds like a dog. And perhaps quite a nice mineral water as well as the eggy sulphury one, I mean. Superb buildings, I understand. The only thing one is nervous about nowadays is that they never seem to put banisters in any up-to-date modern buildings. Flights of marble steps and all that, but nothing to hang on to.'

'I think I know the place you mean,' said Dr Donaldson. 'It's been publicized a good deal, in the press.'

'Well, you know what one is at my age,' said Lady Matilda. 'One likes trying new things. Really, I think it is just to amuse one. It doesn't really make one feel one's health would be any better. Still, you don't think it would be a bad idea, do you, Dr Donaldson?'

Dr Donaldson looked at her. He was not so young as Lady Matilda labelled him in her mind. He was just approaching forty and he was a tactful and kindly man and willing to indulge his elderly patients as far as he considered it desirable, without any actual danger of their attempting something obviously unsuitable.

'I'm sure it wouldn't do you any harm at all,' he said. 'Might be quite a good idea. Of course travel's a bit tiring though one flies to places very quickly and easily nowadays.'

'Quickly, yes. Easily, no,' said Lady Matilda. 'Ramps and moving staircases and in and out of buses from the airport to the plane, and the plane to another airport and from the airport to another bus. All that, you know. But I understand one can have wheelchairs in the airports.'

'Of course you can. Excellent idea. If you promise to do that and not think you can walk everywhere ...'

'I know, I know,' said his patient, interrupting him. 'You do understand. You're really a very understanding man. One has one's pride, you know, and while you can still hobble around with a stick or a little support, you don't really want to look absolutely a crock or bedridden or something. It'd be easier if

I was a man,' she mused. 'I mean, one could tie up one's leg with one of those enormous bandages and padded things as though one had the gout. I mean, gout is all right for the male sex. Nobody thinks anything the worse of them. Some of their older friends think they've been tucking in to the port too much because that used to be the old idea, though I believe that is not really true at all. Port wine does *not* give you gout. Yes, a wheelchair, and I could fly to Munich or somewhere like that. One could arrange for a car or something at the other end.'

'You will take Miss Leatheran with you, of course.'

'Amy? Oh, of course. I couldn't do without her. Anyway, you think no harm would be done?'

'I think it might do you a world of good.'

'You really *are* a nice man.'

Lady Matilda gave him the twinkle from her eyes with which now he was becoming familiar.

'You think it'll amuse me and cheer me up to go somewhere new and see some new faces, and of course you're quite right. But I like to think that I'm taking a Cure, though really there's nothing for me to be cured of. Not really, is there? I mean, except old age. Unfortunately old age doesn't get cured, it only gets more so, doesn't it?'

'The point is really, will you enjoy yourself? Well, I think you will. When you get tired, by the way, when doing anything, stop doing it.'

'I shall still drink glasses of water if the water tastes of rotten eggs. Not because I like them or because frankly I think they do me any good. But it has a sort of mortifying feeling. It's like old women in our village always used to be. They always wanted a nice, strong medicine either coloured black or purple or deep pink, heavily flavoured with peppermint. They thought that did much more good than a nice little pill or a bottle that only appeared to be full of ordinary water without any exotic colouring.'

'You know too much about human nature,' said Dr Donaldson.

'You're very nice to me,' said Lady Matilda. 'I appreciate it. Amy!'

'Yes, Lady Matilda?'

'Get me an atlas, will you. I've lost track of Bavaria and the countries round it.'

'Let me see now. An atlas. There'll be one in the library, I suppose. There must be some old atlases about, dating back to about 1920 or thereabouts, I suppose.'

'I wondered if we had anything a little more modern.'

'Atlas,' said Amy, deep in reflection.

'If not, you can buy one and bring it along tomorrow morning. It's going to be very difficult because all the names are different, the countries are different, and I shan't know where I am. But you'll have to help me with that. Find a big magnifying glass, will you? I have an idea I was reading in bed with one the other day and it probably slipped down between the bed and the wall.'

Her requirements took a little time to satisfy but the atlas, the magnifying glass and an older atlas by which to check, were finally produced and Amy, nice woman that she was, Lady Matilda thought, was extremely helpful.

'Yes, here it is. It still seems to be called Monbrügge or something like that. It's either in the Tyrol or Bavaria. Everything seems to have changed places and got different names –'

II

Lady Matilda looked round her bedroom in the Gasthaus. It was well appointed. It was very expensive. It combined comfort with an appearance of such austerity as might lead the inhabitant to identify herself with an ascetic course of exercises, diet and possibly painful courses of massage. Its furnishings, she thought, were interesting. They provided for all tastes. There was a large framed Gothic script on the wall. Lady Matilda's German was not as good as it had been in her girlhood, but it dealt, she thought, with the golden and enchanting idea of a return to youth. Not only did youth hold the future in its hands but the old were being nicely indoctrinated to feel that they themselves might know such a second golden flowering.

Here there were gentle aids so as to enable one to pursue the doctrine of any of the many paths in life which attracted different classes of people. (Always presuming that they had enough money to pay for it.) Beside the bed was a Gideon Bible such as Lady Matilda when travelling in the United States had often found by her bedside. She picked it up approvingly, opened it at random and dropped a finger on one particular verse. She read it, nodding her head contentedly and made a brief note of it on a note pad that was lying on her bed table. She had often done that in the course of her life – it was her way of obtaining divine guidance at short notice.

I have been young and now am old, yet have I not seen the righteous forsaken.

She made further researches of the room. Handily placed but not too apparent was an *Almanach de Gotha*, modestly situated on a lower shelf on the bedside table. A most invaluable book for those who wished to familiarize themselves with the higher strata of society reaching back for several hundred years and which were still being observed and noted and checked by those of aristocratic lineage or interested in the same. It will come in handy, she thought, I can read up a good deal on that.

Near the desk, by the stove of period porcelain, were paperback editions of certain preachings and tenets by the modern prophets of the world. Those who were now or had recently been crying in the wilderness were here to be studied and approved by young followers with haloes of hair, strange raiment, and earnest hearts. Marcuse, Guevara, Lévi-Strauss, Fanon.

In case she was going to hold any conversations with golden youth she had better read up a little on that also.

At that moment there was a timid tap on the door. It opened slightly and the face of the faithful Amy came round the corner.

Amy, Lady Matilda thought suddenly, would look exactly like a sheep when she was ten years older. A nice, faithful, kindly sheep. At the moment, Lady Matilda was glad to think, she looked still like a very agreeable plump lamb with nice curls of hair, thoughtful and kindly eyes, and able to give kindly baa's rather than to bleat.

'I do hope you slept well.'

'Yes, my dear, I did, excellently. Have you got that thing?'

Amy always knew what she meant. She handed it to her employer.

'Ah, my diet sheet. I see.' Lady Matilda perused it, then said, 'How incredibly unattractive! What's this water like one's supposed to drink?'

'It doesn't taste very nice.'

'No, I don't suppose it would. Come back in half an hour. I've got a letter I want you to post.'

Moving aside her breakfast tray, she moved over to the desk. She thought for a few minutes and then wrote her letter. 'It ought to do the trick,' she murmured.

'I beg your pardon, Lady Matilda, what did you say?'

'I was writing to the old friend I mentioned to you.'

'The one you said you haven't seen for about fifty or sixty years?'

Lady Matilda nodded.

'I do hope –' Amy was apologetic. 'I mean – I – it's such a long time. People have short memories nowadays. I do hope that she'll remember all about you and everything.'

'Of course she will,' said Lady Matilda. 'The people you don't forget are the people you knew when you were about ten to twenty. They stick in your mind for ever. You remember what hats they wore, and the way they laughed, and you remember their faults and their good qualities and everything about them. Now anyone I met twenty years ago, shall we say, I simply can't remember who they are. Not if they're mentioned to me, and not if I saw them even. Oh yes, she'll remember about *me*. And all about Lausanne. You get that letter posted. I've got to do a little homework.'

She picked up the *Almanach de Gotha* and returned to bed, where she made a serious study of such items as might come in useful. Some family relationships and various other kinships of the useful kind. Who had married whom, who had lived where, what misfortunes had overtaken others. Not that the person whom she had in mind was herself likely to be found in the *Almanach de Gotha*. But she lived in a part of the world, had come there deliberately to live in a Schloss belonging to originally noble ancestors, and she had absorbed the local respect and adulation for those above all of good breeding. To good birth, even impaired with poverty, she herself, as Lady Matilda well knew, had no claim whatever. She had had to make do with money. Oceans of money. Incredible amounts of money.

Lady Matilda Cleckheaton had no doubt at all that she herself, the daughter of an eighth Duke, would be bidden to some kind of festivity. Coffee, perhaps, and delicious creamy cakes.

III

Lady Matilda Cleckheaton made her entrance into one of the grand reception rooms of the Schloss. It had been a fifteen-mile drive. She had dressed herself with some care, though somewhat to the disapproval of Amy. Amy seldom offered advice, but she was so anxious for her principal to succeed in whatever she was undertaking that she had ventured this time on a moderate remonstrance.

'You don't think your red dress is really a little *worn*, if you know what I mean. I mean just beneath the arms, and, well, there are two or three very shiny patches –'

'I know, my dear, I know. It is a shabby dress but it is nevertheless a Patou model. It is old but it was enormously expensive. I am not trying to look rich or extravagant. I am an impoverished member of an aristocratic family. Anyone of under fifty, no doubt, would despise me. But my hostess is living and has lived for some years in a part of the world where the rich will be kept waiting for their meal while the hostess will be willing to wait for a shabby, elderly woman of impeccable descent. Family traditions are things that one does not lose easily. One absorbs them, even, when one goes to a new neighbourhood. In my trunk, by the way, you will find a feather boa.'

'Are you going to put on a feather boa?'

'Yes, I am. An ostrich feather one.'

'Oh dear, that must be years old.'

'It is, but I've kept it very carefully. You'll see, Charlotte will recognize what it is. She will think one of the best families in England was reduced to wearing her old clothes that she had kept carefully for years. And I'll wear my sealskin coat, too. That's a little worn, but such a magnificent coat in its time.'

Thus arrayed, she set forth. Amy went with her as a well-dressed though only quietly smart attendant.

Matilda Cleckheaton had been prepared for what she saw. A whale, as Stafford and told her. A wallowing whale, a hideous old woman sitting in a room surrounded with pictures worth a fortune. Rising with some difficulty from a throne-like chair which could have figured on a stage representing the palace of some magnificent prince from any age from the Middle Ages down.

'Matilda!'

'Charlotte!'

'Ah! After all these years. How strange it seems!'

They exchanged words of greeting and pleasure, talking partly in German and partly in English. Lady Matilda's German was slightly faulty. Charlotte spoke excellent German, excellent English though with a strong guttural accent, and occasionally English with an American accent. She was really, Lady Matilda thought, quite splendidly hideous. For a moment she felt a fondness almost dating back to the past although, she reflected the next moment, Charlotte had been a most detestable girl. Nobody had really liked her and she herself had certainly not done so. But there is a great bond, say what we will, in the memories of old schooldays. Whether

Charlotte had liked her or not she did not know. But Charlotte, she remembered, had certainly – what used to be called in those days – sucked up to her. She had had visions, possibly, of staying in a ducal castle in England. Lady Matilda's father, though of most praiseworthy lineage, had been one of the most impecunious of English dukes. His estate had only been held together by the rich wife he had married whom he had treated with the utmost courtesy, and who had enjoyed bullying him whenever able to do so. Lady Matilda had been fortunate enough to be his daughter by a second marriage. Her own mother had been extremely agreeable and also a very successful actress, able to play the part of looking a duchess far more than any real duchess could do.

They exchanged reminiscences of past days, the tortures they had inflicted on some of their instructors, the fortunate and unfortunate marriages that had occurred to some of their schoolmates. Matilda made a few mentions of certain alliances and families culled from the pages of the *Almanach de Gotha* – 'but of course that must have been a terrible marriage for Elsa. One of the Bourbons de Parme, was it not? Yes, yes, well, one knows what that leads to. Most unfortunate.'

Coffee was brought, delicious coffee, plates of millefeuille pastry and delicious cream cakes.

'I should not touch any of this,' cried Lady Matilda. 'No indeed! My doctor, he is most severe. He said that I must adhere strictly to the Cure while I was here. But after all this is a day of holiday, is it not? Of renewal of youth. That is what interests me so much. My great-nephew who visited you not long ago – I forget who brought him here, the Countess – ah, it began with a Z, I cannot remember her name.'

'The Countess Renata Zerkowski –'

'Ah, that was the name, yes. A very charming young woman, I believe. And she brought him to visit you. It was most kind of her. He was so impressed. Impressed, too, with all your beautiful possessions. Your way of living, and indeed, the wonderful things which he had heard about you. How you have a whole movement of – oh, I do not know how to give the proper term. A Galaxy of Youth. Golden, beautiful youth. They flock round you. They worship you. What a wonderful life you must live. Not that I could support such a life. I have to live very quietly. Rheumatoid arthritis. And also the financial difficulties. Difficulty in keeping up the family house. Ah well, you know what it is for us in England – our taxation troubles.'

'I remember that nephew of yours, yes. He was agreeable, a very agreeable man. The Diplomatic Service, I understand?'

'Ah yes. But it is – well, you know, I cannot feel that his talents are being properly recognized. He does not say much. He does not complain, but he feels that he is – well, he feels that he has not been appreciated as he should. The powers that be, those who hold office at present, what are they?'

'*Canaille!*' said Big Charlotte.

'Intellectuals with no *savoir faire* in life. Fifty years ago it would have been different,' said Lady Matilda, 'but nowadays his promotion has been not advanced as it should. I will even tell you, in confidence, of course, that he has been distrusted. They suspect him, you know, of being in with – what shall I call it? – rebellious, revolutionary tendencies. And yet one must realize what the future could hold for a man who could embrace more advanced views.'

'You mean he is not, then, how do you say it in England, in sympathy with the Establishment, as they call it?'

'Hush, hush, we must not say these things. At least *I* must not,' said Lady Matilda.

'You interest me,' said Charlotte.

Matilda Cleckheaton sighed.

'Put it down, if you like, to the fondness of an elderly relative. Staffy has always been a favourite of mine. He has charm and wit. I think also he has ideas. He envisages the future, a future that should differ a good deal from what we have at present. Our country, alas, is politically in a very bad state. Stafford seems to be very much impressed by things you said to him or showed to him. You've done so much for music, I understand. What we need I cannot but feel is the ideal of the super race.'

'There should and could be a super race. Adolf Hitler had the right idea,' said Charlotte. 'A man of no importance in himself, but he had artistic elements in his character. And undoubtedly he had the power of leadership.'

'Ah yes. Leadership, that is what we need.'

'You had the wrong allies in the last war, my dear. If England and Germany now had arrayed themselves side by side, if they had had the same ideals, of youth, strength, two Aryan nations with the right ideals. Think where your country and mine might have arrived today? Yet perhaps even that is too narrow a view to take. In some ways the communists and the others have taught us a lesson. Workers of the world unite? But that is to set one's sights too low. Workers are only our material. It is "Leaders of the world unite!" Young men with the gift of leadership, of good blood. And we must start, not with the middle-aged men set in their ways, repeating themselves like a gramophone record that has stuck. We must seek among the student population, the young men with brave hearts, with great ideas, willing to march, willing to be killed but willing also to kill. To kill without any compunction – because it is certain that without aggressiveness, without violence, without attack – there can be no victory. I must show you something –'

With somewhat of a struggle she succeeded in rising to her feet. Lady Matilda followed suit, underlining a little her difficulty, which was not quite as much as she was making out.

'It was in May 1940,' said Charlotte, 'when Hitler Youth went on to its second stage. When Himmler obtained from Hitler a charter. The charter of the famous SS. It was formed for the destruction of the eastern peoples, the slaves, the appointed slaves of the world. It would make room for the German master race. The SS executive instrument came into being.' Her voice dropped a little. It held for a moment a kind of religious awe.

Lady Matilda nearly crossed herself by mistake.

'The Order of the Death's Head,' said Big Charlotte.

She walked slowly and painfully down the room and pointed

to where on the wall hung, framed in gilt and surmounted with a skull, the Order of the Death's Head.

'See, it is my most cherished possession. It hangs here on my wall. My golden youth band, when they come here, salute it. And in our archives in the castle here are folios of its chronicles. Some of them are only reading for strong stomachs, but one must learn to accept these things. The deaths in gas chambers, the torture cells, the trials at Nuremberg speak venomously of all those things. But it was a great tradition. Strength through pain. They were trained young, the boys, so that they should not falter or turn back or suffer from any kind of softness. Even Lenin, preaching his Marxist doctrine, declared "Away with softness!" It was one of his first rules for creating a perfect State. But we were too narrow. We wished to confine our great dream only to the German master race. But there are other races. They too can attain masterhood through suffering and violence and through the considered practice of anarchy. We must pull down, pull down all the soft institutions. Pull down the more humiliating forms of religion. There is a religion of strength, the old religion of the Viking people. And we have a leader, young as yet, gaining in power every day. What did some great man say? Give me the tools and I will do the job. Something like that. Our leader has already the tools. He will have more tools. He will have the planes, the bombs, the means of chemical warfare. He will have the men to fight. He will have the transport. He will have shipping and oil. He will have what one might call the Aladdin's creation of genie. You rub the lamp and the genie appears. It is all in your hands. The means of production, the means of wealth and our young leader, a leader by birth as well as by character. He has all this.'

She wheezed and coughed.

'Let me help you.'

Lady Matilda supported her back to her seat. Charlotte gasped a little as she sat down.

'It's sad to be old, but I shall last long enough. Long enough to see the triumph of a new world, a new creation. That is what you want for your nephew. I will see to it. Power in his own

161

country, that is what he wants, is it not? You would be ready to encourage the spearhead there?'

'I had influence once. But now –' Lady Matilda shook her head sadly. 'All that is gone.'

'It will come again, dear,' said her friend. 'You were right to come to me. I have a certain influence.'

'It is a great cause,' said Lady Matilda. She sighed and murmured, 'The Young Siegfried.'

'I hope you enjoyed meeting your old friend,' said Amy as they drove back to the Gasthaus.

'If you could have heard all the nonsense I talked, you wouldn't believe it,' said Lady Matilda Cleckheaton.

CHAPTER 16

Pikeaway Talks

'The news from France is very bad,' said Colonel Pikeaway, brushing a cloud of cigar ash off his coat. 'I heard Winston Churchill say that in the last war. There was a man who could speak in plain words and no more than needed. It was very impressive. It told us what we needed to know. Well, it's a long time since then, but I say it again today. The news from France is very bad.'

He coughed, wheezed and brushed a little more ash off himself.

'The news from Italy is very bad,' he said. 'The news from Russia, I imagine, could be very bad if they let much out about it. They've got trouble there too. Marching bands of students in the street, shop windows smashed, Embassies attacked. News from Egypt is very bad. News from Jerusalem is very bad. News from Syria is very bad. That's all more or less normal, so we needn't worry too much. News from Argentine is what I'd call peculiar. Very peculiar indeed. Argentine, Brazil, Cuba, they've all got together. Call themselves the Golden Youth Federated States, or something like that. It's got an army, too. Properly drilled, properly armed, properly commanded. They've got planes, they've got bombs, they've got God-knows-what. And most of them seem to know what to do with them, which makes it worse. There's a singing crowd as well, apparently. Pop songs, old local folk songs, and bygone battle hymns. They go along rather like the Salvation Army used to do – no blasphemy intended – I'm not crabbing the Salvation Army. Jolly good work they did always. And the girls – pretty as Punch in their bonnets.'

He went on:

'I've heard that something's going on in that line in the civilized countries, starting with *us*. Some of us can be called civilized still, I suppose? One of our politicians the other day, I remember, said we were a splendid nation, chiefly because we were permissive, we had demonstrations, we smashed things, we beat up anyone if we hadn't anything better to do, we got rid of our high spirits by showing violence, and our moral purity by taking most of our clothes off. I don't know what he thought he was talking about – politicians seldom do – but they can make it sound all right. That's why they are politicians.'

He paused and looked across at the man he was talking to.

'Distressing – sadly distressing,' said Sir George Packham. 'One can hardly believe – one worries – if one could only – Is that all the news you've got?' he asked plaintively.

'Isn't it enough? You're hard to satisfy. World anarchy well on its way – that's what we've got. A bit wobbly still – not fully established yet, but very near to it – very near indeed.'

'But action can surely be taken against all this?'

'Not so easy as you think. Tear gas puts a stop to rioting for a while and gives the police a break. And naturally we've got plenty of germ warfare and nuclear bombs and all the other pretty bags of tricks – What do you think would happen if we started using those? Mass massacre of all the marching girls and boys, and the housewife's shopping circle, and the old age pensioners at home, and a good quota of our pompous politicians as they tell us we've never had it so good, and in addition you and me – Ha, ha!'

'And anyway,' added Colonel Pikeaway, 'if it's only news you're after, I understand you've got some hot news of your own arriving today. Top secret from Germany, Herr Heinrich Spiess himself.'

'How on earth did you hear that? It's supposed to be strictly –'

'We know everything here,' said Colonel Pikeaway, using his pet phrase – that's what we're for.

'Bringing some tame doctor, too, I understand –' he added.

'Yes, a Dr Reichardt, a top scientist, I presume –'

'No. Medical doctor – Loony-bins –'

'Oh dear – a psychologist?'

'Probably. The ones that run loony-bins are mostly that. With any luck he'll have been brought over so that he can examine the heads of some of our young firebrands. Stuffed full they are of German philosophy, Black Power philosophy, dead French writers' philosophy, and so on and so forth. Possibly they'll let him examine some of the heads of our legal lights who preside over our judicial courts here saying we must be very careful not to do anything to damage a young man's ego because he *might* have to earn his living. We'd be a lot safer if they sent them all round to get plenty of National Assistance to live on and then they could go back to their rooms, not do any work, and enjoy themselves reading more philosophy. However, I'm out of date. I know that. You needn't tell me so.'

'One has to take into account the new modes of thought,' said Sir George Packham. 'One feels, I mean one hopes – well, it's difficult to say –'

'Must be very worrying for you,' said Colonel Pikeaway. 'Finding things so difficult to say.'

His telephone rang. He listened, then handed it to Sir George.

'Yes?' said Sir George. 'Yes? Oh yes. Yes. I agree. I suppose

'- No - no - not the Home Office. No. Privately, you mean. Well, I suppose we'd better use - er -' Sir George looked round him cautiously.

'This place isn't bugged,' said Colonel Pikeaway amiably.

'Code word Blue Danube,' said Sir George Packham in a loud, hoarse whisper. 'Yes, yes. I'll bring Pikeaway along with me. Oh yes, of course. Yes, yes. Get on to him. Yes, say you particularly want him to come, but to remember our meeting has got to be strictly private.'

'We can't take my car then,' said Pikeaway. 'It's too well known.'

'Henry Horsham's coming to fetch us in the Volkswagen.'

'Fine,' said Colonel Pikeaway. 'Interesting, you know, all this.'

'You don't think -' said Sir George and hesitated.

'I don't think what?'

'I mean just really - well, I - mean, if you wouldn't mind my suggesting - a clothes brush?'

'Oh, this.' Colonel Pikeaway hit himself lightly on the shoulder and a cloud of cigar ash flew up and made Sir George choke.

'Nanny,' Colonel Pikeaway shouted. He banged a buzzer on his desk.

A middle-aged woman came in with a clothes brush, appearing with the suddenness of a genie summoned by Aladdin's lamp.

'Hold your breath, please, Sir George,' she said. 'This may be a little pungent.'

She held the door open for him and he retired outside while she brushed Colonel Pikeaway, who coughed and complained:

'Damned nuisance these people are. Always wanting you to get fixed up like a barber's dummy.'

'I should not describe your appearance as quite like that, Colonel Pikeaway. You ought to be used to my cleaning you up nowadays. And you know the Home Secretary suffers from asthma.'

'Well, that's his fault. Not taking proper care to have pollution removed from the streets of London.

'Come on, Sir George, let's hear what our German friend has come over to say. Sounds as though it's a matter of some urgency.'

CHAPTER 17

Herr Heinrich Spiess

Herr Heinrich Spiess was a worried man. He did not seek to conceal the fact. He acknowledged, indeed, without concealment, that the situation which these five men had come together to discuss was a serious situation. At the same time, he brought with him that sense of reassurance which had been his principal asset in dealing with the recently difficult political life in Germany. He was a solid man, a thoughtful man, a man who could bring common sense to any assemblies he attended. He gave no sense of being a brilliant man, and that in itself was reassuring. Brilliant politicians had been responsible for about two-thirds of the national states of crisis in more countries than one. The other third of trouble had been caused by those politicians who were unable to conceal the fact that although duly elected by democratic governments, they had been unable to conceal their remarkably poor powers of judgment, common sense and, in fact, any noticeable brainy qualities.

'This is not in any sense an official visit, you understand,' said the Chancellor.

'Oh quite, quite.'

'A certain piece of knowledge has come to me which I thought is essential we should share. It throws a rather interesting light on certain happenings which have puzzled as well as distressed us. This is Dr Reichardt.'

166

Introductions were made. Dr Reichardt was a large and comfortable-looking man with the habit of saying 'Ach, so' from time to time.

'Dr Reichardt is in charge of a large establishment in the neighbourhood of Karlsruhe. He treats there mental patients. I think I am correct in saying that you treat there between five and six hundred patients, am I not right?'

'Ach, so,' said Dr Reichardt.

'I take it that you have several different forms of mental illness?'

'Ach, so. I have different forms of mental illness, but nevertheless, I have a special interest in, and treat almost exclusively one particular type of mental trouble.' He branched off into German and Herr Spiess presently rendered a brief translation in case some of his English colleagues should not understand. This was both necessary and tactful. Two of them did in part, one of them definitely did not, and the two others were truly puzzled.

'Dr Reichardt has had,' explained Herr Spiess, 'the greatest success in his treatment of what as a layman I describe as megalomania. The belief that you are someone other than you are. Ideas of being more important than you are. Ideas that if you have persecution mania –'

'Ach, no!' said Dr Reichardt. 'Persecution mania, *no*, that I do not treat. There is no persecution mania in my clinic. Not among the group with whom I am specially interested. On the contrary, they hold the delusions that they do because they wish to be happy. And they are happy, and I can keep them happy. But if I cure them, see you, they will not be happy. So I have to find a cure that will restore sanity to them, and yet they will be happy just the same. We call this particular state of mind –'

He uttered a long and ferociously sounding German word of at least eight syllables.

'For the purposes of our English friends, I shall still use my term of megalomania, though I know,' continued Herr Spiess, rather quickly, 'that that is not the term you use nowadays, Dr

Reichardt. So, as I say, you have in your clinic six hundred patients.'

'And at one time, the time to which I am about to refer, I had eight hundred.'

'Eight hundred!'

'It was interesting – most interesting.'

'You have such persons – to start at the beginning –'

'We have God Almighty,' explained Dr Reichardt. 'You comprehend?'

Mr Lazenby looked slightly taken aback.

'Oh – er – yes – er – yes. Very interesting, I am sure.'

'There are one or two young men, of course, who think they are Jesus Christ. But that is not so popular as the Almighty. And then there are the others. I had at the time I am about to mention twenty-four Adolf Hitlers. This you must understand was at the time when Hitler was alive. Yes, twenty-four or twenty-five Adolf Hitlers –' he consulted a small notebook which he took from his pocket – 'I have made some notes here, yes. Fifteen Napoleons. Napoleon, he is always popular, ten Mussolinis, five reincarnations of Julius Caesar, and many other cases, very curious and very interesting. But that I will not weary you with at this moment. Not being specially qualified in the medical sense, it would not be of any interest to you. We will come to the incident that matters.'

Dr Reichardt spoke again at rather shorter length, and Herr Spiess continued to translate.

'There came to him one day a government official. Highly thought of at that time – this was during the war, mind you – by the ruling government. I will call him for the moment Martin B. You will know who I mean. He brought with him his chief. In fact he brought with him – well, we will not beat about the bush – he brought the Führer himself.'

'Ach, so,' said Dr Reichardt.

'It was a great honour, you understand, that he should come to inspect,' went on the doctor. 'He was gracious, mein Führer. He told me that he had heard very good reports of my successes. He said that there had been trouble lately. Cases

168

from the army. There, more than once there had been men believing they were Napoleon, sometimes believing they were some of Napoleon's Marshals and sometimes, you comprehend, behaving accordingly, giving out military orders and causing therefore military difficulties. I would have been happy to have given him any professional knowledge that might be useful to him, but Martin B. who accompanied him said that that would not be necessary. Our great Führer, however,' said Dr Reichardt, looking at Herr Spiess slightly uneasily, 'did not want to be bothered with such details. He said that no doubt it would be better if medically qualified men with some experience as neurologists should come and have a consultation. What he wanted was to – ach, well, he wanted to see round, and I soon found what he was really interested to see. It should not have surprised me. Oh no, because you see, it was a symptom that one recognizes. The strain of his life was already beginning to tell on the Führer.'

'I suppose he was beginning to think he was God Almighty himself at that time,' said Colonel Pikeaway unexpectedly, and he chuckled.

Dr Reichardt looked shocked.

'He asked me to let him know certain things. He said that Martin B. had told him that I actually had a large number of patients thinking, not to put too fine a point on it, that they were themselves Adolf Hitler. I explained to him that this was not uncommon, that naturally with the respect, the worship they paid to Hitler, it was only natural that the great wish to be like him should end eventually by them identifying themselves with him. I was a little anxious when I mentioned this but I was desighted to find that he expressed great signs of satisfaction. He took it, I am thankful to say, as a compliment, this passionate wish to find identity with himself. He next asked if he could meet a representative number of these patients with this particular affliction. We had a little consultation. Martin B. seemed doubtful, but he took me aside and assured me that Herr Hitler actually wished to have this experience. What he himself was anxious to ensure was that Herr Hitler did not meet – well, in short, that Herr Hitler was not to be allowed to run any risks. If any of these so-called Hitlers, believing passionately in themselves as such, were inclined to be a little violent or dangerous ... I assured him that he need have no worry. I suggested that I should collect a group of the most amiable of our Führers and assemble them for him to meet. Herr B. insisted that the Führer was very anxious to interview and mingle with them without my accompanying him. The patients, he said, would not behave naturally if they saw the chief of the establishment there, and if there was no danger ... I assured him again that there was no danger. I said, however, that I should be glad if Herr B. would wait upon him. There was no difficulty about that. It was arranged. Messages were sent to the Führers to assemble in a room for a very distinguished visitor who was anxious to compare notes with them.

'Ach, so. Martin B. and the Führer were introduced into the assembly. I retired, closing the door, and chatted with the two ADC's who had accompanied them. The Führer, I said, was looking in a particularly anxious state. He had no doubt had many troubles of late. This I may say was very shortly before the end of the war when things, quite frankly, were going badly. The Führer himself, they told me, had been greatly distressed of late but was convinced that he could bring the war to a successful close if the ideas which he was continually presenting to his general staff were acted upon, and accepted promptly.'

'The Führer, I presume,' said Sir George Packham, 'was at that time – I mean to say – no doubt he was in a state that –'

'We need not stress these points,' said Herr Spiess. 'He was completely beyond himself. Authority had to be taken for him on several points. But all that you will know well enough from the researches you have made in my country.'

'One remembers that at the Nuremberg trials –'

'There's no need to refer to the Nuremberg trials, I'm sure,' said Mr Lazenby decisively. 'All that is far behind us. We look forward to a great future in the Common Market with your

Government's help, with the Government of Monsieur Gros-jean and your other European colleagues. The past is the past.'

'Quite so,' said Herr Spiess, 'and it is of the past that we now talk. Martin B. and Herr Hitler remained for a very short time in the assembly room. They came out again after seven minutes. Herr B. expressed himself to Dr Reichardt as very well satisfied with their experience. Their car was waiting and he and Herr Hitler must proceed immediately to where they had another appointment. They left very hurriedly.'

There was a silence.

'And then?' asked Colonel Pikeaway. 'Something happened? Or had already happened?'

'The behaviour of one of our Hitler patients was unusual,' said Dr Reichardt. 'He was a man who had a particularly close resemblance to Herr Hitler, which had given him always a special confidence in his own portrayal. He insisted now more fiercely than ever that he *was* the Führer, that he must go immediately to Berlin, that he must preside over a Council of the General Staff. In fact, he behaved with no signs of the former slight amelioration which he had shown in his condition. He seemed so unlike himself that I really could not understand this change taking place so suddenly. I was relieved, indeed, when two days later, his relations called to take him home for future private treatment there.'

'And you let him go,' said Herr Spiess.

'Naturally I let him go. They had a responsible doctor with them, he was a voluntary patient, not certified, and therefore he was within his rights. So he left.'

'I don't see –' began Sir George Packham.

'Herr Spiess has a theory –'

'It's not a theory,' said Spiess. 'What I am telling you is fact. The Russians concealed it, we've concealed it. Plenty of evidence and proof has come in. Hitler, our Führer, *remained in the asylum by his own consent* that day and a man with the nearest resemblance to the real Hitler departed with Martin B. It was that patient's body which was subsequently found in the bunker. I will not beat about the bush. We need not go into unnecessary details.'

'We all have to know the truth,' said Lazenby.

'The real Führer was smuggled by a pre-arranged underground route to the Argentine and lived there for some years. He had a son there by a beautiful Aryan girl of good family. Some say she was an English girl. Hitler's mental condition worsened, and he died insane, believing himself to be commanding his armies in the field. It was the only plan possibly by which he could ever have escaped from Germany. He accepted it.'

'And you mean that for all these years nothing has leaked out about this, nothing has been known?'

'There have been rumours, there are always rumours. If you remember, one of the Czar's daughters in Russia was said to have escaped the general massacre of her family.'

'But that was –' George Packham stopped. 'False – quite false.'

'It was proved false by one set of people. It was accepted by another set of people, both of whom had known her. That Anastasia was indeed Anastasia, or that Anastasia, Grand Duchess of Russia, was really only a peasant girl. Which story was true? Rumours! The longer they go on, the less people believe them, except for those who have romantic minds, who go on believing them. It has often been rumoured that Hitler was alive, not dead. There is no one who has ever said with certainty that they have examined his dead body. The Russians declared so. They brought no proofs, though.'

'Do you really mean to say – Dr Reichardt, do *you* support this extraordinary story?'

'Ach,' said Dr Reichardt. 'You ask me, but I have told you my part. It was certainly Martin B. who came to my sanatorium. It was Martin B. who brought with him the Führer. It was Martin B. who treated him as the Führer, who spoke to him with the deference with which one speaks to the Führer. As for me, I lived already with some hundreds of Führers, of Napoleons, of Julius Caesars. You must understand that the Hitlers who lived in my sanatorium, they looked alike, they could have been, nearly all of them *could* have been, Adolf Hitler. They themselves could never have believed in themselves with the passion, the vehemence with which they knew that they were Hitler, unless they had had a basic resemblance, with make-up, clothing, continual acting, and playing of the part. I had had no personal meeting with Herr Adolf Hitler at any previous time. One saw pictures of him in the papers, one knew roughly what our great genius looked like, but one knew only the pictures that he wished shown. So he came, he was the Führer, Martin B., the man best to be believed on that subject, said he was the Führer. No, I had no doubts. I obeyed orders. Herr Hitler wished to go alone into a room to meet a selection of his – what shall one say? – his plaster copies. He went in. He came out. An exchange of clothing could have been made, not very different clothing in any case. Was it he himself or one of the self-appointed Hitlers who came out? Rushed out quickly by Martin B. and driven away while the real man could have stayed behind, could have enjoyed playing his part, could have known that in this way and in this way only could he manage to escape from the country which at any moment might surrender. He was already disturbed in mind, mentally affected by rage and anger that the orders he gave, the wild fantastic messages sent to his staff, what they were to do, what they were to say, the impossible things they were to attempt, were not, as of old, immediately obeyed. He could feel already that he was no longer in supreme command. But he had a small faithful two or three and they had a plan for him, to get him out of this country, out of Europe, to a place where he could rally round him in a different continent his Nazi followers, the young ones who believed so passionately in him. The swastika would rise again there. He played his part. No doubt, he enjoyed it. Yes, that would be in keeping with a man whose reason was already tottering. He would show these others that he could play the part of Adolf Hitler better than they did. He laughed to himself occasionally, and my doctors, my nurses, they would look in, they would see some slight change. One patient who seemed unusually mentally disturbed, perhaps. Pah, there was nothing in that. It was always happening. With the Napoleons, with the Julius Caesars, with all of them. Some days, as one would say if one was a layman, they are madder than usual. That is the only way I can put it. So now it is for Herr Spiess to speak.'

'Fantastic!' said the Home Secretary.

'Yes, fantastic,' said Herr Spiess patiently, 'but fantastic things can happen, you know. In history, in real life, no matter how fantastic.'

'And nobody suspected, nobody knew?'

'It was very well planned. It was well planned, well thought out. The escape route was ready, the exact details of it are not clearly known, but one can make a pretty good recapitulation of them. Some of the people who were concerned, who passed a certain personage on from place to .place under different disguises, under different names, some of those people, on our looking back and making inquiries, we find did not live as long as they might have done.'

'You mean in case they should give the secret away or should talk too much?'

'The SS saw to that. Rich rewards, praise, promises of high positions in the future and then – death is a much easier answer. And the SS were used to death. They knew the different ways of it, they knew means of disposing of bodies – Oh yes, I will tell you that, this has been inquired into for some time now. The knowledge has come little by little to us, and we have made inquiries, documents have been acquired and the truth has come out. Adolf Hitler certainly reached South America. It is said that a marriage ceremony was performed – that a child was born. The child was branded in the foot with the mark of the swastika. Branded as a baby. I have seen trusted agents whom I can believe. They have seen that branded foot in South America. There that child was brought up, carefully guarded, shielded, prepared – prepared as the Dalai Lama might have been prepared for his great destiny. For that was the idea behind the fanatical young, the idea was greater than the idea

174

that they had started out with. This was not merely a revival of the new Nazis, the new German super race. It was that, yes, but it was many more things besides. It was the young of many other nations, the super race of the young men of nearly every country in Europe, to join together, to join the ranks of anarchy, to destroy the old world, that materialistic world, to usher in a great new band of killing, murdering, violent brothers. Bent first on destruction and then on rising to power. And they had now their leader. A leader with the right blood in his veins and a leader who, though he grew up with no great likeness to his dead father, was – no, *is* – a golden-haired fair Nordic boy, taking presumably after the looks of his mother. A golden boy. A boy whom the whole world could accept. The Germans and the Austrians first because it was the great article of their faith, of their music, the young Siegfried. So he grew up as the young Siegfried who would command them all, who would lead them into the promised land. Not the promised land of the Jews, whom they despised, where Moses led his followers. The Jews were dead under the ground, killed or murdered in the gas chambers. This was to be a land of their own, a land gained by their own prowess. The countries of Europe were to be banded together with the countries of South America. There already they had their spearhead, their anarchists, their prophets, their Guevaras, the Castros, the Guerrillas, their followers, a long arduous training in cruelty and torture and violence and death and after it, glorious life. Freedom! As Rulers of the New World State. The appointed conquerors.'

'Absurd nonsense,' said Mr Lazenby. 'Once all this is put a stop to – the whole thing will collapse. This is all quite ridiculous. What *can* they do?' Cedric Lazenby sounded merely querulous.

Herr Spiess shook his heavy, wise head.

'You may ask. I tell you the answer, which is – *they do not know*. They don't know where they're going. They don't know what is going to be done with them.'

'You mean they're not the real leaders?'

'They are the young marching Heroes, treading their path to glory, on the stepping-stones of violence, of pain, of hatred. They have now their following not only in South America and Europe. The cult has travelled north. In the United States, there too the young men riot, they march, they follow the banner of the Young Siegfried. They are taught his ways, they are taught to kill, to enjoy pain, they are taught the rules of the Death's Head, the rules of Himmler. They are being trained, you see. They are being secretly indoctrinated. They do not know what they're being trained for. But we do, some of us at least. And you? In this country?'

'Four of five of us, perhaps,' said Colonel Pikeaway.

'In Russia they know, in America they have begun to know. They know that there are the followers of the Young Hero, Siegfried, based on the Norse Legends, and that a young Siegfried is the leader. That that is their new religion. The religion of the glorious boy, the golden triumph of youth. In him the old Nordic Gods have risen again.

'But that, of course,' said Herr Spiess, dropping his voice to a commonplace tone, 'that of course is not the simple prosaic truth. There are some powerful personalities behind this. Evil men with first-class brains. A first-class financier, a great industrialist, someone who controls mines, oil, stores of uranium, who owns scientists of the top class, and those are the ones, a committee of men, who themselves do not look particularly interesting or extraordinary, but nevertheless have got control. They control the sources of power, and control through certain means of their own the young men who kill and the young men who are slaves. By control of drugs they acquire slaves. Slaves in every country who little by little progress from soft drugs to hard drugs and who are then completely subservient, completely dependent on men whom they do not even know but who secretly own them body and soul. Their craving need for a particular drug makes them slaves, and in due course, these slaves prove to be no good, because of their dependence on drugs, they will only be capable of sitting in apathy dreaming sweet dreams, and so they will be left to die, or even helped to die. They will not inherit that kingdom in which they believe. Strange religions are being deliberately introduced to them. The gods of the old days disguised.'

'And permissive sex also plays its part, I suppose?'

'Sex can destroy itself. In old Roman times the men who steeped themselves in vice, who were oversexed, who ran sex to death until they were bored and weary of sex, sometimes fled from it and went out into the desert and became Anchorites like St Simeon Stylites. Sex will exhaust itself. It does its work for the time being, but it cannot rule you as drugs rule you. Drugs and sadism and the love of power and hatred. A desire for pain for its own sake. The pleasures of inflicting it. They are teaching themselves the pleasures of evil. Once the pleasures of evil get a hold on you, you cannot draw back.'

'My dear Chancellor – I really can't believe you – I mean, well – I mean if there are these tendencies, they must be put down by adopting strong measures. I mean, really, one – one can't go on pandering to this sort of thing. One must take a firm stand – a firm stand.'

'Shut up, George.' Mr Lazenby pulled out his pipe, looked at it, put it back in his pocket again. 'The best plan, I think,' he said, his *idée fixe* reasserting itself, 'would be for me to fly to Russia. I understand that – well, that these facts are known to the Russians.'

'They know sufficient,' said Herr Spiess. 'How much they will admit they know –' he shrugged his shoulders – 'that is difficult to say. It is never easy to get the Russians to come out in the open. They have their own troubles on the Chinese border. They believe perhaps less in the far advanced stage, into which the movement has got, than we do.'

'I should make mine a special mission, I should.'

'I should stay here if I were you, Cedric.'

Lord Altamount's quiet voice spoke from where he leaned rather wearily back in his chair. 'We need you here, Cedric,' he said. There was gentle authority in his voice. 'You are the head of our Government – you must remain here. We have our

177

trained agents – our own emissaries who are qualified for foreign missions.'

'Agents?' Sir George Packham dubiously demanded. 'What can agents do at this stage? We must have a report from – Ah, Horsham, there you are – I did not notice you before. Tell us – what agents have we got? And what can they possibly do?'

'We've got some very good agents,' said Henry Horsham quietly. 'Agents bring you information. Herr Spiess also has brought you information. Information which *his* agents have obtained for *him*. The trouble is – always has been – (you've only got to read about the last war) *nobody wishes to believe the news the agents bring.*'

'Surely – Intelligence –'

'Nobody wants to accept that the agents *are* intelligent! But they are, you know. They are highly trained and their reports, nine times out of ten, are *true*. What happens then? The High-Ups refuse to believe it, don't want to believe it, go further and refuse to act upon it in any way.'

'Really, my dear Horsham – I can't –'

Horsham turned to the German.

'Even in your country, sir, didn't that happen? True reports were brought in, but they weren't always acted upon. *People don't want to know – if truth is unpalatable.*'

'I have to agree – that can and does happen – not often, of that I assure you – But yes – sometimes –'

Mr Lazenby was fidgeting again with his pipe.

'Let us not argue about information. It is a question of dealing – of acting upon the information we have got. This is not merely a national crises – it is an international crisis. Decisions must be taken at top level – we must act. Munro, the police must be reinforced by the Army – military measures must be set in motion. Herr Spiess, you have always been a great military nation – rebellions must be put down by armed forces before they get out of hand. You would agree with that policy, I am sure –'

'The policy, yes. But these insurrections are already what

you term "out of hand". They have tools, rifles, machine-guns, explosives, grenades, bombs, chemical and other gases –'

'But with our nuclear weapons – a mere threat of nuclear warfare – and –'

'These are not just disaffected schoolboys. With this Army of Youth there are scientists – young biologists, chemists, physicists. To start – or to engage in nuclear warfare in Europe –' Herr Spiess shook his head. 'Already we have had an attempt to poison the water supply at Cologne – Typhoid.'

'The whole position is incredible –' Cedric Lazenby looked round him hopefully – 'Chetwynd – Munro – Blunt?'

Admiral Blunt was, somewhat to Lazenby's surprise, the only one to respond.

'I don't know where the Admiralty comes in – not quite our pigeon. I'd advise you, Cedric, if you want to do the best thing for yourself, to take your pipe, and a big supply of tobacco, and get as far out of range of any nuclear warfare you are thinking of starting as you can. Go and camp in the Antarctic, or somewhere where radio-activity will take a long time catching up with you. Professor Eckstein warned us, you know, and he knows what he's talking about.'

CHAPTER 18

Pikeaway's Postscript

The meeting broke up at this point. It split into a definite rearrangement.

The German Chancellor with the Prime Minister, Sir George Packham, Gordon Chetwynd and Dr Reichardt departed for lunch at Downing Street.

Admiral Blunt, Colonel Munro, Colonel Pikeaway and Henry Horsham remained to make their comments with more freedom of speech than they would have permitted themselves if the VIP's had remained.

The first remarks made were somewhat disjointed.

'Thank goodness they took George Packham with them,' said Colonel Pikeaway. 'Worry, fidget, wonder, surmise – gets me down sometimes.'

'You ought to have gone with them, Admiral,' said Colonel Munro. 'Can't see Gordon Chetwynd or George Packham being able to stop our Cedric from going off for a top-level consultation with the Russians, the Chinese, the Ethiopians, the Argentinians or anywhere else the fancy takes him.'

'I've got other kites to fly,' said the Admiral gruffly. 'Going to the country to see an old friend of mine.' He looked with some curiosity at Colonel Pikeaway.

'Was the Hitler business really a surprise to you, Pikeaway?'

Colonel Pikeaway shook his head.

'Not really. We've known all about the rumours of our Adolf turning up in South America and keeping the swastika flying for years. Fifty-to-fifty chance of its being true. Whoever the chap was, madman, play-acting impostor, or the real thing, he passed in his checks quite soon. Nasty stories about that, too – he wasn't an asset to his supporters.'

'*Whose body was it in the Bunker?* is still a good talking point,' said Blunt. 'Never been any definite identification. Russians saw to that.'

He got up, nodded to the others and went towards the door.

Munro said thoughtfully, 'I suppose Dr Reichardt knows the truth – though he played it cagey.'

'What about the Chancellor?' said Horsham.

'Sensible man,' grunted the Admiral, turning his head back from the doorway. 'He was getting his country the way he wanted it, when this youth business started playing fun and games with the civilized world – Pity!' He looked shrewdly at Colonel Munro.

'What about the Golden-Haired Wonder? Hitler's son? Know all about him?'

'No need to worry,' said Colonel Pikeaway unexpectedly.

The Admiral let go of the door-handle and came back and sat down.

'All my eye and Betty Martin,' said Colonel Pikeaway. 'Hitler never had a son.'

'You can't be sure of that.'

'We *are* sure – Franz Joseph, the Young Siegfried, the idolized Leader, is a common or garden fraud, a rank impostor. He's the son of an Argentinian carpenter and a good-looking blonde, a small-part German opera singer – inherited his looks and his singing voice from his mother. He was carefully chosen for the part he was to play, groomed for stardom. In his early youth he was a professional actor – he was branded in the foot with a swastika – a story made up for him full of romantic details. He was treated like a dedicated Dalai Lama.'

'And you've proof of this?'

'Full documentation,' Colonel Pikeaway grinned. 'One of my best agents got it. Affidavits, photostats, signed declaration, including one from the mother, and medical evidence as to the date of the scar, copy of the original birth certificate of Karl Aguileros – and signed evidence of his identity with the so-called Franz Joseph. The whole bag of tricks. My agent got away with it just in time. They were after her – might have got her if she hadn't had a bit of luck at Frankfurt.'

'And where are these documents now?'

'In a safe place. Waiting for the right moment for a spectacular debunking of a first-class impostor –'

'Do the Government know this? – the Prime Minister?'

'I never tell all I know to politicians – not until I can't avoid it, or until I'm quite sure they'll do the right thing.'

'You *are* an old devil, Pikeaway,' said Colonel Munro.

'Somebody has to be,' said Colonel Pikeaway, sadly.

CHAPTER 19

Sir Stafford Nye Has Visitors

Sir Stafford Nye was entertaining guests. They were guests with whom he had previously been unacquainted except for one of them whom he knew fairly well by sight. They were good-looking young men, serious-minded and intelligent, or so he should judge. Their hair was controlled and stylish, their clothes were well cut though not unduly old-fashioned. Looking at them, Stafford Nye was unable to deny that he liked the look of them. At the same time he wondered what they wanted with him. One of them he knew was the son of an oil king. Another of them, since leaving the university, had interested himself in politics. He had an uncle who owned a chain of restaurants. The third one was a young man with beetle brows who frowned and to whom perpetual suspicion seemed to be second nature.

'It's very good of you to let us come and call upon you, Sir Stafford,' said the one who seemed to be the blond leader of the three.

His voice was very agreeable. His name was Clifford Bent.

'This is Roderick Ketelly and this is Jim Brewster. We're all anxious about the future. Shall I put it like that?'

'I suppose the answer to that is, aren't we all?' said Sir Stafford Nye.

'We don't like things the way they're going,' said Clifford Bent. 'Rebellion, anarchy, all that. Well, it's all right as a philosophy. Frankly I think we may say that we all seem to go through a phase of it but one does come out the other side. We want people to be able to pursue academic careers without their being interrupted. We want a good sufficiency of demonstrations but not demonstrations of hooliganism and violence. We want intelligent demonstrations. And what we want, quite frankly, or so I think, is a new political party. Jim Brewster here has been paying serious attention to entirely new ideas and plans concerning trade union matters. They've tried to shout him down and talk him out, but he's gone on talking, haven't you, Jim?'

'Muddle-headed old fools, most of them,' said Jim Brewster.

'We want a sensible and serious policy for youth, a more economical method of government. We want different ideas to obtain in education but nothing fantastic or high-falutin'. And we shall want, if we win seats, and if we are able finally to form a government – and I don't see why we shouldn't – to put these ideas into action. There are a lot of people in our movement. We stand for youth, you know, just as well as the violent ones do. We stand for moderation and we mean to have a sensible government, with a reduction in the number of MP's, and we're noting down, looking for the men already in politics no matter what their particular persuasion is, if we think they're men of sense. We've come here to see if we can interest you in our aims. At the moment they are still in a state of flux but we have got as far as knowing the men we want. I may say that we don't want the ones we've got at present and we don't want the ones who might be put in instead. As for the third party, it seems to have died out of the running, though there are one or two good people there who suffer now for being in a minority, but I think they would come over to our way of thinking. We want to interest you. We want, one of these days, perhaps not so far distant as you might think – we want someone who'd understand and put out a proper, successful foreign policy. The rest of the world's in a worse mess than we are now. Washington's razed to the ground, Europe has continual military actions, demonstrations, wrecking of airports. Oh well, I don't need to write you a news letter of the past six months, but our aim is not so much to put the world on its legs again as to put England on its legs again. To have the right men to do it. We want young men, a great many young men and we've got a great many young men who aren't revolutionary, who aren't anarchistic, who will be willing to try and make a country run profitably. And we want some of the older men –

I don't mean men of sixty-odd, I mean men of forty or fifty – and we've come to you because, well, we've heard things about you. We know about you and you're the sort of man we want.'

'Do you think you are wise?' said Sir Stafford.

'Well, *we*, think we are.'

The second young man laughed slightly.

'We hope you'll agree with us there.'

'I'm not sure that I do. You're talking in this room very freely.'

'It's your sitting-room.'

'Yes, yes, it's my flat and it's my sitting-room. But what you are saying, and in fact what you might be going to say, might be unwise. That means both for you as well as me.'

'Oh! I think I see what you're driving at.'

'You are offering me something. A way of life, a new career and you are suggesting a breaking of certain ties. You are suggesting a form of disloyalty.'

'We're not suggesting your becoming a defector to any other country, if that's what you mean.'

'No, no, this is not an invitation to Russia or an invitation to China or an invitation to other places mentioned in the past, but I think it is an invitation connected with some foreign interests.' He went on: 'I've recently come back from abroad. A very interesting journey. I have spent the last three weeks in South America. There is something I would like to tell you. I have been conscious since I returned to England that I have been followed.'

'Followed? You don't think you imagined it?'

'No, I don't think I've imagined it. Those are the sort of things I have learned to notice in the course of my career. I have been in some fairly far distant and – shall we say? – interesting parts of the world. You chose to call upon me to sound me as to a proposition. It might have been safer, though, if we had met elsewhere.'

He got up, opened the door into the bathroom and turned the tap.

'From the films I used to see some years ago,' he said, 'if you wished to disguise your conversation when a room was bugged, you turned on taps. I have no doubt that I am somewhat old-fashioned and that there are better methods of dealing with these things now. But at any rate perhaps we could speak a little more clearly now, though even then I still think we should be careful. South America,' he went on, 'is a very interesting part of the world. The Federation of South American countries (Spanish Gold has been one name for it), comprising by now Cuba, the Argentine, Brazil, Peru, one or two others not quite settled and fixed but coming into being. Yes. Very interesting.'

'And what are your views on the subject,' the suspicious-looking Jim Brewster asked. 'What have you got to say about things?'

'I shall continue to be careful,' said Sir Stafford. 'You will have more dependence on me if I do not talk unadvisedly. But I think that can be done quite well after I turn off the bath water.'

'Turn it off, Jim,' said Cliff Bent.

Jim grinned suddenly and obeyed.

Stafford Nye opened a drawer at the table and took out a recorder.

'Not a very practised player yet,' he said.

He put it to his lips and started a tune. Jim Brewster came back, scowling.

'What's this? A bloody concert we're going to put on?'

'Shut up,' said Cliff Bent. 'You ignoramus, you don't know anything about music.'

Stafford Nye smiled.

'You share my pleasure in Wagnerian music, I see,' he said. 'I was at the Youth Festival this year and enjoyed the concerts there very much.'

Again he repeated the tune.

'Not any tune I know,' said Jim Brewster. 'It might be the Internationale or the Red Flag or God Save the King or Yankee Doodle or the Star-Spangled Banner. What the devil is it?'

'It's a motif from an opera,' said Ketelly. 'And shut your mouth. We know all we want to know.'

'The horn call of a young Hero,' said Stafford Nye.

He brought his hand up in a quick gesture, the gesture from the past meaning 'Heil Hitler'. He murmured very gently,

'The new Siegfried.'

All three rose.

'You're quite right,' said Clifford Bent. 'We must all, I think, be very careful.'

He shook hands.

'We are glad to know that you will be with us. One of the things this country will need in its future – its great future, I hope – will be a first-class Foreign Minister.'

They went out of the room. Stafford Nye watched them through the slightly open door go into the lift and descend.

He gave a curious smile, shut the door, glanced up at the clock on the wall and sat down in an easy chair – to wait ...

His mind went back to the day, a week ago now, when he and Mary Ann had gone their separate ways from Kennedy Airport. They had stood there, both of them finding it difficult to speak. Stafford Nye had broken the silence first.

'Do you think we'll ever meet again? I wonder ...'

'Is there any reason why we shouldn't?'

'Every reason, I should think.'

She looked at him, then quickly away again.

'These partings have to happen. It's – part of the job.'

'The job! It's always the job with you, isn't it?'

'It has to be.'

'You're a professional. I'm only an amateur. You're a –' he broke off. 'What are you? Who are you? I don't really know, do I?'

'No.'

He looked at her then. He saw sadness, he thought, in her face. Something that was almost pain.

'So I have to – wonder ... You think I ought to trust you, I suppose?'

'No, not that. That is one of the things that I have learnt, that life has taught me. There is nobody that one can trust. Remember that – always.'

'So that is your world? A world of distrust, of fear, of danger.'

'I wish to stay alive. I am alive.'

'I know.'

'And I want *you* to stay alive.'

'*I* trusted you – in Frankfurt ...'

'You took a risk.'

'It was a risk well worth taking. You know that as well as I do.'

'You mean because –?'

'Because we have been together. And now – That is my flight being called. Is this companionship of ours which started in an airport, to end here in another airport? You are going where? To do what?'

'To do what I have to do. To Baltimore, to Washington, to Texas. To do what I have been told to do.'

'And I? I have been told nothing. I am to go back to London – and do what there?'

'Wait.'

'Wait for what?'

'For the advances that almost certainly will be made to you.'

'And what am I to do then?'

She smiled at him, with the sudden gay smile that he knew so well.

'Then you play it by ear. You'll know how to do it, none better. You'll like the people who approach you. They'll be well chosen. It's important, very important, that we should know who they are.'

'I must go. Goodbye, Mary Ann.'

'*Auf Wiedersehen.*'

In the London flat, the telephone rang. At a singularly apposite moment, Stafford Nye thought, bringing him back from his past memories just at that moment of their farewell. '*Auf Wiedersehen,*' he murmured, as he rose to his feet, crossed to take the receiver off, 'let it be so.'

A voice spoke whose wheezy accents were quite unmistakable.

'Stafford Nye?'

He gave the requisite answer: 'No smoke without fire.'

'My doctor says I should give up smoking. Poor fellow,' said Colonel Pikeaway, 'he might as well give up hope of that. Any news?'

'Oh yes. Thirty pieces of silver. Promised, that is to say.'

'Damned swine!'

'Yes, yes, keep calm.'

'And what did you say?'

'I played them a tune. Siegfried's Horn motif. I was following an elderly aunt's advice. It went down very well.'

'Sounds crazy to me!'

'Do you know a song called Juanita? I must learn that too, in case I need it.'

'Do you know who Juanita is?'

'I think so.'

'H'm, I wonder – heard of in Baltimore last.'

'What about your Greek girl, Daphne Theodofanous? Where is she now, I wonder?'

'Sitting in an airport somewhere in Europe waiting for you, probably,' said Colonel Pikeaway.

'Most of the European airports seem to be closed down because they've been blown up or more or less damaged. High explosive, hi-jackers, high jinks.

> 'The boys and girls come out to play
> The moon doth shine as bright as day –
> Leave your supper and leave your sleep
> And shoot your playfellow in the street.'

'The Children's Crusade à la mode.'

'Not that I really know much about it. I only know the one that Richard Coeur de Lion went to. But in a way this whole business is rather like the Children's Crusade. Starting with idealism, starting with ideas of the Christian world delivering he holy city from pagans, and ending with death, death and gain, death. Nearly all the children died. Or were sold into lavery. This will end the same way unless we can find some neans of getting them out of it ...'

CHAPTER 20

The Admiral Visits An Old Friend

Thought you must all be dead here,' said Admiral Blunt with a snort.

His remark was addressed not to the kind of butler which he would have liked to see opening this front door, but to the young woman whose surname he could never remember but whose Christian name was Amy.

'Rung you up at least four times in the last week. Gone abroad, that's what they said.'

'We have been abroad. We've only just come back.'

'Matilda oughtn't to go rampaging about abroad. Not at her time of life. She'll die of blood pressure or heart failure or something in one of these modern airplanes. Cavorting about, full of explosives put in them by the Arabs or the Israelis or somebody or other. Not safe at all any longer.'

'Her doctor recommended it to her.'

'Oh well, we all know what doctors are.' .

'And she has really come back in very good spirits.'

'Where's she been, then?'

'Oh, taking a Cure. In Germany or – I never can quite remember whether it's Germany or Austria. That new place, you know, the Golden Gasthaus.'

'Ah yes, I know the place you mean. Costs the earth, doesn't it?'

'Well, it's said to produce very remarkable results.'

'Probably only a different way of killing you quicker,' said
Admiral Blunt. 'How did *you* enjoy it?'

'Well, not really very much. The scenery was very nice
but –'

An imperious voice sounded from the floor above.

'Amy. Amy! What are you doing, talking in the hall all this
time? Bring Admiral Blunt up here. I'm waiting for him.'

'Gallivanting about,' said Admiral Blunt, after he had
greeted his old friend. 'That's how you'll kill yourself one of
these days. You mark my words –'

'No, I shan't. There's no difficulty at all in travelling
nowadays.'

'Running about all those airports, ramps, stairs, buses.'

'Not at all. I had a wheelchair.'

'A year or two ago when I saw you, you said you wouldn't
hear of such a thing. You said you had too much pride to admit
you needed one.'

'Well, I've had to give up some of my pride, nowadays,
Philip. Come and sit down here and tell me why you wanted to
come and see me so much all of a sudden. You've neglected me
a great deal for the last year.'

'Well, I've not been so well myself. Besides, I've been
looking into a few things. You know the sort of thing. Where
they ask your advice but don't mean in the least to take it. They
can't leave the Navy alone. Keep on wanting to fiddle about
with it, drat them.'

'You look quite well to me,' said Lady Matilda.

'You don't look so bad yourself, my dear. You've got a nice
sparkle in your eye.'

'I'm deafer than when you saw me last. You'll have to speak
up more.'

'All right. I'll speak up.'

'What do you want, gin and tonic or whisky or rum?'

'You seem ready to dispense strong liquor of any kind. If it's
all the same to you, I'll have a gin and tonic.'

Amy rose and left the room.

'And when she brings it,' said the Admiral, 'get rid of her

gain, will you? I want to talk to you. Talk to you particularly
what I mean.'

Refreshment brought, Lady Matilda made a dismissive
wave of the hand and Amy departed with the air of one who is
pleasing herself, not her employer. She was a tactful young
woman.

'Nice girl,' said the Admiral, 'very nice.'

'Is that why you asked me to get rid of her and see she shut
the door? So that she mightn't overhear you saying something
nice about her?'

'No. I wanted to consult you.'

'What about? Your health or where to get some new servants
or what to grow in the garden?'

'I want to consult you very seriously. I thought perhaps you
might be able to remember something for me.'

'Dear Philip, how touching that you should think I can
remember *anything*. Every year my memory gets worse. I've
come to the conclusion one only remembers what's called the
"friends of one's youth". Even horrid girls one was at school
with one remembers, though one doesn't want to. That's where
've been now, as a matter of fact.'

'Where've you been now? Visiting schools?'

'No, no, no, I went to see an old school friend whom I
haven't seen for thirty – forty – fifty – that sort of time.'

'What was she like?'

'Enormously fat and even nastier and horrider than I
remembered her.'

'You've got very queer tastes, I must say, Matilda.'

'Well, go on, tell me. Tell me what it is you want me to
remember?'

'I wondered if you remembered another friend of yours.
Robert Shoreham.'

'Robbie Shoreham? Of course I do.'

'The scientist feller. Top scientist.'

'Of course. He wasn't the sort of man one would ever forget.
I wonder what put him into you head.'

'Public need.'

191

'Funny you should say that,' said Lady Matilda. 'I though[t] the same myself the other day.'

'You thought what?'

'That he was needed. Or someone like him – if there i[s] anyone like him.'

'There isn't. Now listen, Matilda. People talk to you a bit. They tell you things. I've told you things myself.'

'I've always wondered why, because you can't believe tha[t] I'll understand them or be able to describe them. And that wa[s] even more the case with Robbie than with you.'

'I don't tell you naval secrets.'

'Well, he didn't tell me scientific secrets. I mean, only in [a] very general way.'

'Yes, but he used to talk to you about them, didn't he?'

'Well, he liked saying things that would astonish m[e] sometimes.'

'All right, then, here it comes. I want to know if he eve[r] talked to you, in the days when he could talk properly, poo[r] devil, about something called Project B.'

'Project B.' Matilda Cleckheaton considered thoughtfully. 'Sounds vaguely familiar,' she said. 'He used to talk abou[t] Project this or that sometimes, or Operation that or this. Bu[t] you must realize that none of it ever made any kind of *sense* t[o] me, and he knew it didn't. But he used to like – oh, how shal[l] I put it? – astonishing me rather, you know. Sort of describing it the way that a conjuror might describe how he takes thre[e] rabbits out of a hat without your knowing how he did it. Projec[t] B? Yes, that was a good long time ago ... He was wildly excite[d] for a bit. I used to say to him sometimes "How's Project [B] going on?"'

'I know, I know, you've always been a tactful woman. You can always remember what people were doing or interested in. And even if you don't know the first thing about it you'd show an interest. I described a new kind of naval gun to you once and you must have been bored stiff. But you listened as brightly a[s] though it was the thing you'd been waiting to hear about all your life.'

192

'As you tell me, I've been a tactful woman and a good listener, even if I've never had much in the way of brains.'

'Well, I want to hear a little more what Robbie said about Project B.'

'He said – well, it's very difficult to remember now. He mentioned it after talking about some operation that they used to do on people's brains. You know, the people who were terribly melancholic and who were thinking of suicide and who were so worried and neurasthenic that they had awful anxiety complexes. Stuff like that, the sort of thing people used to talk of in connection with Freud. And he said that the side effects were impossible. I mean, the people were quite happy and meek and docile and didn't worry any more, or want to kill themselves, but they – well I mean they didn't worry *enough* and therefore they used to get run over and all sorts of things like that because they weren't thinking of any danger and didn't notice it. I'm putting it badly but you do understand what I mean. And anyway, he said, that was going to be the trouble, he thought, with Project B.'

'Did he describe it at all more closely than that?'

'He said I'd put it into his head,' said Matilda Cleckheaton unexpectedly.

'What? Do you mean to say a scientiest – a top-flight scientist like Robbie actually said to you that you had put something into his scientific brain? You don't know the first thing about science.'

'Of course not. But I used to try and put a little common sense into people's brains. The cleverer they are, the less common sense they have. I mean, really, the people who matter are the people who thought of simple things like perforations on postage stamps, or like somebody Adam, or whatever his name was – No – MacAdam in America who put black stuff on roads so that farmers could get all their crops from farms to the coast and make a better profit. I mean, they do much more good than all the high-powered scientists do. Scientists can only think of things for destroying you. Well, that's the sort of thing I said to Robbie. Quite nicely, of course, as a kind of joke.

He'd been just telling me that some splendid things had been done in the scientific world about germ warfare and experiments with biology and what you can do to unborn babies if you get at them early enough. And also some peculiarly nasty and very unpleasant gases and saying how silly people were to protest against nuclear bombs because they were really a kindness compared to some of the other things that had been invented since then. And so I said it'd be much more to the point if Robbie, or someone clever like Robbie, could think of something really sensible. And he looked at me with that, you know, little twinkle he has in his eye sometimes and said, "Well, what would you consider sensible?" And I said, "Well, instead of inventing all these germ warfares and these nasty gases, and all the rest of it, why don't you just invent something that makes people feel happy?" I said it oughtn't to be any more difficult to do. I said, "You've talked about this operation where, I think you said, they took out a bit of the front of your brain or maybe the back of your brain. But anyway it made a great difference in people's dispositions. They'd become quite different. They hadn't worried any more or they hadn't wanted to commit suicide. But," I said, "well, if you can change people like that just by taking a little bit of bone or muscle or nerve or tinkering up a gland or taking out a gland or putting in more of a gland," I said, "if you can make all that difference in people's dispositions, why can't you invent something that will make people pleasant or just sleepy perhaps? Supposing you had something, not a sleeping draught, but just something that people sat down in a chair and had a nice dream. Twenty-four hours or so and just woke up to be fed now and again." I said it would be a much better idea.'

'And is that what Project B was?'

'Well, of course he never told me what it was exactly. But he was excited with an idea and he said I'd put it into his head, so it must have been something rather pleasant I'd put into his head, mustn't it? I mean, I hadn't suggested any ideas to him of any nastier ways for killing people and I didn't want people even – you know – to cry, like tear gas or anything like that.

Perhaps laughing – yes, I believe I mentioned laughing gas. I said well if you have your teeth out, they give you three sniffs of it and you laugh, well, surely, surely you could invent something that's as useful as that but would last a little longer. Because I believe laughing gas only lasts about fifty seconds, doesn't it? I know my brother had some teeth out once. The dentist's chair was very near the window and my brother was laughing so much, when he was unconscious, I mean, that he stretched his leg right out and put it through the dentist's window and all the glass fell in the street, and the dentist was very cross about it.'

'Your stories always have such strange side-kicks,' said the Admiral. 'Anyway, this is what Robbie Shoreham had chosen to get on with, from your advice.'

'Well, I don't know what it was exactly. I mean, I don't think it was sleeping or laughing. At any rate, it was *something*. It wasn't really Project B. It had another name.'

'What sort of a name?'

'Well, he did mention it once I think, or twice. The name he'd given it. Rather like Benger's Food,' said Aunt Matilda, considering thoughtfully.

'Some soothing agent for the digestion?'

'I don't think it had anything to do with the digestion. I rather think it was something you sniffed or something, perhaps it was a gland. You know we talked of so many things that you never quite knew what he was talking about at the moment. Benger's Food. Ben – Ben – it did begin with Ben. And there was a pleasant word associated with it.'

'Is that all you can remember about it?'

'I think so. I mean, this was just a talk we had once and then, quite a long time afterwards, he told me I'd put something into his head for Project Ben something. And after that, occasionally, if I remembered, I'd ask him if he was still working on Project Ben and then sometimes he'd be very exasperated and say no, he'd come up against a snag and he was putting it all aside now because it was in – in – well, I mean the next eight words were pure jargon and I couldn't remember them and you wouldn't understand them if I said them to you. But in the end, I think – oh dear, oh dear, this is all about eight or nine years ago – in the end he came one day and he said, "Do you remember Project Ben?" I said, "Of course I remember it. Are you still working on it?" And he said no, he was determined to lay it all aside. I said I was sorry. Sorry if he'd given it up and he said, "Well, it's not only that I can't get what I was trying for. I know now that it *could* be got. I know where I went wrong. I know just what the snag was, I know just how to put that snag right again. I've got Lisa working on it with me. Yes, it could work. It'd require experimenting on certain things but it could work." "Well," I said to him, "what are you worrying about?" And he said, "Because I don't know what it would really do to people." I said something about his being afraid it would kill people or maim them for life or something. "No," he said, "it's not like that." He said, it's a – oh, of course, now I remember. He called it Project Benvo. Yes. And that's because it had to do with *benevolence*.'

'Benevolence!' said the Admiral, highly surprised. 'Benevolence? Do you mean charity?'

'No, no, no. I think he meant simply that you could make people benevolent. *Feel* benevolent.'

'Peace and good will towards men?'

'Well, he didn't put it like that.'

'No, that's reserved for religious leaders. They preach that to you and if you did what they preach it'd be a very happy world. But Robbie, I gather, was not preaching. He proposed to do something in his laboratory to bring about this result by purely physical means.'

'That's the sort of thing. And he said you can never tell when things *are* beneficial to people or when they're not. They are in one way, they're not in another. And he said things about – oh, penicillin and sulphonamides and heart transplants and things like pills for women, though we hadn't got "The Pill" then. But you know, things that seem all right and they're wonder-drugs or wonder-gases or wonder-something or other, and then there's something about them that makes them go wrong as

196

well as right, and then you wish they weren't there and had never been thought of. Well, that's the sort of thing that he seemed to be trying to get over to me. It was all rather difficult to understand. I said, "Do you mean you don't like to take the risk?" and he said, "You're quite right. I don't like to take the risk. That's the trouble because, you see, I don't know in the least what the risk will be. That's what happens to us poor devils of scientists. We take the risks and the risks are not in what we've discovered, it's the risks of what the people we'll have to tell about it will do with what we've discovered." I said, "Now you're talking about nuclear weapons again and atom bombs," and he said, "Oh, to Hell with nuclear weapons and atomic bombs. We've gone far beyond that."

'"But if you're going to make people nice-tempered and benevolent," I said, "what have you got to worry about?" And he said, "You don't *understand*, Matilda. You'll never understand. My fellow scientists in all probability would not understand either. And no politicians would ever understand. And so, you see, it's too big a risk to be taken. At any rate one would have to think for a long time."

'"But," I said, "you could bring people out of it again, just like laughing gas, couldn't you? I mean, you could make people benevolent just for a short time, and then they'd get all right again – or all wrong again – it depends which way you look at it, I should have thought." And he said, "No. This will be, you see, permanent. Quite permanent because it affects the –" and then he went into jargon again. You know, long words and numbers. Formulas, or molecular changes – something like that. I expect really it must be something like what they do to cretins. You know, to make them stop being cretins, like giving them thyroid or taking it away from them. I forget which it is. Something like that. Well, I expect there's some nice little gland somewhere and if you take it away or smoke it out, or do something drastic to it – but then, the people are permanently –'

'Permanently *benevolent*? You're sure that's the right word? Benevolence?'

'Yes, because that's why he nicknamed it *Benvo*.'

'But what did his colleagues think, I wonder, about his backing out?'

'I don't think he had many who knew. Lisa what's-her-name, the Austrian girl; she'd worked on it with him. And there was one young man called Leadenthal or some name like that, but he died of tuberculosis. And he rather spoke as though the other people who worked with him were merely assistants who didn't know exactly what he was doing or trying for. I see what you're getting at,' said Matilda suddenly. 'I don't think he ever told anybody, really. I mean, I think he destroyed his formulas or notes or whatever they were and gave up the whole idea. And then he had his stroke and got ill, and now, poor dear, he can't speak very well. He's paralysed one side. He can hear fairly well. He listens to music. That's his whole life now.'

'His life's work's ended, you think?'

'He doesn't even see friends. I think it's painful to him to see them. He always makes some excuse.'

'But he's alive,' said Admiral Blunt. 'He's alive still. Got his address?'

'It's in my address book somewhere. He's still in the same place. North Scotland somewhere. But – oh, do understand – he was such a wonderful man once. He isn't now. He's just almost dead. For all intents and purposes.'

'There's always hope,' said Admiral Blunt. 'And belief,' he added. 'Faith.'

'And benevolence, I suppose,' said Lady Matilda.

CHAPTER 21

Project Benvo

Professor John Gottlieb sat in his chair looking very steadfastly at the handsome young woman sitting opposite him. He scratched his ear with a rather monkey-like gesture which was characteristic of him. He looked rather like a monkey anyway. A prognathous jaw, a high mathematical head which make a slight contrast in terms, and a small wizened frame.

'It's not every day,' said Professor Gottlieb, 'that a young lady brings me a letter from the President of the United States. However,' he said cheerfully, 'Presidents don't always know exactly what they're doing. What's this all about? I gather you're vouched for on the highest authority.'

'I've come to ask you what you know or what you can tell me about something called Project Benvo.'

'Are you really Countess Renata Zerkowski?'

'Technically, possibly, I am. I'm more often known as Mary Ann.'

'Yes, that's what they wrote me under separate cover. And you want to know about Project Benvo. Well, there was such a thing. Now it's dead and buried and the man who thought of it also, I expect.'

'You mean Professor Shoreham.'

'That's right. Robert Shoreham. One of the greatest geniuses of our age. Einstein, Niels Bohr and some others. But Robert Shoreham didn't last as long as he should. A great loss to science – what is it Shakespeare says of Lady Macbeth: "*She should have died hereafter.*"'

'He's not dead,' said Mary Ann.

'Oh. Sure of that?' Nothing's been heard of him for a long time.'

'He's an invalid. He lives in the north of Scotland. He is paralysed, can't speak very well, can't walk very well. He sits most of the time listening to music.'

'Yes, I can imagine that. Well, I'm glad about that. If he can do that he won't be too unhappy. Otherwise it's a pretty fair hell for a brilliant man who isn't brilliant any more. Who's, as it were, dead in an invalid chair.'

'There *was* such a thing as Project Benvo?'

'Yes, he was very keen about it.'

'He talked to you about it?'

'He talked to some of us about it in the early days. You're not a scientist yourself, young woman, I suppose?'

'No, I'm –'

'You're just an agent, I suppose. I hope you're on the right side. We still have to hope for miracles these days, but I don't think you'll get anything out of Project Benvo.'

'Why not? You said he worked on it. It would have been a very great invention, wouldn't it? Or discovery, or whatever you call these things?'

'Yes, it would have been one of the greatest discoveries of the age. I don't know just what went wrong. It's happened before now. A thing goes along all right but in the last stages somehow, it doesn't click. Breaks down. Doesn't do what's expected of it and you give up in despair. Or else you do what Shoreham did.'

'What was that?'

'He destroyed it. Every damn bit of it. He told me so himself. Burnt all the formulas, all the papers concerning it, all the data. Three weeks later he had his stroke. I'm sorry. You see, I can't help you. I never knew any details about it, nothing but its main idea. I don't even remember that now, except for one thing. Benvo stood for Benevolence.'

CHAPTER 22

Juanita

Lord Altamount was dictating.

The voice that had once been ringing and dominant was now reduced to a gentleness that had still an unexpectedly special appeal. It seemed to come gently out of the shadows of the past, but to be emotionally moving in a way that a more dominant tone would not have been.

James Kleek was taking down the words as they came, pausing every now and then when a moment of hesitation came, allowing for it and waiting gently himself.

'Idealism,' said Lord Altamount, 'can arise and indeed usually does so when moved by a natural antagonism to injustice. That is a natural revulsion from crass materialism. The natural idealism of youth is fed more and more by a desire to destroy those two phases of modern life, injustice and crass materialism. That desire to destroy what is evil, sometimes leads to a love of destruction for its own sake. It can lead to a pleasure in violence and in the infliction of pain. All this can be fostered and strengthened from outside by those who are gifted by a natural power of leadership. This original idealism arises in a non-adult stage. It should and could lead on to a desire for a new world. It should lead also towards a love of all human beings, and of goodwill towards them. But those who have once learnt to love violence for its own sake will never become adult. They will be fixed in their own retarded development and will so remain for their lifetime.'

The buzzer went. Lord Altamount gestured and James Kleek lifted it up and listened.

'Mr Robinson is here.'

'Ah yes. Bring him in. We can go on with this later.'

James Kleek rose, laying aside his notebook and pencil.

Mr Robinson came in. James Kleek set a chair for him, one sufficiently widely proportioned to receive his form without discomfort. Mr Robinson smiled his thanks and arranged himself by Lord Altamount's side.

'Well,' said Lord Altamount. 'Got anything new for us? Diagrams? Circles? Bubbles?'

He seemed faintly amused.

'Not exactly,' said Mr Robinson imperturbably, 'it's more like plotting the course of a river –'

'River?' said Lord Altamount. 'What sort of a river?'

'A river of money,' said Mr Robinson, in the slightly apologetic voice he was wont to use when referring to his speciality. 'It's really just like a river, money is – coming from somewhere and definitely going to somewhere. Really very interesting – that is, if you are interested in these things – It tells its own story, you see –'

James Kleek looked as though he didn't see, but Altamount said, 'I understand. Go on.'

'It's flowing from Scandinavia – from Bavaria – from the USA – from South-east Asia – fed by lesser tributaries on the way –'

'And going – where?'

'Mainly to South America – meeting the demands of the now securely established Headquarters of Militant Youth –'

'And representing four of the five interwined Circles you showed us – Armaments, Drugs, Scientific and Chemical Warfare Missiles as well as Finance?'

'Yes – we think we know now fairly accurately who controls these various groups –'

'What about Circle J – Juanita?' asked James Kleek.

'As yet we cannot be sure.'

'James has certain ideas as to that,' said Lord Altamount. 'I hope he may be wrong – yes, I hope so. The initial J is interesting. What does it stand for – Justice? Judgment?'

'A dedicated killer,' said James Kleek. 'The female of the species is more deadly than the male.'

'There are historical precedents,' admitted Altamount. 'Jael setting butter in a lordly dish before Sisera – and afterwards driving the nail through his head. Judith executing Holofernes, and applauded for it by her countrymen. Yes, you may have something there.'

'So you think you know who Juanita is, do you?' said Mr Robinson. 'That's interesting.'

'Well, perhaps I'm wrong, sir, but there have been things that made me think –'

'Yes,' said Mr Robinson, 'we have all had to think, haven't we? Better say who you think it is, James.'

'The Countess Renata Zerkowski.'

'What makes you pitch upon her?'

'The places she's been, the people she's been in contact with.

202

There's been too much coincidence about the way she has been turning up in different places, and all that. She's been in Bavaria. She's been visiting Big Charlotte there. What's more, she took Stafford Nye with her. I think that's significant –'

'You think they're in this together?' asked Altamount.

'I wouldn't like to say that. I don't know enough about him, but …' He paused.

'Yes,' said Lord Altamount, 'there have been doubts about him. He was suspected from the beginning.'

'By Henry Horsham?'

'Henry Horsham for one, perhaps. Colonel Pikeaway isn't sure, I imagine. He's been under observation. Probably knows it too. He's not a fool.'

'Another of them,' said James Kleek savagely. 'Extraordinary, how we can breed them, how we trust them, tell 'em our secrets, let them know what we're doing, go on saying: "If there's one person I'm absolutely sure of it's – oh, McLean, or Burgess, or Philby, or any of the lot." And now – Stafford Nye.'

'Stafford Nye, indoctrinated by Renata alias Juanita,' said Mr Robinson.

'There was that curious business at Frankfurt airport,' said Kleek, 'and there was the visit to Charlotte. Stafford Nye, I gather, has since been in South America with her. As for she herself – do we know where she is now?'

'I dare say Mr Robinson does,' said Lord Altamount. 'Do you, Mr Robinson?'

'She's in the United States. I've heard that after staying with friends in Washington or near it, she was in Chicago, then in California and that she went from Austin to visit a top-flight scientist. That's the last I've heard.'

'What's she doing there?'

'One would presume,' said Mr Robinson, in his calm voice, 'that she is trying to obtain information.'

'What information?'

Mr Robinson sighed.

'That is what one wishes one knew. One presumes that it is

the same information that *we* are anxious to obtain and that she is doing it on our behalf. But one never knows – it may be for the other side.'

He turned to look at Lord Altamount.

'Tonight, I understand, you are travelling to Scotland. Is that right?'

'Quite right.'

'I don't think he ought to, sir,' said James Kleek. He turned an anxious face to his employer. 'You've not been so well lately, sir. It'll be a very tiring journey whichever way you go. Air or train. Can't you leave it to Munro and Horsham?'

'At my age it's a waste of time to take care,' said Lord Altamount. 'If I can be useful I would like to die in harness, as the saying goes.'

He smiled at Mr Robinson.

'You'd better come with us, Robinson.'

CHAPTER 23

Journey To Scotland

The Squadron Leader wondered a little what it was all about. He was accustomed to being left only partly in the picture. That was Security's doing, he supposed. Taking no chances. He'd done this sort of thing before more than once. Flying a plane of people out to an unlikely spot, with unlikely passengers, being careful to ask no questions except such as were of an entirely factual nature. He knew some of his passengers on this flight but not all of them. Lord Altamount he recognized. An ill man, a very sick man, he thought, a man who, he judged, kept himself alive by sheer willpower. The keen hawk-faced man with him was his special guard dog, presumably. Seeing not so much to his safety as to his welfare.

A faithful dog who never left his side. He would have with him restoratives, stimulants, all the medical box of tricks. The Squadron Leader wondered why there wasn't a doctor also in attendance. It would have been an extra precaution. Like a death's head, the old man looked. A noble death's head. Something made of marble in a museum. Henry Horsham the Squadron Leader knew quite well. He knew several of the Security lot. And Colonel Munro, looking slightly less fierce than usual, rather more worried. Not very happy on the whole. There was also a large, yellow-faced man. Foreigner, he might be. Asiatic? What was he doing, flying in a plane to the North of Scotland? The Squadron Leader said deferentially to Colonel Munro:

'Everything laid on, sir? The car is here waiting.'

'How far exactly is the distance?'

'Seventeen miles, sir, roughish road but not too bad. There are extra rugs in the car.'

'You have your orders? Repeat, please, if you will, Squadron Leader Andrews.'

The Squadron Leader repeated and the Colonel nodded satisfaction. As the car finally drove off, the Squadron Leader looked after it, wondering to himself why on earth those particular people were here on this drive over the lonely moor to a venerable old castle where a sick man lived as a recluse without friends or visitors in the general run of things. Horsham knew, he supposed. Horsham must know a lot of strange things. Oh well, Horsham wasn't likely to tell him anything.

The car was well and carefully driven. It drew up at last over a gravel driveway and came to a stop before the porch. It was a turreted building of heavy stone. Lights hung at either side of the big door. The door itself opened before there was any need to ring a bell or demand admittance.

An old Scottish woman of sixty-odd with a stern, dour face, stood in the doorway. The chauffeur helped the occupants out.

James Kleek and Horsham helped Lord Altamount to alight

and supported him up the steps. The old Scottish woman stood aside and dropped a respectful curtsy to him. She said:

'Good evening, y'r lordship. The master's waiting for you. He knows you're arriving, we've got rooms prepared and fires for you in all of them.'

'Another figure had arrived in the hall now. A tall lean woman between fifty and sixty, a woman who was still handsome. Her black hair was parted in the middle, she had a high forehead, an aquiline nose and a tanned skin.

'Here's Miss Neumann to look after you,' said the Scottish woman.

'Thank you, Janet,' said Miss Neumann. 'Be sure the fires are kept up in the bedrooms.'

'I will that.'

Lord Altamount shook hands with her.

'Good evening, Miss Neumann.'

'Good evening, Lord Altamount. I hope you are not too tired by your journey.'

'We had a very good flight. This is Colonel Munro, Miss Neumann. This is Mr Robinson, Sir James Kleek and Mr Horsham, of the Security Department.'

'I remember Mr Horsham from some years ago, I think.'

'I hadn't forgotten,' said Henry Horsham. 'It was at the Leveson Foundation. You were already, I think, Professor Shoreham's secretary at that time?'

'I was first his assistant in the laboratory, and afterwards his secretary. I am still, as far as he needs one, his secretary. He also has to have a hospital nurse living here more or less permanently. There have to be changes from time to time – Miss Ellis who is here now took over from Miss Bude only two days ago. I have suggested that she should stay near at hand to the room in which we ourselves shall be. I thought you would prefer privacy, but that she ought not to be out of call in case she was needed.'

'Is he in very bad health?' asked Colonel Munro.

'He doesn't actually suffer,' said Miss Neumann, 'but you

must prepare yourself, if you have not seen him, that is, for a long time. He is only what is left of a man.'

'Just one moment before you take us to him. His mental processes are not too badly depleted? He can understand what one says to him?'

'Oh, yes, he can understand perfectly, but as he is semi-paralysed, he is unable to speak with much clarity, though that varies, and is unable to walk without help. His brain, in my opinion, is as good as ever it was. The only difference is that he tires very easily now. Now, would you like some refreshment first?'

'No,' said Lord Altamount. 'No, I don't want to wait. This is a rather urgent matter on which we have come, so if you will take us to him now – he expects us, I understand?'

'He expects you, yes,' said Lisa Neumann.

She led the way up some stairs, along a corridor and opened a room of medium size. It had tapestries on the wall, the heads of stags looked down on them, the place had been a one-time shooting-box. It had been little changed in its furnishing or arrangements. There was a big record-player on one side of the room.

The tall man sat in a chair by the fire. His head trembled a little, so did his left hand. The skin of his face was pulled down one side. Without beating about the bush, one could only describe him one way, as a wreck of a man. A man who had once been tall, sturdy, strong. He had a fine forehead, deep-set eyes, and a rugged, determined-looking chin. The eyes, below the heavy eyebrows, were intelligent. He said something. His voice was not weak, it made fairly clear sounds but not always recognizable ones. The faculty of speech had only partly gone from him, he was still understandable.

Lisa Neumann went to stand by him, watching his lips, so that she could interpret what he said if necessary.

'Professor Shoreham welcomes you. He is very pleased to see you here, Lord Altamount, Colonel Munro, Sir James Kleek, Mr Robinson and Mr Horsham. He would like me to tell you that his hearing is reasonably good. Anything you say to him he will be able to hear. If there is any difficulty I can assist. What he wants to say to you he will be able to transmit through me. If he gets too tired to articulate, I can lip-read and we also converse in a perfected sign language if there is any difficulty.'

'I shall try,' said Colonel Munro, 'not to waste your time and to tire you as little as possible, Professor Shoreham.'

The man in the chair bent his head in recognition of the words.

'Some questions I can ask of Miss Neumann.'

Shoreham's hand went out in a faint gesture towards the woman standing by his side. Sounds came from his lips, again not quite recognizable to them, but she translated quickly.

'He says he can depend on me to transcribe anything you wish to say to him or I to you.'

'You have, I think, already received a letter from me,' said Colonel Munro.

'That is so,' said Miss Neumann. 'Professor Shoreham received your letter and knows its contents.'

A hospital nurse opened the door just a crack – but she did not come in. She spoke in a low whisper:

'Is there anything I can get or do, Miss Neumann? For any of the guests or for Professor Shoreham?'

'I don't think there is anything, thank you, Miss Ellis. I should be glad, though, if you could stay in your sitting-room just along the passage, in case we should need anything.'

'Certainly – I quite understand.' She went away, closing the door softly.

'We don't want to lose time,' said Colonel Munro. 'No doubt Professor Shoreham is in tune with current affairs.'

'Entirely so,' said Miss Neumann, 'as far as he is interested.'

'Doess he keep in touch with scientific advancements and such things?'

Robert Shoreham's head shook slightly from side to side. He himself answered.

'I have finished with all that.'

'But you know roughly the state the world is in? The success of what is called the Revolution of Youth. The seizing of power by youthful fully-equipped forces.'

Miss Neumann said, 'He is in touch entirely with everything that is going on – in a political sense, that is.'

'The world is now given over to violence, pain, revolutionary tenets, a strange and incredible philosophy of rule by an anarchic minority.'

A faint look of impatience went across the gaunt face.

'He knows all that,' said Mr Robinson, speaking unexpectedly. 'No need to go over a lot of things again. He's a man who knows everything.'

He said:

'Do you remember Admiral Blunt?'

Again the head bowed. Something like a smile showed on the twisted lips.

'Admiral Blunt remembers some scientific work you had done on a certain project – I think project is what you call these things? Project Benvo.'

They saw the alert look which came into the eyes.

'Project Benvo,' said Miss Neumann. 'You are going back quite a long time, Mr Robinson, to recall that.'

'It was *your* project, wasn't it?' said Mr Robinson.

'Yes, it was his project.' Miss Neumann now spoke more easily for him, as a matter of course.

'We cannot use nuclear weapons, we cannot use explosives or gas or chemistry, but *your* project, Project Benvo, we *could* use.'

There was silence and nobody spoke. And then again the queer distorted sounds came from Professor Shoreham's lips.

'He says, of course,' said Miss Neumann, 'Benvo *could* be used successfully in the circumstances in which we find ourselves –'

The man in the chair had turned to her and was saying something to her.

'He wants me to explain it to you,' said Miss Neumann. 'Project B, later called Project Benvo, was something that he worked upon for many years but which at last he laid aside for reasons of his own.'

'Because he had failed to make his project materialize?'

'No, he had not failed,' said Lisa Neumann. 'We had not failed. I worked with him on this project. He laid it aside for certain reasons, but he did not fail. He succeeded. He was on the right track, he developed it, he tested it in various laboratory experiments, and it worked.' She turned to Professor Shoreham again, made a few gestures with her hand, touching her lips, ear, mouth in a strange kind of code signal.

'I am asking if he wants me to explain just what Benvo does.'

'We do want you to explain.'

'And he wants to know how you learnt about it.'

'We learnt about it,' said Colonel Munro, 'through an old friend of yours, Professor Shoreham. Not Admiral Blunt, he could not remember very much, but the other person to whom you had once spoken about it, Lady Matilda Cleckheaton.'

Again Miss Neumann turned to him and watched his lips. She smiled faintly.

'He says he thought Matilda was dead years ago.'

'She is very much alive. It is she who wanted us to know about this discovery of Professor Shoreham's.'

'Professor Shoreham will tell you the main points of what you want to know, though he has to warn you that this knowledge will be quite useless to you. Papers, formulae, accounts and proofs of this discovery were all destroyed. But since the only way to satisfy your questions is for you to learn the main outline of Project Benvo, I can tell you fairly clearly of what it consists. You know the uses and purpose of tear gas as used by the police in controlling riot crowds; violent demonstrations and so on. It induces a fit of weeping, painful tears and sinus inflammation.'

'And this is something of the same kind?'

'No, it is not in the least of the same kind but it can have the same purpose. It came into the heads of scientists that one can change not only men's principal reactions and feeling, but also mental characteristics. You can change a man's character. The qualities of an aphrodisiac are well known. They lead to a condition of sexual desire, there are various drugs or gases or glandular operations – any of these things can lead to a change in your mental vigour, increased energy as by alterations to the thyroid gland, and Professor Shoreham wishes to tell you that there is a certain process – he will not tell you now whether it is glandular, or a gas that can be manufactured, but there is something that can change a man in his outlook on life – his reaction to people and to life generally. He may be in a state of homicidal fury, he may be pathologically violent, and yet, by the influence of Project Benvo, he turns into something, or rather *someone*, quite different. He becomes – there is only one word for it, I believe, which is embodied in its name – he becomes *benevolent*. He wishes to benefit others. He exudes kindness. He has a horror of causing pain or inflicting violence. Benvo can be released over a big area, it can affect hundreds, thousands of people if manufactured in big enough quantities, and if distributed successfully.'

'How long does it last?' said Colonel Munro. 'Twenty-four hours? Longer?'

'You don't understand,' said Miss Neumann. 'It is *permanent*.'

'Permanent? You've changed a man's nature, you've altered a component, a physical component, of course, of his being which has produced the effect of a permanent change in his nature. And you cannot go back on that? You cannot put him back to where he was again. It has to be accepted as a permanent change?'

'Yes. It was, perhaps, a discovery more of medical interest at first, but Professor Shoreham had conceived of it as a deterrent to be used in war, in mass risings, riotings, revolutions, anarchy. He didn't think of it as merely medical. It does not produce happiness in the subject, only a great wish for others to be happy. That is an effect, he says, that everyone feels in their life at one time or another. They have a great wish to make someone, one person ·or many people – to make them comfortable, happy, in good health, all these things. And since

211

people can and do feel these things, there is, we both believed, a component that controls that desire in their bodies, and if you once put that component in operation it can go on in perpetuity.'

'Wonderful,' said Mr Robinson.

He spoke thoughtfully rather than enthusiastically.

'Wonderful. What a thing to have discovered. What a thing to be able to put into action if – but why?'

The head resting towards the back of the chair turned slowly towards Mr Robinson. Miss Neumann said:

'He says you understand better than the others.'

'But it's the answer,' said James Kleek. 'It's the *exact* answer! It's wonderful.' His face was enthusiastically excited.

Miss Neumann was shaking her head.

'Project Benvo,' she said, 'is not for sale and not for a gift. It has been relinquished.'

'Are you telling us the answer is no?' said Colonel Munro incredulously.

'Yes. Professor Shoreham says the answer is no. He decided that it was against –' she paused a minute and turned to look at the man in the chair. He made quaint gestures with his head, with one hand, and a few guttural sounds came from his mouth. She waited and then she said, 'He will tell you himself, he was afraid. Afraid of what science has done in its time of triumph. The things it has found out and known, the things it has discovered and given to the world. The wonder drugs that have not always been wonder drugs, the penicillin that has saved lives and the penicillin that has taken lives, the heart transplants that have brought disillusion and the disappointment of a death not expected. He has lived in the period of nuclear fission; new weapons that have slain. The tragedies of radioactivity; the pollutions that new industrial discoveries have brought about. He has been afraid of what science could do, used indiscriminately.'

'But this is a benefit. A benefit to everyone,' cried Munro.

'So have many things been. Always greeted as great benefits to humanity, as great wonders. And then come the side effects, and worse than that, the fact that they have sometimes brought not benefit but disaster. And so he decided that he would give up. He says' – she read from a paper she held, whilst beside her he nodded agreement from his chair – ' *"I am satisfied that I have done what I set out to do, that I made my discovery. But I decided not to put it into circulation. It must be destroyed. And so it has been destroyed. And so the answer to you is no. There is no benevolence on tap. There could have been once, but now all the formulae, all the know-how, my notes and my account of the necessary procedure are gone – burnt to ashes – I have destroyed my brain child."'*

Robert Shoreham struggled into raucous difficult speech.

'I have destroyed my brain child and nobody in the world knows how I arrived at it. One man helped me but he is dead. He died of tuberculosis a year after we had come to success. You must go away again. I cannot help you.'

'But this knowledge of yours means you could save the world!'

The man in the chair made a curious noise. It was laughter. Laughter of a crippled man.

'Save the world. Save the world! What a phrase! That's what your young people are doing, they think! They're going ahead in violence and hatred to save the world. But they don't know how! They will have to do it *themselves*, out of their own hearts, out of their own minds. We can't give them an artificial way of doing it. No. An artificial goodness? An artificial kindness? None of that. It wouldn't be *real*. It wouldn't *mean* anything. It would be against Nature.' He said slowly: '*Against God.*'

The last two words came out unexpectedly, clearly enunciated.

He looked round at his listeners. It was as though he pleaded with them for understanding, yet at the same time had no real hope of it.

'I had a right to destroy what I had created –'

'I doubt it very much,' said Mr Robinson, 'knowledge is

213

knowledge. What you have given birth to – what you have made come to life, you should not destroy.'

'You have a right to your opinion – but the fact you will have to accept.'

'No,' Mr Robinson brought the word out with force.

Lisa Neumann turned on him angrily.

'What do you mean by "No"?'

Her eyes were flashing. A handsome woman, Mr Robinson thought. A woman who had been in love with Robert Shoreham all her life probably. Had loved him, worked with him, and now lived beside him, ministering to him with her intellect, giving him devotion in its purest form without pity.

'There are things one gets to know in the course of one's lifetime,' said Mr Robinson. 'I don't suppose mine will be a long life. I carry too much weight to begin with.' He sighed as he looked down at his bulk. 'But I do know some things. I'm right, you know, Shoreham. You'll have to admit I'm right, too. You're an honest man. You wouldn't have destroyed your work. You couldn't have brought yourself to do it. You've got it somewhere still, locked away, hidden away, not in this house, probably. I'd guess, and I'm only making a guess, that you've got it somewhere in a safe deposit or a bank. She knows you've got it there, too. You trust her. She's the only person in the world you do trust.'

Shoreham said, and this time his voice was almost distinct: 'Who are *you*? Who the devil are you?'

'I'm just a man who knows about money,' said Mr Robinson, 'and the things that branch off from money, you know. People and their idiosyncrasies and their practices in life. If you liked to, you could lay your hand on the work that you've put away. I'm not saying that you could do the same work now, but I think it's all there somewhere. You've told us your views, and I wouldn't say they were all wrong,' said Mr Robinson.

'Possibly you're right. Benefits to humanity are tricky things to deal with. Poor old Beveridge, freedom from want, freedom from fear, freedom from whatever it was, he thought he was making a heaven on earth by saying that and planning for it and

214

getting it done. But it hasn't made heaven on earth and I don't suppose your benvo or whatever you call it (sounds like a patent food) will bring heaven on earth either. Benevolence has its dangers just like everything else. What it will do is save a lot of suffering, pain, anarchy, violence, slavery to drugs. Yes, it'll save quite a lot of bad things from happening, and it *might* save something that was important. It might – just *might* – make a difference to people. Young people. This Benvoleo of yours – now I've made it sound like a patent cleaner – is going to make people benevolent and I'll admit perhaps that it's going to make them condescending, smug and pleased with themselves, but there's just a chance, too, that if you change people's natures by force and they have to go on using that particular kind of nature until they die, one or two of them – not many – might discover that they had a natural vocation, in humility, not pride, for what they were being forced to do. *Really* change themselves, I mean, before they died. Not be able to get out of a new habit they'd learnt.'

Colonel Munro said, 'I don't understand what the hell you're all talking about.'

Miss Neumann said, 'He's talking nonsense. You have to take Professor Shoreham's answer. He will do what he likes with his own discoveries. You can't coerce him.'

'No,' said Lord Altamount. 'We're not going to coerce you or torture you, Robert, or force you to reveal your hiding-places. You'll do what you think right. That's agreed.'

'Edward?' said Robert Shoreham. His speech failed him slightly again, his hands moved in gesture, and Miss Neumann translated quickly.

'Edward? He says you are Edward Altamount?'

Shoreham spoke again and she took the words from him.

'He asks you, Lord Altamount, if you are definitely, with your whole heart and mind, asking him to put Project Benvo in your jurisdiction. He says –' she paused, watching, listening – 'he says you are the only man in public life that he ever trusted. If it is *your* wish –'

215

James Kleek was suddenly on his feet. Anxious, quick to move like lightning, he stood by Lord Altamount's chair.

'Let me help you up, sir. You're ill. You're not well. Please stand back a little, Miss Neumann. I – I must get to him. I – I have his remedies here. I know what to do –'

His hand went into his pocket and came out again with a hypodermic syringe.

'Unless he gets this at once it'll be too late –' He had caught up Lord Altamount's arm, rolling up his sleeve, pinching the flesh between his fingers, he held the hypodermic ready.

'But someone else moved. Horsham was across the room, pushing Colonel Munro aside: his hand closed over James Kleek's as he wrenched the hypodermic away. Kleek struggled but Horsham was too strong for him. And Munro was now there, too.

'So it's been *you*, James Kleek,' he said. 'You who've been the traitor, a faithful disciple who wasn't a faithful disciple.'

Miss Neumann had gone to the door – had flung it open and was calling.

'Nurse! Come quickly. Come.'

The nurse appeared. She gave one quick glance to Professor Shoreham, but he waved her away and pointed across the room to where Horsham and Munro still held a struggling Kleek. Her hand went into the pocket of her uniform.

Shoreham stammered out, 'It's Altamount. A heart attack.'

'Heart attack, my foot,' roared Munro. 'It's attempted murder.' He stopped.

'Hold the chap,' he said to Horsham, and leapt across the room.

'Mrs Cortman? Since when have you entered the nursing profession? We'd rather lost sight of you since you gave us the slip in Baltimore.'

Milly Jean was still wrestling with her pocket. Now her hand came out with the small automatic in it. She glanced towards Shoreham but Munro blocked her, and Lisa Neumann was standing in front of Shoreham's chair.

James Kleek yelled, 'Get Altamount, Juanita – quick – get Altamount.'

Her arm flashed up and she fired.

James Kleek said,

'Damned good shot!'

Lord Altamount had had a classical education. He murmured faintly, looking at James Kleek,

'Jamie? *Et tu Brute?*' and collapsed against the back of his chair.

Dr McCulloch looked round him, a little uncertain of what he was going to do or say next. The evening had been a somewhat unusual experience for him.

Lisa Neumann came to him and set a glass by his side.

'A hot toddy,' she said.

'I always knew you were a woman in a thousand, Lisa.' He sipped appreciatively.

'I must say I'd like to know what all this has been about – but I gather it's the sort of thing that's so hush-hush that nobody's going to tell me anything.'

'The Professor – he's all right, isn't he?'

'The Professor?' He looked at her anxious face, kindly. 'He's fine. If you ask me, it's done him a world of good.'

'I thought perhaps the shock –'

'I'm quite all right,' said Shoreham. 'Shock treatment is what I needed. I feel – how shall I put it – *alive* again.' He looked surprised.

McCulloch said to Lisa, 'Notice how much stronger his voice is? It's apathy really that's the enemy in these cases – what *he* wants is to work again – the stimulation of some brain work. Music is all very well – it's kept him soothed and able to enjoy life in a mild way. But he's really a man of great intellectual power – and he misses the mental activity that was the essence of life to him. Get him started on it again if you can.'

He nodded encouragingly at her as she looked doubtfully at him.

'I think, Dr McCulloch,' said Colonel Munro, 'that we owe you a few explanations of what happened this evening, even though, as you surmise, the powers-that-be will demand a hush-hush policy. Lord Altamount's death –' He hesitated.

'The bullet didn't actually kill him,' said the doctor, 'death was due to shock. That hypodermic would have done the trick – strychnine. The young man –'

'I only just got it away from him in time,' said Horsham.

'Been the nigger in the woodpile all along?' asked the doctor.

'Yes – regarded with trust and affection for over seven years. The son of one of Lord Altamount's oldest friends –'

'It happens. And the lady – in it together, do I understand?'

'Yes. She got the post here by false credentials. She is also wanted by the police for murder.'

'Murder?'

'Yes. Murder of her husband, Sam Cortman, the American Ambassador. She shot him on the steps of the Embassy – and told a fine tale of young men, masked, attacking him.'

'Why did she have it in for him? Political or personal?'

'He found out about some of her activities, we think.'

'I'd say he suspected infidelity,' said Horsham. 'instead he discovered a hornets' nest of espionage and conspiracy, and his wife running the show. He didn't know quite how to deal with it. Nice chap, but slow-thinking – and she had the sense to act quickly. Wonderful how she registered grief at the Memorial Service.'

'Memorial –' said Professor Shoreham.

Everyone, slightly startled, turned round to look at him.

'Difficult word to say, memorial – but I mean it. Lisa, you and I are going to have to start work again.'

'But, Robert –'

'I'm alive again. Ask the doctor if I ought to take things easy.'

Lisa turned her eyes inquiringly on McCulloch.

'If you do, you'll shorten your life and sink back into apathy –'

'There you are,' said Shoreham. 'Fash-fashion – medical

'Suppose sl
'She'll com
'I feel – I
'That's be
foie gras. Y
much, Staff
all right wh
'That re
'You ha
'No, no
you, Aunt
'That's
'You s
'Yes,
'I've
'Real
get hin
'Bav
'We
'He
'W
'H
'O
moth
I'm
'
wo

ch
dr
a

fashion today. Make everyone, even if they're – at – death's
door – go on working –'

Dr McCulloch laughed and got up.

'Not far wrong. I'll send you some pills along to help.'

'I shan't take them.'

'You'll do.'

At the door the doctor paused. 'Just want to know – how did
you get the police along so quickly?'

'Squadron Leader Andrews,' said Munro, 'had it all in hand.
Arrived on the dot. We knew the woman was around
somewhere, but had no idea she was in the house already.'

'Well – I'll be off. Is all you've told me true? Feel I shall
wake up any minute, having dropped off to sleep half way
through the latest thriller. Spies, murders, traitors, espionage,
scientists –'

He went out.

'There was a silence.

Professor Shoreham said slowly and carefully:

'Back to work –'

Lisa said as women have always said:

'You must be *careful*, Robert –'

'Not – not careful. Time might be short.'

He said again:

'Memorial –'

'What *do* you mean? You said it before.'

'Memorial? Yes. To Edward. His Memorial! Always used to
think he had the face of a martyr.'

Shoreham seemed lost in thought.

'I'd like to get hold of Gottlieb. May be dead. Good man to
work with. With him and with you, Lisa – get the stuff out of
the bank –'

'Professor Gottlieb is alive – in the Baker Foundation,
Austin, Texas,' said Mr Robinson.

'What are you talking of doing?' said Lisa.

'Benvo, of course! Memorial to Edward Altamount. H

Fontana Paperbacks: Fiction

Fontana is a leading paperback publisher of both non-fiction, popular and academic, and fiction. Below are some recent fiction titles.

- ☐ THE ROSE STONE Teresa Crane £2.95
- ☐ THE DANCING MEN Duncan Kyle £2.50
- ☐ AN EXCESS OF LOVE Cathy Cash Spellman £3.50
- ☐ THE ANVIL CHORUS Shane Stevens £2.95
- ☐ A SONG TWICE OVER Brenda Jagger £3.50
- ☐ SHELL GAME Douglas Terman £2.95
- ☐ FAMILY TRUTHS Syrell Leahy £2.95
- ☐ ROUGH JUSTICE Jerry Oster £2.50
- ☐ ANOTHER DOOR OPENS Lee Mackenzie £2.25
- ☐ THE MONEY STONES Ian St James £2.95
- ☐ THE BAD AND THE BEAUTIFUL Vera Cowie £2.95
- ☐ RAMAGE'S CHALLENGE Dudley Pope £2.95
- ☐ THE ROAD TO UNDERFALL Mike Jefferies £2.95

You can buy Fontana paperbacks at your local bookshop or newsagent. Or you can order them from Fontana Paperbacks, Cash Sales Department, Box 29, Douglas, Isle of Man. Please send a cheque, postal or money order (not currency) worth the purchase price plus 22p per book for postage (maximum postage required is £3.00 for orders within the UK).

NAME (Block letters) _____

ADDRESS _____

_____

_____

While every effort is made to keep
them at short notice.